"I want to follow you around for six weeks," Judy said.

Paul looked at her as if she'd just expressed a desire to become his mail-order bride. "No."

For a moment she could only stare at him. She couldn't think of any reason for his refusal. Until now, everyone in Grateful Bend had been exceptionally warm and helpful. "I don't see the problem."

"The problem," he told her, "is that I don't have the time to play nursemaid to an American tourist with a camera."

Judy squared her shoulders ever so slightly. "You won't be playing nursemaid. It'll be as if I'm not there."

Paul's eyes slid over her slowly. There was no way a man could ignore a woman like her. "I suggest you find yourself another man."

"You are a Royal Canadian Mounted Policeman, aren't you?" she asked.

"Yes."

Judy smiled. "Then I want *you....*"

Dear Reader:

Romance readers have been enthusiastic about the Silhouette Special Editions for years. And that's not by accident: Special Editions were the first of their kind and continue to feature realistic stories with heightened romantic tension.

The longer stories, sophisticated style, greater sensual detail and variety that made Special Editions popular are the same elements that will make you want to read book after book.

We hope that you enjoy this Special Edition today, and will enjoy many more.

Please write to us:

Jane Nicholls
Silhouette Books
PO Box 236
Thornton Road
Croydon
Surrey
CR9 3RU

MARIE FERRARELLA

She Got Her Man

Silhouette Special Edition

Originally Published by Silhouette Books
a division of
Harlequin Enterprises Ltd.

*First published in Great Britain in 1994
by Silhouette Books, Eton House, 18-24 Paradise Road,
Richmond, Surrey TW9 1SR*

© Marie Rydzynski-Ferrarella 1993

*Silhouette, Silhouette Special Edition and Colophon are
Trade Marks of Harlequin Enterprises B.V.*

ISBN 0 373 59128 4

23-9403

Made and printed in Great Britain

To Tara Gavin,
for the opportunity,
and
to Dr. J.G. Miller
for input.
(and being a great doctor, as well)

MARIE FERRARELLA

was born in Europe, raised in New York City and now
lives in Southern California. She describes herself as the
tired mother of two overenergetic children and the
contented wife of one wonderful man. She is thrilled to
be following her dream of writing full-time.

Other Silhouette Books by Marie Ferrarella

Silhouette Special Edition

It Happened One Night
A Girl's Best Friend
Blessing in Disguise
Someone To Talk To
World's Greatest Dad
Family Matters

Books by Marie Ferrarella writing as Marie Nicole

Silhouette Desire

Tried and True   Chocolate Dreams
Buyer Beware   No Laughing Matter
Through Laughter and Tears
Grand Theft: Heart
A Woman of Integrity
Country Blue
Last Year's Hunk
Foxy Lady

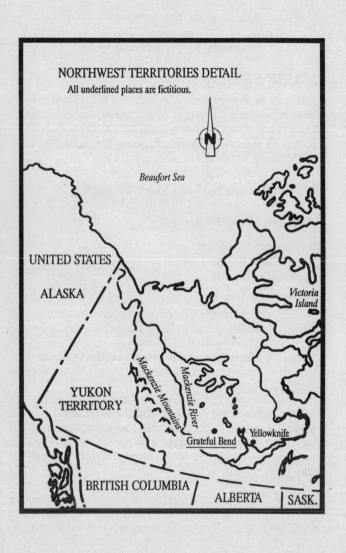

NORTHWEST TERRITORIES DETAIL

All underlined places are fictitious.

N

Beaufort Sea

UNITED STATES

ALASKA

Victoria Island

Mackenzie Mountains

Mackenzie River

YUKON TERRITORY

Grateful Bend

Yellowknife

BRITISH COLUMBIA

ALBERTA

SASK.

Chapter One

The mournful howling embraced the small wood-framed house on all sides, seeping through its very walls. He tossed restlessly, attempting to ignore the incessant moaning of the wind. Defeated, he sat up in bed and ran a hand through his hair as a particularly intense gust rattled the windows and doors in a symbolic gesture of victory.

The wind. It was the wind, he thought, as he quickly shook off the last threads of tenuous sleep. No need to be alarmed. It was just the wind.

He took a long, deep breath, attempting to steady the pulse that hammered in his throat, and exhaled slowly. Control returned. Beyond his window, near-naked branches, just coming to terms with spring, were caught in the wind's grip, scraping long, pointy fingers against the predawn sky.

Sgt. Paul Monroe swung his long, sturdy legs out from beneath the warm covers, the bite of a cold spring greeting his body. He was oblivious to it. For a long moment, all he did was listen and stare out the window. The wind spoke to him. The sound it made was the sound of loneliness, echoing in the wilderness. There was nothing to separate today from yesterday or tomorrow.

That was just the way he liked it.

Anonymity.

Anonymity of self, of his day-to-day world, it was all he asked for, all he needed to sustain himself.

It was still early, but he knew there was no use in trying to recapture sleep. Once he was awake, that was the end of the matter. He might as well get ready.

Paul stretched and rose, then found his way into the bathroom in the dark.

There was little to get in his way. It was a Spartan bedroom, even by Grateful Bend's standards, with a double brass bed that seemed, at times, too small to accommodate his fitful nights, a nightstand and a scatter rug thrown before it on a scarred and creaking wooden floor. The room's sparse decor matched that found in the living room and small kitchen. Paul allowed himself few luxuries. He was completely self-contained, and that was the way he liked it.

A cold shower in the tiny bathroom completed what the sound of the wind had started—he was now totally awake. Being alert was part of his job description, though he knew firsthand that what was required of him did not match what was needed from his counterparts in Toronto and Montreal. They had constant crime to deal with. He had the snow and the wilderness. And the desolation.

He was surrounded by desolation, yet there were others here, sharing it with him. They were his responsibility. His duty was seeing to the various needs of the scattered populace that lived in and around Grateful Bend. At times he found himself a cross between an old-time sheriff, a father confessor and a handyman. The people here had to be exceedingly independent to live in the recesses of the Northwest Territories. Yet everyone had a time of need, a time when outside help—or, as they saw it, outside intervention—was necessary. That was his role.

Though there was no one who could intervene for him.

As he walked out of the bathroom, he glanced at the framed photograph of his graduating class on the wall, one of the few ornamental trappings in the room, and wondered what had happened to the men in it. He had lost touch with them all. His own fault, actually. He had been the one who had broken communication with them and with the world outside of Grateful Bend.

He had come to escape, to find peace while trying to preserve it among the six hundred or so citizens of Grateful Bend. The last part had been easy. The people were a peaceful lot, too busy struggling against the elements, struggling to survive, to be troublesome. It was finding his own peace that had eluded him.

He had been out here for five years. Five years away from his past. It still overtook him at times—in his dreams. Those were the only dreams he had. Dreams of her. Dreams of his partner. Dreams of the incident. They overtook him in unguarded moments as well, when something familiar would trigger a memory and cause it to flash through his mind like a racing bullet. But that was happening with less frequency now, he thought as he got dressed quickly. Perhaps someday he would find peace.

If he lived long enough.

He turned on the light in the kitchen as he entered, and a pale yellow cast washed over the cheerless room. There was an old-fashioned stove, a small refrigerator and a table just large enough for two. But there was no one to use the second chair.

Mechanically, he began to brew coffee, the dented coffeepot rattling slightly as he placed it on the warming burner. Inside, the hot water slowly dripped through the coffee grounds, forming a deep brown liquid that hit the metal bottom, making a noise like summer rain against a tin roof. He dropped two slices of bread into the toaster Hayes's wife had given him upon his arrival.

Paul waited, his cup in hand, consciously making his mind embrace nothing. It was easier that way.

He had found a shred of solace in maintaining the peace here in Grateful Bend. It was a different world here than in Montreal, where he had grown up. Where he had been young, he thought with a fleeting sting of remorse. His patrol encompassed the town, the Inuit settlement and the snow-covered lands between and beyond. A large chunk for a man to handle, even with help. But usually, it handled itself. Mankind, at least this small segment of it, seemed bent on peace, beyond the occasional squabble that he resolved.

The only real enemy to the townspeople was the long, merciless winter.

Paul poured the single cup of coffee he took before departing for work each morning, watching the steam rise as he filled the cup. He stared at the shimmering liquid, mesmerized for a moment. Black, like the interior of his soul. But that, too, was his fault. If only he had been somewhere else at the time.

If only...

There was no wishing it away, no forgetting. It had happened, and there wasn't anything he could do to change that.

He drank the coffee, letting the hot liquid burn its way through his system, emptying his mind of everything except the details of the day that lay ahead. Preoccupied, he didn't realize that the toast was burning until the acrid smell assaulted his nostrils and stung his eyes, making them smart.

"Damn!"

Paul pulled the lever, popping the toast manually. Two pieces of charcoal peered out at him from the slots, bearing only faint resemblance to bread. He bit off a curse and lifted them out, burning his fingertips as he did so. He dropped them on the napkin next to the toaster and frowned. He didn't believe in waste. Stoically, he scraped off what he could and coated the rest in margarine. It would have to do. If he had wanted to pamper himself, he wouldn't have been out here to begin with.

After forcing down the burnt toast, Paul glanced at the clock on the mantel. Seven o'clock. It was time to go through the motions of living another day. He strapped on his revolver, made certain the fire was completely out and then left.

It was a beautiful day, absolutely, breathtakingly beautiful. Judith Tara Treherne pulled her rented red four-wheel-drive vehicle to the side of the deserted highway and just stared in wonder at the scenery for a moment. It made her feel wonderfully alive.

She had to capture this.

She slid her jeans-clad legs out of the car and opened the rear door on the driver's side. Her camera equipment filled the back seat. As she lifted out her camera, the dog sitting patiently on the passenger side barked at her.

"Hold your horses, Raymond. This is too terrific to pass up, even if we are behind schedule." The dog barked again, as if in agreement.

These photographs would be for her own album, she thought as she looked along both sides of the highway leading to Grateful Bend. On second thought, they could probably fit in very well with the project she was currently working on.

She grinned, moving her blond hair away from her face with the back of her wrist. She brought the camera to her eye, framing a wilderness that was shedding the crystal jewels of winter in preparation for the green finery of a not-too-distant summer.

The camera whirled as she shot photograph after photograph. The dog in the car remained silent, as if somehow knowing better than to intrude upon this private communion his mistress was having with her subject.

This was nature at its finest, Judy thought. Pure, clean, wonderful. She felt as if the sun shining overhead were actually smiling down on the land, on her.

It was wonderful, she thought as the camera rewound its film, to be high on life. And there was no reason not to be. She was doing exactly what she wanted to do.

Satisfied, she capped her lens and snapped the leather cover over it. Raymond yipped his approval.

Judy was quite aware of the image she projected. A California beach bunny come to life—her only ambition being to sit out in the sun, get a perfect tan, surf and talk. The talking part, she thought with a smile, she had down to a science. But the rest couldn't have interested her less. Unless, of course, it was to photograph it for a beach layout.

She fed her soul and her bank account, in that order, by immortalizing moments of life, freezing them forever on film. She had produced three coffee-table specials that way and was determined to make a name for herself with the next. The one she was working on now.

The oldest of five, Judith Tara Treherne had grown up spinning stories for her younger brothers and sisters to wile away the lonely nights in Eugene, Oregon. She had the ability to fabricate a story at a moment's notice and the gift to see a story almost anywhere—in the flight of a sparrow; in the eyes of an old woman sitting on a bench, waiting for a bus; in a scrap of newspaper blowing end over end on a dirty, crowded street. And with her camera, she could make others see it, too.

She slid back into the car, giving the camera an affectionate pat before turning on the ignition. She was very proud of the fact that she could make her camera speak eloquently. She had Uncle Harry to thank for that. A ne'er-do-well uncle who popped in and out of her young life to entertain her and then disappear until the next time, it was Harry who had given her that first camera, plunking down twenty dollars in a thrift shop to purchase a very used portrait camera. It was for her ninth birthday.

And the rest, Judy mused as she stepped on the gas, is history.

The pulsating green numbers of the digital clock on the dashboard drew her attention to the fact that it was growing late. She had been traveling from Yellowknife since early that morning. The plan had been to reach Grateful Bend by noon. It was less than half an hour away from that now, and

by her calculations she was going to have to stop admiring
and really hustle if she wanted to get there by noon.

There was no one on the highway as far as the eye could
see. Perfect.

"Hang on to your dog collar, Raymond. Here we go."
Judy stepped on the gas, easing the speedometer up to the
seventy mark as she took the curves of the lonesome highway.

The sound of a car engine broke the tranquillity of the
morning air. The wind had all but abated, and Paul could
see the car from a distance, tearing down the road as if the
driver were in some sort of a race against who knew what.

He didn't recognize the vehicle. Paul shook his head.
Someone else in a hurry to meet their destiny, not realizing
that the journey was all there was, he thought with a sigh.
He positioned himself in full view, ready to stop the driver
as he approached.

The driver didn't stop, though. The red car whipped right
by Paul's as if he weren't even there. Stepping on the gas
pedal, Paul gave chase. Pursuit lasted for over a mile, making him more annoyed with each passing moment.

Judy was so caught up in her own world, so enthused with
what she saw in front of her, she had no idea what was behind her.

Until the siren caught her attention.

Startled that there was another living being so close without her having noticed, Judy looked up into her rearview
mirror.

"Oh-oh, Raymond, looks like we're in for it." She slowed
down. With a quick turn of her wrist, she pulled the car over
to the side of the road again.

Raymond's contribution to the conversation was to
thump his tail rhythmically against the light beige uphol-
stery several times. Of dubious parentage, Raymond looked
a lot like a miniature, slightly mixed version of Lassie. He
had caught her heart the day she'd found him scrounging

through garbage pails in an alley in Los Angeles. She'd recognized him from the neighborhood. It turned out his owner didn't want him any longer. Said he was too much trouble and had just abandoned him, moving away soon afterward. Judy took the dog home with her, cleaned him up, fed him and most important, loved him. She took Raymond with her whenever possible. Off on assignment for most of the year, Judy couldn't bear the idea of Raymond languishing away in some kennel. And the one time she had left the animal with her sister Sharon, her niece and nephew had almost been Raymond's undoing.

So she took him with her and found a way to manage each time. It was a matter of priorities and determination. A sunny smile didn't hurt, either.

Somehow, she doubted that a sunny smile would help this time. The man who approached Judy's red car was the portrait of sternness, and he filled his uniform well.

Judy got out of her car. "Good morning, Officer." She attempted to keep her voice cheerful, in contrast to the somber expression on this tall giant. It suddenly occurred to her that she wasn't certain how to address him. "It is Officer, isn't it?"

He had a youthful face, she decided, not hard. But it looked as if it had been cast in granite instead of flesh. Was this his official face? Did he laugh when he was alone, when he made love to his wife, held a child in his arms? Judy wondered.

She flushed, pulling herself back to the present. "I'm sorry, I don't know. What does one call a Mountie?"

"Sir," he informed her dryly. There was no smile to offset the tone. Paul put out his hand. "May I see your license, please?"

Well, this certainly wasn't starting out on the right foot, Judy thought. Maybe she should have begun in Montreal instead of here. But Montreal was on the opposite coast. With most of her family still living in Oregon, she had thought this a perfect opportunity to swing by and visit with them before plunging into her assignment. The two weeks she had allotted herself had passed much too quickly and she hadn't been able to do nearly as much as she had hoped. But each day had been filled with memories and the stuff that memories were made of and she was content with that.

She was content with a lot of things. Unlike this dour-looking man, she noted.

Nudging Raymond aside, she bent over to get her purse from the floor of the car, then took out her wallet. She flipped it open to her driver's license.

"Take it out, please."

She did as she was told, handing it to him. "Was I speeding, sir? I had no idea I was going too fast."

Paul glanced at the address. American. From Los Angeles—it figured. That made her a tourist. But if she was one, she was certainly off the beaten path. He looked at the photograph in the corner of the license just below his thumb. She looked like the type to lose her way. Blond and vacant, relying on others to help her through.

Paul raised his eyes to her face and amended his assessment a notch. Perhaps not so vague. There seemed to be a lot going on just behind the eyes. "That depends."

Judy slid her tongue over her lower lip, eyeing her license. He was still holding it, but he wasn't writing anything yet. There was hope. "Depends on what?"

He took out his ticket book. "On whether you were driving a car or flying a plane."

Judy felt her heart sink. Oh, well, it served her right, she supposed. She was going fast, but there hadn't been anyone in sight. Wrong, she reminded herself, she just hadn't noticed anyone in sight.

She pretended to look at the length of the car, hoping the man had a sense of humor. "Yep, it's a car."

Paul squinted to make out her zip code as he wrote. "Not the way you were handling it."

She shrugged, accepting her fate. "I guess I got kind of carried away."

He glanced at her, then went on to write out the citation. "You could have been. If the car had gone out of control at this speed, you would have had six men carrying you away in short order."

Cheerful man, she thought. She clasped her hands behind her and rocked slightly on her toes. The air was so crisp, it was stinging her cheeks. "Would it help to say I'm sorry and that it won't happen again?"

Paul signed his name and then stopped writing. "You mean, in lieu of a ticket?"

Maybe he was human after all. She looked at him hopefully. "Yes."

"No." He handed her the book. "Sign here." He pointed to the space.

"Oh." She took the pen from him and complied. "Well, it couldn't hurt to try." She returned the pen and book to him. It wasn't her first ticket, she thought, but it was her first international one.

Paul flipped his book closed and looked at her again. She seemed in incredibly good spirits for someone who had just gotten a ticket.

Though he didn't generally issue traffic tickets, the fact that she was doing a good twenty kilometers over the speed limit had prompted him to get tougher than he normally would. People around Grateful Bend didn't usually hurry. They took their time, knowing that tomorrow would be here soon enough.

Paul took a step away from her car and touched his fingers to his hat. "Drive carefully."

Well, at least he hadn't told her to have a nice day. That would have added insult to injury. She folded the ticket and put it into her purse. Her first souvenir of Canada, she thought dryly.

Raymond's tail thumped against the seat madly. She gave the dog a disparaging look as she got behind the wheel again.

"My hero," she murmured.

Raymond placed a paw on her thigh. She glanced at the soulful eyes that looked up at her. If she had any sense, she'd quit all this running around, hang up her camera and devote herself to making a canine star out of Raymond.

"Know all the right moves, don't you, boy?" She laughed, scratching the dog behind the ear. "Sure hope the rest of the Royal Canadian Mounted Police aren't like Mr. Grim."

Tilting her head, Judy looked into her rearview mirror. The Mountie was still sitting in his car, obviously waiting for her to drive away.

"Probably hoping to give me another ticket for bad roadside etiquette or something like that." She turned on her ignition. "I guess that happens when you have no real crime to sink your teeth into."

Raymond barked his agreement.

Determined to be the soul of cooperation, Judy signaled before pulling away from the side of the road, even though there wasn't a single vehicle besides the Mountie's automobile to reckon with in either direction.

Glancing in her rearview mirror, she saw the Mountie's car grow smaller and smaller in the distance. Ticket or no ticket, she was determined to remain in a good mood. She already had her incentive.

It felt wonderful just to be alive and working. Four years after her life-threatening accident, and the euphoria hadn't dissipated one iota. If anything, it had increased. Four years ago she had been lying in a hospital bed, her body racked with pain. All because a man had celebrated the Memorial Day weekend a little too early and plowed his car into her van.

She had spent a week crying, feeling sorry for herself. Seven days. And then Uncle Harry had shown up.

She had been in no mood for his wit, his light-hearted stories, envisioning herself a cripple for the rest of her life. It was the first time she had seen her uncle angry. He had dared her to rally, to get well, goaded her until she was screaming at him. He had called her a coward, a quitter. He had told her that he had expected more of her than to follow in his footsteps.

Judy's mother had always shaken her head when her younger brother's name came up in the conversation. While he was growing up, Harry had everyone dreaming dreams for him, burdening him with a measure of success he felt too intimidated to live up to. So he didn't even try. Instead, Harry had wrapped himself up in his sense of humor and drifted from place to place and in and out of their lives.

His demands that day on a crippled girl had made Judy angry. And then she understood. Her uncle had seen all his best qualities embodied within her, without the fear, the chains that dragged him down and kept him from taking the risk and daring to become someone.

He had stayed with her. More than the rest of her family, he had worked with her until, six months later, she walked out of the hospital where, a broken doll, she had been carried in.

Uncle Harry, as was his way, disappeared soon afterward. He left another camera in his wake. A beautiful one. The one in the leather case she kept with her. And she went on with her life.

She had rallied and won. And nothing had looked gloomy or hopeless to her ever since. Judy looked upon life now as a second chance to do everything she wanted. With that in mind, she gave up her teaching position at the elementary school and threw herself into her first love, photography. She seized life with both hands and became what she had always dreamed about becoming. A photojournalist.

"And a damn good one," Judy said aloud as she neared the town. A newly painted sign proclaimed: You Are Entering Grateful Bend. Stay.

She laughed. At least the town was friendlier than the local Mountie.

"This must be the place, Raymond."

The manila envelope on her dashboard contained a letter from the director of public relations for the Royal Canadian Mounted Police. Her publisher had pulled strings and gotten complete approval from the man. She was to present the letter to the captain in charge of the post at Grateful

Bend. He, in turn, would assign her to a Mountie of her very own.

She grinned at the way that sounded. Her own Mountie. The idea was to follow the man around for six weeks, living his life, seeing the wilderness through his eyes. In time he and the Mountie she would be assigned to in Montreal would find themselves profiled and captured forever in the book Taylor Press was putting out the following year.

On first sight, Grateful Bend hardly qualified for the title of town. There were two rows of weather-beaten buildings facing one another like aging participants in a Virginia reel. It reminded her of something she would see in a book of photographs of the Old West, she mused, delighted. She had purposely chosen this area because of its isolation. It would contrast splendidly with Montreal.

She looked around as she drove slowly. The contrast would probably be a lot more romantic, she decided, given the majestic scenery and the closeness that undoubtedly had to develop among the citizens.

"Except for Mr. Stiff Upper Lip," she mused.

She wondered if the man ever cracked a smile. And then one began to form on her lips as a thought began to suggest itself to her.

Why not?

Her smile grew. She was going to make it her business to find out if the man was as gruff as he seemed. He was the one she was going to ask to be assigned to. She stopped the car in front of the outpost.

The next six weeks, she decided, were going to be a challenge.

Chapter Two

As was his habit, Paul drove into town a little after twelve to check in. He passed the red car at the curb just before he guided the squad car between the Royal Canadian Mounted Police building and Sam's Emporium. It was that woman's car. Even if he hadn't gotten a look at the license plate, he would have recognized the dog. The animal was in the front seat, running his long tongue along the side window just below the opening.

What was she doing here?

She was an American, he remembered. She was probably contesting the ticket he'd just given her. The more he thought about it, the more likely it seemed to be. He squared his broad shoulders beneath the navy blue uniform jacket and walked into the RCMP building.

Warmth and the scent of wood and lemon oil drifted vaguely by him as he shut the door against the cold. It was Tuesday. Mrs. McGillis was cleaning again, waxing and polishing everything in sight so that the tired wood shone as if it were still new. He took another whiff.

And then he heard her voice, low, melodious. And constant. Mechanically, he pushed aside the half gate that separated the reception area from the inner office. He barely nodded at the officer at work at his desk. Paul's attention was on the woman as he walked through. The American.

She was sitting at the captain's desk and, from the expression on Captain Reynolds's lined face, she was charming the regulation boots off the old man. A grandfather three times over, the tall, distinguished Captain Reynolds had a fondness for conversations with pretty young women. Said it kept him forever young.

In a population of just over six hundred, there weren't all that many young, available women to be found in Grateful Bend, Paul mused. He knew firsthand. In one way or another, he had been approached by most of them in his five years here. Loneliness and boredom bred needs like a fire consuming dry grass on the plains of summer.

Except sometimes, he thought, loneliness just bred more of the same, no matter how many people there were around.

Paul was in no hurry to have words over the woman's grievance, so he stayed where he was, studying her animated face as she spoke. It was as if her whole body were engaged in the conversation. There was a wealth of hand gestures going on and a cavalcade of expressions that winked over her face like fireflies flying through the July air. He had never seen so much energy expended in simply speaking. Perhaps she felt she needed that extra touch because she was appealing her ticket.

Appeal would be the word for it. She had that going for her, Paul thought with only a smattering of his customary disinterest. With light blond hair curling about her face like a chrysanthemum just beginning to flower, and eyes the color of the first shoots of spring grass, she was the most appealing-looking woman he had seen in a long time.

But it wouldn't do her any good, not with him or with Reynolds. While the captain might enjoy the platonic company of a lovely woman, he was first and foremost a staunch law-and-order man, and she had broken the law.

The gate creaked behind Paul as it shut, clapping against the back of his legs. The woman at the captain's desk looked in his direction, her green eyes opening wide in momentary surprise. Paul wasn't prepared for the pleased smile that spread over her generous mouth.

Nor was he prepared for his own reaction to it. It was, he thought, like watching the sun come out after a particularly heavy snowstorm. It seemed to almost fill him for a moment, completely mesmerizing him as it generated strangely warm sensations throughout. It wasn't just a smile, it was something more, something that defied description. Something almost tangible that he could swear he actually felt.

And undoubtedly, he thought, shaking off its effects, something that hid a devious mind.

"That's him!" Judy told the captain, amazed at how easy it was to find him. She was afraid that the Mountie had driven off to some faraway corner of the territory after ticketing her and that she would have to wait several days before seeing him again.

Reynolds turned, his deep-set brown eyes glancing over to Paul. He already knew the man Judy had been referring to was Sgt. Paul Monroe from the illegible signature on the ticket.

"How about Corporal Hayes over there?" he said, gesturing across the room.

Paul was just not the right man for what this young woman had in mind. Sgt. Paul Monroe was a very good Royal Canadian Mounted Police officer. The man worked long and hard and was exemplary in every fashion. But there was no getting around the fact that he just wasn't a social creature by any stretch of the imagination. He didn't initiate or even participate in private conversations. It was understood among the men that one didn't invite Monroe to get-togethers and expect him to appear. The invitations were still tendered, but simply for form's sake.

Paul Monroe was a loner in every sense of the word. Although the most dependable of Reynolds's men, when his hours on duty were up and no extra effort was required, Monroe simply went home. To do whatever it was that he did until the next day. Reynolds knew no more about his silent sergeant now than he had the first time the man had stood in front of his desk with his transfer orders in hand. A man's privacy was to be respected in these parts. It went without saying.

Reynolds looked at Judy, waiting for her to reconsider her hasty choice. He fingered the ticket she had handed him. On his desk lay the check she had given him to cover the fine. Why would she want to be in the constant company of a man who had just given her a ticket?

Judy smiled, her eyes lightly skimming over the tall, stern Mountie standing near the front door. "No, I'm sure. I want him."

Want?

The word echoed in Paul's head as he came forward. Was the woman protesting her ticket or ordering a lackey? Just what was going on here?

Captain Reynolds sighed and shook his head. He was sure this woman was going to regret her choice. Although, by the smile on her face, she obviously seemed convinced otherwise.

"Very well." A finely veined, thin hand beckoned Paul forward. "Sergeant Monroe, would you mind coming here?"

"I am here, sir," Paul pointed out quietly.

He stood at attention, though his eyes were on the woman in the chair. Judith Treherne. Her name swam before Paul's mind's eye as it had appeared on the license. From Los Angeles. He raised a brow slightly as he looked in the captain's direction. Maybe she was going to get out of her ticket, after all.

"So you are. At ease, Monroe." Reynolds didn't have to look to know that to Paul at ease was only marginally more relaxed than standing at attention. "Miss—it is miss, isn't it?"

Judy smiled. "Yes, it's miss."

The captain nodded, warming to her smile. "Miss Treherne has a letter from the director of public relations in Ottawa—"

Paul frowned slightly at the title. What did a letter from the director have to do with him? He had never met the man, nor had he the slightest desire to. The only desire that burned within his chest had to do with preserving his solitude.

And, perhaps eventually, atonement.

Reynolds noted Paul's frown and knew that there was going to be a bumpy road ahead. He coughed uncomfortably, his Adam's apple jiggling up and down the long white column of his throat.

"She's doing a book—umm." Reynolds looked at Judy. "Perhaps you would like to finish this for me, Miss Treherne?"

"Judy," she corrected easily.

She slipped into a familiar footing with the man as effortlessly as if she enjoyed being on a first-name basis with the rest of the immediate world, Paul noted with a twinge of annoyance as well as just the slightest bit of foreboding.

"It's really very simple. I've been contracted to take a series of photographs and write up the initial copy for a book my publisher is putting together on the Mount—" Judy stopped, instinct telling her that formality, at least in the beginning, might make getting along with the man a little easier. "On the Royal Canadian Mounted Police." She smiled, hoping to elicit a look in kind from the sergeant. She was disappointed, but undaunted. "A twentieth-century update, if you will, on the romance of the Mountie." She studied his face to see if he would forgive her this shortened, affectionate term. At first glance, he didn't look like a forgiving man.

Paul raised a brow. He thought of the merciless winters. Of the endless days that fed into one another with no change. Of the people who lived and died without ever leaving the area. "What romance?"

Decidedly a toughie, she thought with an inward sigh. "I'm speaking figuratively."

This woman is speaking gibberish, he thought, *if she thinks that any of this has something remotely to do with me.*

Judy pushed on, encouraged in a challenging sort of way by the scowl on the younger Mountie's face. "I would like to follow you around for six weeks—"

He looked at her as if she had just expressed a desire to become his mail-order bride. "No."

The word fairly ricocheted about the wood-paneled room like a trapped sparrow searching for a way out.

For a moment, Judy could only stare at Paul's stony expression. "Oh. Do you have a vacation coming?"

She couldn't think of another reason for such a strongly voiced refusal. So far, everyone she had dealt with regarding this was exceptionally warm, helpful and enthusiastic. She shifted her eyes toward the captain for confirmation.

Reynolds steepled his fingertips as he leaned back in his chair. He was beginning to enjoy this. "Sergeant Monroe doesn't take vacations."

The captain was going to add something to make Judy relent in her quest, but he decided against it. Let them hash this out for themselves. It might prove diverting, and there was precious little entertainment to be had as it was. Normally he would have placed his money on Monroe to win. But there was that letter from the director ordering full cooperation, and that did override any personal preferences that might arise.

Judy was heartened by the information. A man dedicated to his duties. Perfect. "Well, if you don't take vacations and I'm not interrupting any plans, there should be no problem."

She was beginning to set his teeth on edge. "The problem, Miss Treherne," Paul told her sternly, "is that I don't have the time to play nursemaid to an American tourist with a camera."

Reynolds stifled a chuckle as he watched Judy square her shoulders ever so slightly. War had been quietly declared.

Judy wasn't going to take no for an answer. It was now a matter of pride. "You won't be playing nursemaid. It will be as if I'm not there."

Paul's eyes slid over her slowly. There was no way a man could ignore a woman like her. She was trouble. He could smell it. "But you will be."

Judy knew she had only to ask Reynolds to step in and intervene and he would, but she chose for the moment to reckon with this herself. She tapped a short, rounded nail on the envelope on Reynolds's desk, drawing Paul's reluctant attention to it.

"Sergeant Monroe, I do have a letter from the director, asking for full cooperation on this project."

He set his chin stubbornly. "It doesn't name me specifically, does it?"

"No." He had her there, but it wasn't going to make a bit of difference.

"Then I suggest you find yourself another man. What about Hayes, who's just sitting there?" He waved in the man's direction. Hayes looked up, a smile from ear to glasses-rimmed ear. "Or Keller, or—" *Anyone but me.*

Why was he so adamant? Was he just possessive of his privacy, or was there more to the sergeant's story than met the eye?

Intrigued, Judy pressed on. "You are a Royal Canadian Mounted Policeman, aren't you, Sergeant?"

She was playing word games with him. It would be like this the entire time they'd be together. He wasn't going to stand for it. Paul looked toward his superior for help and found only an amused smile. He gritted his teeth together. "Yes."

Judy spread her hands, palms up, in the air. "Then I want you."

His eyes narrowed to small gray slits. It made no sense. "Why?"

The answer was so simple, it could be easily overlooked. "Because you won't try to show off." Judy glanced at Reynolds. "No offense, Captain Reynolds, but I find it much easier to do my work when the subject tends to try to ignore me. It makes the photographs I take look far more natural."

This time, Reynolds did laugh. "I'm sure Sergeant Monroe will ignore you to your complete satisfaction, Miss Treherne. Possibly even more than you will find bearable, given the harsh conditions we find ourselves in."

Subject. The word she had used echoed in Paul's head. She made him sound like something found in a petri dish in a science lab. He wasn't about to allow himself to be treated that way, or saddled with a charge he didn't want.

Paul turned to face Reynolds, completely blocking Judy out. There had to be a way around this. "Captain, with all due respect, I would really rather decline the...honor." The last word was fairly growled.

No, this was something Reynolds wanted to see played through. It would be very, very interesting to see what six weeks was going to bring about. He gave Paul his most fatherly smile.

"Sergeant Monroe, when each of us signed on, we knew that there would be times during the execution of our duties that we would find trying."

Judy could see that Reynolds was doing his best not to laugh.

"And the director—" he nodded toward the envelope "—is quite emphatic in his orders. Since our outpost has been chosen, he would like us to represent the service with honor and present the proper image of the RCMP to the world. And I myself would be curious to see just what Miss—umm, Judy—is capable of doing."

Both with a camera and with a reticent, frozen-hearted Mountie, Reynolds added silently. Monroe was close-mouthed and allowed no trespassers into his life. Reynolds would have been lying if he had said that he wasn't curious to see the effect this very lively woman would have on his stoic sergeant.

"It would be excellent for public relations," Reynolds added.

He rose and placed a hand on Paul's shoulder. They were almost the same height, but it was evident that the younger man filled out his uniform far more solidly. Reynolds had watched Paul silently rebuff the advances of all the young women in Grateful Bend, including his youngest daughter, Diana. The next six weeks should prove to be very interesting, indeed.

"Think of it as serving your fellow officer, Monroe. Judy, I place Sergeant Monroe into your hands. Sergeant," he directed with a tinge of formality, "for the next six weeks, you are to assist Miss Treherne in whatever manner she may request."

Judy stood up, hooking her purse over her shoulder. The strap snagged in the deep-piled fur of her white jacket. She pulled it free, her eyes on Paul.

"Oh, no, I want him to go about his daily routine as if I'm not here." She came around the desk to stand next to the two men. She had the momentary impression of a sapling in the presence of two fully grown trees. "I want a complete record of your life. I want to go where you go, see what you see." Without being fully conscious of it, she had edged out the captain and was standing toe-to-toe with Paul. "In essence, I want to be your shadow."

Paul's eyes locked with hers. "Then you should have been taller."

She could see how this man might be intimidating. But not to her. Judy merely grinned in response, enjoying the conflict. "Maybe I'll stretch as the time goes on." She turned and offered her hand to the captain. He quickly swallowed it up within the cave formed by both his own. "You've been most helpful, Captain."

"My pleasure." And he meant that sincerely. Grant Reynolds had a feeling that he had been present at the start of something unique.

"Now then—" she hiked up her purse strap again "—I'll be needing a place to stay." Judy had always made the best of a given situation. At various times on assignment, that meant having to camp out and use a sleeping bag. It was too cold for that here, but there had to be someplace for her to stay for the next few weeks. "Is there a hotel or a rooming house or..." She let her voice trail off, inviting either man to fill in the answer.

There was no hotel in the real sense of the word, but the woman didn't look like the type to demand luxuries. "There's a boarding house. Hattie's. Sergeant—" Reynolds quirked a brow in Paul's direction "—would you mind taking Judy to Hattie's?"

Paul resigned himself as best he could to the situation. The captain was right. There would always be duties that he would find trying. The only way to handle them was to put up with them and wait them out. If nothing else, he had learned patience in Grateful Bend. At times, there was nothing else but patience to be had.

"Might as well."

Reynolds cleared his throat, obviously embarrassed for Judy, but Judy was unaffected by the stoic response. She was certain she had made the right choice. Besides, Paul Monroe did look dashing, and she had a feeling that the man was positively stunning in his dress uniform. Seeing him in it was something she was going to insist on before she left. It would be the only actually posed photograph. Perhaps it would appear on the cover.

That should send ladies' hearts palpitating, she mused, looking at him appreciatively.

"We'll get along just fine," she promised Paul. He had never doubted anything more in his life. "Thank you again for all your help, Captain."

Reynolds had done little more than stand aside and let her go to work, but he reacted congenially to her words. "If there's anything I can do, don't hesitate to call." He gave Paul a benevolent look. "I'm sure that Sergeant Monroe will represent the RCMP in his customary, flawless manner."

"I'm sure." She turned, ready to leave. "Sergeant, I'm all yours."

Lucky me, Paul thought as he held the front door open for her.

The air outside was still brisk and bracing, but it felt warm in comparison to the look Paul gave her. "Hattie's probably isn't what you're used to."

Think I'm a cream puff, don't you? Judy only smiled, amused. She stopped just outside of the one-story building. "You'd be surprised at what I'm used to, Sergeant Monroe. Compared to having to sleep in the center of the South American jungle, I'm sure Hattie's is a veritable paradise. I do have a problem, though." She paused.

He knew it. She was probably going to ask about cable television or where she could get a manicure, neither of which were available in any manner, shape or form in Grateful Bend. "What is it?"

"Does Hattie's allow dogs?"

"Dogs?" he repeated, surprised.

He was cute when he was confused, she thought. And wouldn't he just love to hear that assessment. "Dogs," she echoed, holding up her hands, limp at the wrist, as if they were paws. "You know, furry creatures—teeth, tail, lovable eyes."

He didn't appreciate being made sport of. "I know what a dog is, Miss Treherne."

"I have one with me. You might have noticed," she reminded him. "In the car," she added, pointing to it at the curb when he looked at her mutely.

Though animals provided needed company for the residents in the area, Paul couldn't see anyone taking a dog along with them while they traveled the way she did. "Why?"

It was an honest enough question, she supposed, though he didn't sound very friendly when he asked. "Because I didn't want to leave him in a kennel, and Jolienne and Andy almost did him in last time."

"Jolienne and Andy?" A nagging headache began to form just behind his left temple. He was right. The woman was trouble. And the trouble so far seemed to be aimed exclusively at him.

He took her by the arm—commandeered her, actually—and escorted her to the end of the sidewalk. She felt as if she were being hustled along. Did he realize that his legs were a lot longer than hers? She did her best to keep up.

"My niece and nephew," she explained.

He nodded, discarding the information as unimportant. "I don't think Hattie allows animals." He pointed toward the three-story building across the street. "I never thought to ask."

The boarding house looked as if it had been standing in that exact same spot since the trees in the forest directly behind it had been just seedlings. A veranda surrounded the building on all sides like faded lace trimming a Victorian lady's dress. A new roof topped it, but the wooden structure was wearing the coat of the scores of winters it had weathered.

Judy had been hoping for something just a little more detached. Something more in the way of a motel, where each individual room had its own entrance. It would have made keeping Raymond with her a lot easier, even if she had to resort to sneaking him in. She chewed on her lip thoughtfully.

"Probably not," she agreed. Judy turned toward Paul suddenly, inspired and hopeful. "Do you have children, Sergeant?"

He kept his expression impassive, though feelings raged inside, stirred by her question. "I'm not married."

Good, so far, she thought. "Do you live by yourself?"

"Yes." The answer came out slowly as he studied her face. What was she up to?

Since no information followed, Judy pushed on. "In an apartment?"

He folded his arms across his chest and looked twice as formidable. "There are no apartments here. I live in a house."

Bingo. She had enough restraint to keep from clapping her hands together, although she felt like it. "Perfect."

Paul's eyes narrowed, pulling curved, dark brows together in a tight, annoyed line that united over the bridge of his straight nose. He knew where she was going with this. "A very *small* house."

She looked toward the car. The dog was busy licking his side of the windshield. "Raymond is small. Very small."

Another name she was tossing at him with the carelessness of someone yanking tissues from a box. "Raymond?"

The corners of her mouth raised in an innocent smile that cautioned him to be wary. "My dog."

That was a ridiculous name for a dog. "Who calls their dog Raymond?"

She knew better than to get defensive over small things, despite the sergeant's disparaging tone. "I do," she said, opening the car door to let the dog out. Raymond barked his gratitude.

Judy held the dog up for Paul's closer inspection. Paul vainly tried to ignore the madly wagging tail and darting tongue. "It was a rhetorical question. It's just that it's a very strange name for a dog that won't be staying with me," he ended staunchly as he turned toward Hattie's again.

If he thought that was the end of the matter, he was sorely mistaken.

"Sergeant, he won't be any trouble at all." Like a coal-burning locomotive, she began building up steam as she progressed. They tramped across the patches of melting snow toward Hattie's. "I can feed him each morning when I come by—"

Paul stopped abruptly. "Why will you be coming by?"

She shifted Raymond to her other side, wishing Paul had given her enough time to attach Raymond's leash. "So that I can be ready to leave when you are."

Was he to have no peace from this woman? The last thing he wanted was to have her underfoot first thing in the morning. "My day starts before sunrise."

She expected as much. "No problem."

Paul tried again. "Way before sunrise."

Judy lifted her shoulders beneath the heavy jacket and let them drop again. "I'm prepared."

He let out a short, annoyed breath. "You might be, but I'm not."

Judy wet her lips. "Paul—"

There were barriers to be maintained. If she was to annoy him for the next six weeks, she would have to follow the rules. "I prefer Sergeant."

Holding Raymond in both arms, she looked at Paul, her expression serious.

"All right, Sergeant, have it your way." For now. "This arrangement is only for about six weeks." She saw a pained expression spread across his face as she said the word *about.* "Then I move on to Montreal. It'll be a lot easier on both of us if you try to get along with me." Her serious expression melted like the first spring thaw during an onslaught of the hot, dry Chinook winds, and she smiled. "I do have a tendency to grow on people."

So did moss, but he didn't much care for that, either. He said the only thing he could. "The captain made it clear to me that he wanted me to cooperate, and I will do exactly that."

Even if it kills you, huh? she wondered.

For now, she accepted his response. There was time enough to turn him into a friend as they went along. "That's all I ask."

No, he thought as he opened the front door to Hattie's for her and waited until she stepped inside, she was asking a great deal more than that. She was asking to invade his space, his sanctuary, for exactly six weeks. There was no *about* about it. He was going to make sure of that. And in the interim, he was going to have to do his best to ignore the intrusion.

Chapter Three

Hattie Matthews had run the local boarding house, the *only* boarding house in Grateful Bend, for the last twenty-six years. Before then, her mother had been behind the small, crudely fashioned desk in the front room that housed an elaborate guest book, which all the boarding-house patrons signed.

For a time, there had been a husband for Hattie to round out the family portrait. Citizens around the area said he arrived one day from Yellowknife and remained long enough to beget three daughters before he got behind the wheel of a four by four and drove himself into a tree. People thought it was a foiled attempt to get away from Hattie. No one really knew if they were legally married. Some said an Indian elder had performed the ceremony. Others claimed it was a passing minister. Most thought that Hattie and Jake had just said a few words and married themselves.

Hattie didn't talk about him very much. As most residents were fond of saying, Jake Matthews was the only thing

Hattie *didn't* talk about. Every other topic was fair and open game as far as she was concerned.

Armed with a near-empty bottle of lemon oil, Hattie had just finished massaging the last of the banister when the front door opened, admitting a cool draft and that evening's topic of conversation around the dinner table.

Hattie's green eyes glowed like june bugs caught in the sunlight as she watched the small, blond woman in the expensive winter wear walk through her door. The fact that the stranger was followed by the strong, silent Sergeant Monroe—who had so patiently ignored her only unmarried daughter, Cynthia—only added fuel to her imagination.

Hattie's curiosity was close to exploding as she eyed the dog the sergeant was carrying. The man held it as if the animal were about to relieve himself on his freshly pressed uniform at any moment.

The older woman would have rubbed her hands together in gleeful anticipation if there hadn't been an oil-soaked cloth in one and the bottle in the other. She left these standing on the small table beside the newly reupholstered love seat and wiped the oil residue from her hands onto her wide, faded apron.

Without thinking, Hattie smacked her lips. Fresh material. "And what is it that I can do for you?" Hattie studied Judy like a hungry terrier watching the butcher carve up a side of beef.

It was cosy in here, Judy thought. Warm and cosy. And full of stories. She could almost hear them. Her mind began to race, framing photographs as she looked around. It was with effort that she pulled her thoughts back to the heavy-set woman in front of her.

"I'd like a room, please."

One hand fisted on her waist, Hattie cocked her head. The bun that she'd haphazardly affixed to the top of her head tilted like a henna-colored Slinky.

"For how long?"

"For the next six weeks."

It wasn't hard to guess at Hattie's thoughts. She had obviously coupled Judy with the sergeant. Her appraisal was all but scathing as she looked at Judy. "Just you?"

"And Raymond," Judy put in hopefully.

Hattie knew the sergeant's first name. She still harbored hopes of being able to address him as Paul when he finally became her son-in-law. More curious by the moment, Hattie rocked forward on her toes, trying to peer through the window and see someone on the street. "Your husband?" Hattie wanted to know.

Judy glanced at the dog Paul was holding. Raymond's expression looked particularly sorrowful. "No, my dog."

Hattie's sharp eyes slid down to Judy's hands as Judy stripped off the fur-lined leather gloves. No ring. Just what the area needed. A single woman for the men to fight over.

Hattie snorted, looking at the dog again. She had no use for any animal that couldn't earn his own keep. For Hattie, that meant only huskies, and this dog wasn't a husky by any stretch of the imagination.

The older woman frowned. "Sorry. You're more than welcome to stay—the dog isn't."

Judy turned to Paul, hope highlighting her eyes.

Oh, no, he wasn't about to be sucked in that easily, Paul thought. His expression was stony, impenetrable. "No."

As if on cue, Raymond began to lick Paul's hand, the long, sloppy tongue all but bathing his fingers.

Judy grinned. "Look, Raymond likes you. You can't just turn your back on him."

He wondered if the dog was her alter ego. "I already told you that I don't have room for a dog."

How small could his cabin be? He had said he didn't live with anyone. "Raymond's small," Judy persisted. "He won't take up much room, Sergeant." She saw no indication that she was winning him over. Her voice picked up momentum. "And he's very well behaved." She petted the dog's head. Raymond licked her hand. "He won't be any trouble at all."

The dog might not, but Paul knew *she* would before the six weeks were up. Hell, she was giving him trouble already, and he had just met her.

"Please, I don't have anywhere else to leave him."

He didn't like having a woman ask him for a favor. It made it difficult to refuse. Paul felt trapped.

His eyes shifted toward Hattie. The woman took out a handkerchief from the deep recesses of her large apron pocket.

"I've got my allergies." Hattie ended the protest by covering her nose and taking a dramatic step back from the dog. The small, sharp eyes darted back and forth between Judy and Paul, like someone seated in the front row of a tennis match.

Paul looked down at the animal he was holding. He had no idea what was preventing him from turning on his heel and walking out—out of the boarding house and away from the problem. Perhaps it was because he didn't have it in him to ignore a plea or a needy animal. He knew Hattie well enough to realize that the older woman would stand by her decision. If she said she wouldn't have the dog staying on the premises, then she wouldn't. That left the perky pain in the neck with a dilemma, and according to the captain, any dilemma of hers was a dilemma of his for the next eternally long six weeks.

He shifted the animal and blew out a long sigh. Paul nudged his hat back on his head with his thumb and studied the friendly dog. She was right. The dog was small. Basically.

He supposed, all things considered, he could bear up to the minor inconvenience. He'd had a dog once. The thought sent bittersweet memories spilling through his mind like marbles on a collision course. His father had given him a husky one year for Christmas. Windwalker, Paul had named him. The dog had been his only source of consolation when his father had died. The following year, his new stepfather had taken the dog away as punishment for the first infraction of the man's rules Paul had committed.

He remembered pleading with his stepfather to keep Windwalker, but to no avail. The dog was sold. Paul hadn't allowed himself to get attached to another animal after that. It was pointless. As were all attachments.

The broad shoulders beneath the blue uniform rose and fell in a careless shrug.

"All right, I suppose I could take him since it's for a short duration." He emphasized the word *short*.

His surliness didn't fool her. Judy had known that Paul would take the dog in. There was something beyond the chiseled exterior and rigid jaw muscles, something in his eyes, that hinted at the real human being who lived within the uniform.

Still, it was better not to appear overly confident. "Thank you, Sergeant. I really appreciate this."

Paul didn't care for the way Hattie was taking all this in, as if she had plunked down her money at a play that was now being performed solely for her pleasure. "I'm sure you do."

"This way, dearie." Hattie beckoned Judy to the guest book and presented her with a pen. She stood watching, unabashedly inquisitive, as Judy wrote her name on the parchmentlike page.

"Judith Tara Treherne," Hattie read aloud, as if she were trying Judy's name on for size. "Los Angeles." Hattie looked up. "California, eh?"

Judy smiled in affirmation.

Hattie turned the book around, skimmed over the neat lettering again, then closed it. She eyed Judy, as if to draw out her innermost secrets. "So, six weeks, you said?"

"Yes, ma'am."

Hattie came around the desk again. It was plain that her curiosity was far from satisfied. "We don't get many people who stay that length of time. They're either just passing through or staying on." She crossed her arms before her wide, ample bosom. "Six weeks seems like an odd time to pick."

Judy was enjoying herself. She knew that Hattie would pick at her until she had what she wanted, like a squirrel trying to crack a nut to get at the meat. "I'm putting together a book."

Hattie's penciled-in brows rose to touch the henna-colored bangs that hung over her eyes. "A book? What kind of book?" Excitement grew within her like rice in a pressure cooker. "About Canada?"

Judy shook her head. Before she had a chance to tell the woman, Hattie had jumped in with another guess. "Small towns?"

Judy looked at Paul and saw his scowl darkening. Here was a man who wanted no recognition whatsoever. She couldn't help wondering why. He didn't strike her as overly modest and he certainly wasn't shy. Just foreboding.

"Mounties," she told Hattie. "Specifically, I'm contrasting the life of a Mountie in a small town in the Northwest Territories with the life of a Mountie in one of the larger cities, like Montreal."

Hattie's mouth fell open. She looked Paul up and down in an exaggerated show of disbelief. "And you're going to use *him?*"

Judy didn't bother to hide her smile. She was certain that if she hadn't been wearing a parka, Paul's frosty glare would have frozen her on the spot. "Yes."

Hattie snorted again as she turned toward the table and picked up her rag. She scooped up the bottle of polish with her other hand. "Honey, you might as well be getting an interview with one of those old-fashioned cigar-store Indians." She chuckled at her own joke and began to amble away.

"Oh, almost forgot." She shifted her cleaning tools to one hand and pulled open the desk drawer. An assortment of keys, all with different tags, lay before her. She handed one to Judy. "This fits the first door on your left at the top of the stairs. Dinner's at seven. Breakfast's at eight. You get your own lunch. Bathroom's down the hall."

With that, she shuffled off to attack an easy chair that was warming itself by the fire. She began to slowly oil and rub the ornately carved arms. She was fooling no one. Both Paul and Judy knew that the woman's complete attention was focused on them and not her task.

But Judy had something more interesting on her mind than an overly nosy woman with a cleaning rag. She looked at Paul, amused as she thought of Hattie's evaluation of the tall Mountie. "So you give everyone the silent treatment. I thought maybe it was just me," she said to Paul.

That would make it personal, and he had long since ceased making anything personal. It was far less complicated that way. "Why should it be just you?"

Judy shrugged. Several possibilities had occurred to her. "Because I'm an American." He looked at her oddly, and she hurried to add, "I thought perhaps you didn't care for Americans." Or blondes with green eyes and cameras around their necks, she added silently.

Nationality had never had anything to do with it. The world, as Paul saw it, was divided into them and him. Beyond that, there was nothing. "Labels don't make much of a difference to me."

Judy heard the floor creaking above them and wondered who she would be sharing the house with besides the venerable Hattie. "An equal-opportunity hermit?" Judy guessed.

He didn't like the way her lips curved when she smiled. There was something all too warming about it. He liked distance. Appreciated distance. And right now, he wished he had some between them. "If I was a hermit, I'd be a lot farther from civilization than I am now."

She pretended to retreat. "Sorry. My mistake."

As if suddenly wanting attention, Raymond began to wag his tail, thumping it against Paul's wrist. There was no reason to continue holding this ridiculous animal, Paul thought irritably. He bent over to set Raymond down on the floor.

Hattie sprang to life like a lioness guarding an injured cub. "Don't put that animal on my nice, clean floor! I just polished it this morning!'' Her squeaky voice rose in an ominous warning.

Paul thrust Raymond into Judy's arms, where the mutt belonged. ''Why don't you get settled in, and I'll see you tomorrow?'' He ended his suggestion by turning away and walking toward the door.

Three strides had Paul halfway across the room and to his goal. He wasn't destined to reach it alone. Judy moved faster and caught up quickly, still holding the infernal dog in her arms.

''I've got a better idea,'' Judy said pleasantly. ''Why don't I follow you to your house so I can find out where you live?'' Because her hands were full of dog, she indicated the stairs with a nod. ''I can always settle in later.''

''I'm not going to be able to get rid of you, am I?''

Judy's delight was evident in her laugh. She shook her head in answer to his question. ''For the next six weeks, Sergeant, I'm going to be sticking to you like glue.''

He only sighed as he opened the door and walked out onto the veranda. He held the door open for her and waited until she passed through with her burden. She set the dog down immediately, and Raymond's tail went into double time.

Protests and pleas to her common sense, Paul felt certain, would be to no avail. This was a woman who did as she pleased. And it was for damn sure that whatever she did do, it wasn't going to please him. He headed for his vehicle.

Paul's gait didn't allow for the fact that he had about ten inches on her leg-wise. Judy had to hustle to keep up. She thought of it as exercise. ''One more thing.''

He wondered how many times he was going to hear that in the next six weeks. ''Yes?''

''Since we are going to be together for the next six weeks, don't you think I should call you Paul?''

Paul stopped and looked down at her just as she caught up. He took his time with the answer. ''No.''

Nothing ventured, nothing gained. ''Well, at least you're honest,'' she acknowledged, undaunted.

Paul had resumed walking and glanced over his shoulder at her comment. He wondered if she was always this annoyingly cheerful. It threatened to set his teeth on edge. A few more hours in her company and he'd probably tell her that. "That's not a trait you might find favorable."

"I admire honesty, Sergeant," she said seriously. She caught up again and began walking next to him. "I'll let you know when I don't."

He had no doubt of that. The way he saw it, for the next six weeks she was going to make his life a living hell, letting him know about *everything* that crossed her mind. As if she thought he needed to know.

Paul's house was on the edge of the wilderness. She knew it would be. A log cabin that looked as if time had forgotten it, leaving it in place for the last hundred years or so. It was humble and picturesque and very, very isolated, as if daring nature to do something about its being there.

It suited him.

She drove up right behind him and pulled up her hand brake, but remained in the car.

Paul got out of his vehicle. The air felt pregnant with another snowfall. Perhaps it would come soon and make Judy change her mind about all this.

He felt like a man walking his last mile. Except he was walking it alone. She was still in her car. Had she had a change of heart already? He doubted it. Paul turned and looked expectantly over his shoulder in her direction. "Well, what are you waiting for?"

That was when he saw it. Her camera. Its wide-angle lens was aimed right at him. Before he could utter a word of protest, she had snapped three frames through the window. Paul strode toward her like a man whose territory had been senselessly violated. His hand on the camera, he pulled it down until it rested in her lap.

"Just what the hell do you think you're doing?" His eyes were dark and fierce. They gave her pause. But she knew if she didn't stand up to him now, she might as well turn around and go home.

"My job."

The absolute gall of her intrusion stunned Paul so that for a moment, he couldn't find the words. "My house." He bit off the retort.

She didn't understand what he was driving at. "Yes, I know." She tried to raise her camera again, but he kept his hand on it. The camera remained where it was, immobile in her lap.

"No, I don't think you do. My house," he repeated with all the territorial pride that united beggars and kings. "My privacy." His eyes pinned her in place, daring her to voice any sort of protest. "I don't want it invaded for some over-size book that's going to collect dust on coffee tables around the country, no matter what words you used to con the RCMP director or the captain."

Now she was angry. Just because he didn't like her being here was no reason to denigrate either her or her work. "I didn't con. I requested." Paul continued to look at her, unconvinced. "Strongly," she allowed after a beat. Her eyes held his. "You're pressing the camera into my thighs. I'd rather not be permanently dented there."

He released the camera. Judy got out of her car. The camera remained around her neck.

Paul was already walking away from her. Talk about pigheaded. She tried to hurry after him, but the snow on the ground made it difficult. Unlike the tiny town, here no one had even attempted to clear off a path.

She caught up to him and laid a hand on his arm. "I don't see the problem."

He spared her one impersonal look. He expected as much. "No, you wouldn't."

Because she could never remain angry for more than a few minutes at a time, her passion cooled. "So explain it to me," she coaxed.

It was so simple, he had no idea how she could be oblivious to it. He inserted his key, but didn't turn the knob. "I don't want my privacy invaded."

She nodded. "Your space."

It sounded trivialized on her tongue. But it was all he had left. "My house, my life. It's bad enough you're invading my work."

He still didn't understand, did he? She shook her head. "No, Sergeant, not just your work. *All* of you is the subject."

No way, no how. His eyes said as much as the words burned in his brain. "We need some rules."

Judy looked up at him, unintimidated, her smile engaging. She held up her right hand, her eyes teasing him. "I promise not to take pictures of you coming out of the shower."

There was something about the way her mouth curved, something that got in the way of his anger. But he held on to it as his only defense. "Has anyone ever tried to strangle you?"

"No."

He couldn't be the only one she'd ever irritated to distraction. "Odd." Paul turned the knob and opened the door. But then he stepped in the doorway and barred Judy's entrance. "The lens cap stays on."

It was too cold to stand out there and argue. For now, Judy let the matter drop. He wasn't going to be an easy subject, but then, if she had wanted easy subjects, she would have set up a studio and photographed weddings. The photographs she was going to capture of Sgt. Paul Monroe would mean that much more to her because of the effort involved once she got them.

Judy held her hands up, fingertips pointing toward the clouded sky. "Look, no hands."

No mouth would be something to celebrate, he thought as he turned and walked inside.

The living room was small and Spartan. Its focal point was the flagstone fireplace. A single chair was set in front of it. She looked slowly around. There were absolutely no homey touches. No photograph on the mantel, nothing over it. No identifying marks anywhere, and that branded it even more than a score of scattered knickknacks would.

Paul Monroe was hiding something or someone. Possibly himself, Judy thought, turning slowly toward him. "Your space doesn't look lived-in."

He could have sworn he detected a trace of sympathy or pity in her voice. He wanted neither. "Now you're an interior decorator as well?"

"No," she said easily. "An observer."

Judy moved slowly around the room, making herself more at home in three minutes than he had in five years. She could see an even tinier kitchen off to the left. The bedroom had to be just beyond that, she guessed. "There're no photographs here." It was more of a question than a statement.

He should have found a way to dissuade her from coming inside. He didn't like being scrutinized, and that was exactly what she was doing. "I don't like clutter."

It was lonely in this house, not because of what wasn't here, but because of what was. She suddenly shivered, turning to look at him. "How about memories? Don't you like them?"

"No." He hoped that was the end of her twenty questions. But he had a feeling that there would never be an end.

"What *do* you like, Sergeant?"

He gave subtlety another try. "Peace and quiet," his voice rumbled out.

She glanced at the walls again. People made their own prisons, she mused. She wondered if this cabin was his. "Doesn't it ever get too quiet for you?"

Yes, it did. In the middle of the night, when the memories would jump up at him out of darkened corners. And with them, the pain. But she had no business knowing any of that. "No, it doesn't."

Judy ran her hands up and down her arms. It was cold in this cabin. Colder than the weather warranted. Raymond nudged her with his nose, reminding her that she wasn't alone. It helped. "It would for me."

A brass band was probably too quiet for her. "No doubt."

She heard the censure in his voice and could only laugh. Did he realize how dour he sounded? She couldn't believe that he was really like that, not down deep. "I like peace and quiet," she admitted. "But I like noise, too. I guess that makes me eclectic."

He watched the dog sniff around as if marking off his space. He was under siege, pure and simple, Paul thought. "That's your word for it."

She had humor on her side, and optimism, but sometimes it was best to attack the heart of the problem quickly. "Why don't you like me, Sergeant?"

Though he was direct, he didn't like being placed on the spot. "I don't even know you."

"That's just my point." She placed her hand on his chest as if to anchor him in place. "You seem to have prejudged me before I even opened my mouth."

He raised a brow, but refrained from removing her hand, although he didn't like her touching him. It felt far more personal than he wanted to be with this woman. He preferred physical contact with people to be maintained at a minimum. And she had exceeded her minimum within an hour.

"That would have hardly seemed humanly possible," he said dryly. "I don't think that fast."

She surprised him by laughing and appearing delighted at his comment rather than being insulted. She kept her hand where it was a moment longer. He felt solid, like a statue of a hero.

"It won't be nearly as bad as you think, Sergeant. I promise not to rattle any of your cages or open up any closets. I don't like skeletons."

She meant it as a joke to lessen the tension that was humming between them. The sudden sharp look in his eyes told her that she had struck a nerve. Somehow, she had rattled a cage already without meaning to.

Bordering just a little on self-consciousness, Judy let her hand drop.

For now, it was business. Later she could satisfy her curiosity about this man. "And this will be a lot easier if we try to get along." She said "we," but they both knew she meant "you." Judy put out her hand. "I'm willing—" she looked up at him "—how about you?"

Grudgingly, he took her hand in his, knowing that to do anything less would be classified as unreasonable. And although he didn't feel the least bit like being reasonable about having his privacy invaded, he had no choice in the matter.

That bothered him most of all, not having a choice.

But then, he hadn't done all that well with the choices he had made in life, Paul thought cynically. The distant memory pricked at his conscience like the edge of a sharp splinter. It was having her here that did it, he thought, looking at Judy. She made him remember.

Judy smiled as her fingers curled within his, gripping his hand firmly. He had a strong hand, she thought. A capable hand. The kind of hand a woman could depend on. She wondered vaguely if it could be gentle, as well. She had her thoughts on that matter.

"There, that wasn't so bad, was it?"

He broke contact, pulling his hand from hers as if he had touched an ember. "That all depends."

"On what?" God, but he had beautiful, expressive eyes, she thought. Blue eyes that seemed to change color with his thoughts, from indigo to midnight in less than a moment. She was going to love taking his photograph, filling her camera's eye with his face.

She could envision him in his red dress uniform, and her heart did an involuntary backward flip. She wondered how long it would take her to talk him into it.

"On what comes after," Paul told her.

That part was easy. "Only me, Sergeant. Only me."

And that, Paul thought, was exactly what he was afraid of.

Chapter Four

He had all but ushered her physically out the door after she had given him some cursory instructions regarding the dog's feeding. Judy absolutely refused to be put off by Paul's manner. If he thought she was going to fade back and disappear just because he was putting his worst foot forward, he would be sorely disappointed.

Judy turned to face him as soon as she was outside his cabin. "Well, now that I know where you live, I don't expect to have any trouble finding you in the morning."

One could always hope, Paul thought. He glanced back at the dog. The animal had settled down for a nap. If Paul was lucky, the dog would stay right where he was until evening.

Paul merely grunted in response to her words. Eventually, he reasoned, her incessant cheeriness was going to have to dissolve, like a soap bubble reaching the end of its life expectancy.

He hoped it would be soon.

Judy smiled to herself. If grunts could be interpreted, she had the distinct feeling this one would not translate in her favor. Still, she was completely confident that Sgt. Paul Monroe would come around in time. Judy had never met anyone who hadn't been transformed into a friend by the time she moved on. Life was hard enough as it was. It was her firm belief that it could be far more easily endured with a feeling of well-being and friendship permeating each day.

Paul looked like a man in itchy underwear who wanted nothing more than to escape and change. "So, where do we go first?"

He pulled the cabin door closed behind him and locked it, then dropped the key into his pocket. "I'm going to continue on my rounds." He said each word slowly, as if it were a building block in the wall he was constructing between them.

"Perfect."

Not so perfect. He nodded toward her car. "Why don't you settle in at Hattie's first?"

She would have been disappointed if he hadn't said that. She was beginning to second-guess him. "You keep suggesting that."

Paul had no idea what to make of the amusement in her face. "Maybe it's because you haven't done it yet," he pointed out.

Judy paused and rolled the thought over in her head for a second. She was going to need background shots, and there was no disputing the fact that Grateful Bend was picturesque with or without the good sergeant looming at her side. All right, she'd give him a little leeway. Maybe he deserved it.

But she couldn't resist some good-natured teasing. "Need a little time to get used to the idea of having me around?" She caught her lower lip between her teeth as she looked at him.

Paul sincerely doubted that there was enough time available before Armageddon, no matter how far off into the future that was. And if it bought him some time, he was willing to give her the truth, even if it wasn't all that flattering to either one of them. "Yes."

Judy nodded. You didn't break the shell of a hard-boiled egg by smashing it against the wall. You removed it with care.

To Paul's surprise, she put out her hand. When he took it warily, like a man trying to decide how best to pick up a live lobster, she shook it firmly and grinned. "Done. I'll be by in the morning. Is seven all right?"

He wouldn't go so far as to say that. It wasn't all right at all. But he had no choice. "Seven'll do."

His inference was not lost on Judy. She maintained a straight face as she offered, "I can be here earlier if you like."

What he'd have liked was for her not to be here at all. Then he could just go about doing what he had been doing for the last five years. Patrolling in peace. He knew if he acted indifferent to her suggestion, the woman would be here at two in the morning.

"No, seven'll be fine."

Judy opened her car door, then stopped. "Don't forget, his name's Raymond." She saw impatience create creases along his chiseled face. She knew by his blank stare that he'd forgotten.

"Whose name?"

"My dog's." She gestured toward the cabin. "He'll only come if you call him by name. Raymond," she repeated clearly, raising her voice. She doubted that he was actually paying attention to her. He had a rather vague, faraway look in his eyes.

Paul shrugged at the information. "That's all right, I won't be calling him."

Judy pretended she didn't hear him. He might not be a dog person, but she had a feeling that he wouldn't really neglect the animal. He just didn't seem to want to let anyone know that he could care about anything. Again, she couldn't help wondering why. People weren't born apathetic and withdrawn. Something made them that way.

Finding out was going to be as challenging as putting together the book she was commissioned to create.

She continued as if he hadn't said a word. "And Raymond likes to be scratched at night just before he falls asleep."

"Don't we all?" The sarcastic remark had risen to his lips without thought.

Undaunted, Judy grinned as she seated herself behind the wheel of the four by four. "Do you like to be scratched, Sergeant?"

He had every intention of just getting into his car and pulling away. Instead, he strode over to hers. "I don't have any itches." He said it emphatically, lest she get any wrong ideas.

Oh, I don't know about that, Sergeant. There was something in his eyes, a glimmer of a need that contradicted his words. "Lucky you."

"If I was really lucky," Paul said, emphasizing each word, "I would have drawn Featherman's assignment in the Yukon."

She had no idea who Featherman was, but she did know that she had made the right choice in selecting Paul. It was up to her to make him feel that way, as well. "Cheer up, Sergeant. You might even get to like this."

He spared one dark look at her camera, the ultimate voyeur, intruding into people's lives and secrets. The hell he would. "When caribou fly."

She nodded, accepting his assessment as if it were an event that would take place next week, instead of never. "Very picturesque. See you tomorrow."

Paul sighed resignedly as he stepped away from her vehicle. As he watched, the woman's car disappeared down the barely visible road.

Paul let out a sigh of relief. He wondered what the chances were of Hattie's getting snowed in by the morning. The only snowplow in the area was now lying in several dismembered, intimidating heaps on Humphrey's garage floor. He'd seen it there the other day. Humphrey worked on it in his spare time. To the mechanic it was like a giant jigsaw puzzle that could only be worked on for so long before his patience ran out. Bets in town were going that Humphrey'd have the plow reassembled by early summer.

Judy's smile was still intact as she brought the four by four to a stop before the boarding house. She had no reason *not* to be cheerful. True, the noble sergeant was going to be a challenge. But it wasn't anything that she didn't feel she was up to.

It might even be fun, finding the right buttons to push in order to bring him back among the living. At the moment, she had the distinct impression that he was just going through the motions of being alive because it was only a slightly better option than the alternative. There had to be more to life than that, and she was going to show him.

She had sworn to herself, since the day she walked out of the hospital on her own power, that she wasn't going to do anything that wasn't fun. Life was too precious and too short to do otherwise. She was going to enjoy making the sergeant aware that life could be fun if only he got the right slant on it. That's all it was. Like the difference between a good photograph and a bad one, it was all a matter of perspective.

Judy stretched her legs as she got out of the car. Turning, she became aware of a willowy young girl standing on the veranda. She had pine-needle-straight blond hair that hung down past the waist of her light green parka, and she was watching Judy. There was the unmistakable air of uncertainty mingled with excitement about her.

The girl bit her lower lip, as if undecided about whether or not to say something to Judy.

Judy ended the girl's indecision by addressing her first. "Hi." She waved. "I'm Judy Treherne."

The girl on the veranda hooked her fingers together before her as if, so linked, they provided a source of support for her.

"Yes, I know. I'm Cynthia Matthews, Hattie's daughter," she added quickly, as if her mother's name gave her the right to be standing here, talking to Judy.

Cynthia looked hesitantly at the four by four, working her lower lip again.

Judy turned and looked at it herself. She didn't see anything amiss. "Something wrong?"

Cynthia took a deep, fortifying breath. Judy guessed that she was about eighteen or nineteen. A shaky age at times, she recalled.

"Ma doesn't like people leaving their vehicles in front of the house," Cynthia blurted out in a rush. "Says it's tacky." She waited, as if wanting to see if her words would make Judy angry.

The vehicle looked about as well kept as the house, but Judy knew better than to argue with the natives. "Can't have that."

More important than where she parked was who she encountered. Judy wanted to do nothing that would affront any of the inhabitants. All of them, Hattie and Cynthia included, were possible subjects to be captured in her camera's eye.

Still, she didn't want to leave the car out overnight, subjected to the elements. She believed in taking care of things, even if they weren't her own. "Do you have a garage?"

Cynthia nodded. She wrapped her long fingers around the post as she leaned forward. "But it's full. Mr. Evans and Mr. Simpson have their cars in it. And there's Ma's old Jeep. That takes up an awful lot of space."

She had no doubts. Judy looked at Cynthia hopefully. "Any suggestions?"

Cynthia thought a minute. "You could try Humphrey."

Was that the name of a person or a store? "Humphrey?"

Cynthia nodded vigorously. "He has a place just down the road a ways. He's a mechanic." Cynthia suddenly came down the steps quickly, eagerness lighting the pale, thin features of her face like a candle. Judy decided that she had to look like her father. There was nothing of Hattie about the girl. "I could show you."

That sounded good to Judy. "All right. Why don't I get my things out of the back and then you can show me where Humphrey's shop is."

Cynthia was beside her. She reminded Judy of a colt that hadn't quite figured out how to coordinate all four legs at the same time yet.

"It's not a shop, exactly," she warned Judy. "It's really an old barn with a sign out front. But you could keep your car in it," she added quickly, afraid that Judy would change her mind and perhaps leave town altogether. They were so hopelessly out-of-date here.

A barn was as good as a shop, as long as it was closed off from the elements, she thought. "Whatever it takes."

Judy took out the suitcase with her camera accessories first. The rest of her things, chemicals and developing equipment, were being shipped and would get here within a few days. The suitcase contained the very basics, without which she couldn't function.

Cynthia's long, thin hands were reaching for the suitcase before Judy had a chance to set it down. Judy smiled her thanks, then took out the case with her clothing in it.

Cynthia peered into the interior of the car, her eager expression fading. She had envisioned the latest fashions coming into her life through this woman. She looked at Judy. "Is that all?"

Judy slammed the door with her hip. "I travel light." She indicated the case Cynthia was holding. "This is mostly camera equipment."

Cynthia's disappointment mounted, but she struggled not to let it show. She was far from successful. Her disdain for the area shone through even more clearly. "Why do you wanna take pictures here for?"

The girl was too close to it to see, Judy thought. "Because it's beautiful."

The pale brows drew together as Cynthia looked around. She saw nothing but patches of melting snow and the dirt beneath. It was the same thing she always saw. "Grateful Bend?"

Judy laughed at the unabashed surprise in the girl's voice. "It's picturesque." She had used that word a lot today, Judy thought, but there was no better way to describe the area.

Cynthia frowned. Picturesque was New York, Los Angeles, New Orleans. Grateful Bend was none of those and never would be. "It's boring." She pouted as she walked up the stairs in front of Judy. "I can't wait to get out of here."

Judy heard the futility and the yearning in Cynthia's voice. It all but vibrated like a freshly struck tuning fork. "Oh? Where are you going?"

The warm air inside of Hattie's felt like the caress of a welcoming friend along her face. Judy's cold cheeks stung as Cynthia closed the door behind them.

Cynthia shrugged. She hadn't made up her mind yet. "Someplace bigger."

She looked about ripe to fly out of the nest, Judy mused. "When?"

That hadn't been decided on, either. But Cynthia had her dreams. "I dunno. Someday. When I save enough." She grinned ruefully. "Or marry my way out."

Judy followed the girl up the stairs that led from the front room to the second floor. Hattie was nowhere in sight, but Judy could smell the lemon polish. The older woman had been around recently.

Inserting the key into the first door on her left, Judy turned to look at the tall girl. "Marriage seems a rather drastic step to take just to get out of town."

Cynthia set Judy's suitcase down gingerly inside the door with all the reverence of someone handling the crown jewels.

"I don't want to die here, Ms. Treherne." Her young face took on a glow as her mind raced to places she had only visited vicariously through books and dreams. Cynthia wrapped her arms around herself, as if to seal the feelings in. "I want to see something big, something important." She looked directly at Judy. "I want to meet people."

At the zenith of her optimism, Judy doubted if she had ever been that young, that innocent. She left her suitcase on the big brass bed that dominated the room. It looked like a holdover from the last century. Judy hoped that the mattress wasn't.

"People are just people, Cynthia, no matter where they are. They're just a little ruder sometimes in the bigger cities." She thought of her last stay in Los Angeles. It had ceased feeling like home. "They're so busy running around, they tend to forget what life's about."

Cynthia's expression told Judy that she was utterly unconvinced. "It's gotta be better than this."

Judy compassionately slipped an arm around Cynthia's narrow shoulders. The girl would learn things soon enough. Happiness only grew in fertile soil it found within, not without. "The grass is never, ever greener on the other side, Cynthia. It just looks that way."

Cynthia stuck out her lower lip in a pout. "We don't even have grass here for most of the year."

Judy laughed. Maybe the best cure for Cynthia would be a stay in the city. Who knew, she might be completely suited to it. And if not, there was always the boarding house to return to.

"C'mon—" Judy nodded toward the door "—take me to Humphrey's."

Humphrey's was exactly what Cynthia had led her to believe it was. A converted barn suffering from slight disrepair. Like an aging mistress, it was badly in the need of a new coat of paint. Judy's camera was out and working practically before she pulled up the hand brake on the four by four.

Cynthia slipped out of the car with more agility than enthusiasm. She worked her lower lip as she tried to see what it was that Judy saw here. She failed to understand what could possibly warrant any attention at all, much less half a dozen photographs. She tugged at the end of her hair and looked at Judy quizzically. "Why d'you want to take a picture of this place for? It's just an old barn." She spat the word out as if it were one of the cardinal sins.

Judy capped her lens and slung the camera strap over her shoulder. "I like old barns. They remind me of home."

The pale brows knitted together and rose. "Ma told me you lived in Hollywood."

"Your mother misunderstood. I wrote down Los Angeles."

"There's a difference?" Cynthia had envisioned movie stars on every corner and glamour spilling out of every home.

"A big one. But I'm not from Los Angeles originally. I was born twenty miles outside of Eugene, Oregon." Even as she said it, a fond smile curved Judy's mouth. "My family still lives back there. My dad and brothers run a dairy farm."

"Oh." A dairy farm? A little of the stardust that Cynthia had immediately attached to Judy floated to the ground.

Judy could almost read the girl's thoughts and smiled to herself. A great deal more than ten years separated them, she thought.

A tall, rubbery-faced giant in stained, faded bib overalls appeared at the entrance just at the moment that Judy raised her hand to knock. He was working something round beneath his large hands, rubbing a dirty rag over it methodically as if he were wiping away grime from a lump of gold. Hair not quite rust colored, not quite brown, fell into his eyes like untended grass that hadn't been mowed in too long a time.

After a moment, tiny, close-set eyes looked down at the women. Recognition flickered through them as they passed over Cynthia, and then they came to rest on Judy.

She was being sized up, Judy thought. She withstood it with good humor. He had the right; she was doing the same with him.

The overalled giant nodded at her vehicle, still working his rag. "Car not running?"

"Oh, it's just fine," Judy said quickly, afraid that he might start taking it apart before she could stop him. She saw the scattered innards of the snowplow on the floor just inside the door. She had no wish for her car's parts to be mingled with the snowplow's. "Cynthia tells me I might be able to park my vehicle here at night."

"Might." The large melon head bobbed up and down once. "For a fee."

Judy adopted the giant's curt tone. "Reasonable?"

Humphrey hesitated for a moment, trying to decide whether the small blond woman was making sport of him. There were those in town who did because of his lumbering size. They thought just because he was slow-footed, he was slow-witted as well.

The genial smile on her lips that accompanied the single word made up Humphrey's mind for him. His wide cheeks rose like the jowls of a basset hound and he smiled back. "As the day is long."

Judy turned toward Cynthia. "What month are we in, Cynthia?"

"It's the end of April." Cynthia looked at Judy, wondering if the woman in the expensively tooled boots was serious. How could you lose track of the months?

Judy winked at Humphrey. "Well, considering that the days are extra long here, that sounds like a good deal to me."

She put out her hand. Humphrey scrubbed his own quickly with the rag. He took her hand and shook it as if it were a fragile vase that would shatter when it came in contact with his big paw.

"My name's Judy Treherne, and I'll be staying in Grateful Bend for the next six weeks. I'm going to need a place to leave my vehicle overnight for that length of time. Will that work out?"

He'd see to it that it would. Humphrey looked over his shoulder. The parts of the dismembered snowplow were taking up a large portion of the floor. Beyond were several cars he was working on. But if he reshuffled some things, there was room available in the back. "I think I can squeeze it in."

Another problem solved. "Perfect." She handed him the car keys and wrote out a check against future boarding charges.

Yeah, Humphrey thought, slipping the check into his pocket without looking at it. His eyes followed the sway of her hips as she walked away with Cynthia. *Perfect.* That was the word.

Paul almost tripped over the damned mutt when he let himself in that evening. The day had been overly long. There had been a nasty dispute at the Indian reservation that he'd had to mediate before blows were exchanged.

Relieved to be alone, exhausted, Paul had completely forgotten that he had a four-legged housemate staying with him and had walked into the animal in the dark. Biting off a curse, Paul turned on the light. The dog raised his head from his front paws and looked at Paul with eyes that danced with eagerness and hope. Raymond's long tongue lolled out of the side of his mouth as he scrambled to feet he had never quite grown into.

The bark of greeting ended in a whimper as the animal circled Paul and sniffed him over.

"Sorry, she's not here," Paul told the dog as he unzipped his jacket.

And wasn't he grateful for that small boon? he thought as he laid his jacket across the back of the sofa. He began to coax a fire in the hearth. There had been a moment this afternoon when he thought she was going to accompany him on his rounds right then and there.

He leaned back on his heels as the fire took, spreading orange fingers out to nudge awake friends to come join in the revelry. Paul knew he couldn't avoid the assignment indefinitely, that it was going to be breathing down his neck possibly as soon as tomorrow, but he wanted to keep it at bay for as long as possible.

Keep *her* at bay as long as possible.

He didn't like people in his space. He had gotten used to the fact that solitude was his only companion and he liked it that way. He wouldn't have transferred here from Montreal if he couldn't have put up with it. Now he was saddled with a pint-size blond shadow who made noises as if she had jumped straight out of a Cracker Jack box. And if that wasn't bad enough, he had her dog as a roommate.

Paul rose and leaned the poker against the wall. The dog had slipped up next to him as silently as a cloud. He stood now, eyeing Paul expectantly. "I suppose you're hungry."

Raymond pricked up his ears as if in assent. The tail wagged, thumping on the floor.

Dogs were always hungry, Paul thought. Windwalker had been. Dumb dog would have burst if he'd been allowed to eat as much as he wanted to. "Well, you'll have table scraps and like it. I don't have anything fancy like dog food to feed you."

Paul walked into his kitchen. Raymond trotted after him, his clumsy paws gliding along the unpolished floor. Every third step, one of the dog's nails clicked against the wood.

"You know," Paul said, looking down at the dog, "if she cares so much about you, she should have left a supply of food for you." Paul made a mental note to discuss the matter with Judy. He wasn't about to feed her dog as well as play nursemaid to her. A man had his limits.

And his limits had been reached a long time ago, Paul thought. Involuntarily, he remembered the framed miniature of his father on the wall.

A long time ago.

Paul shook off the memory. He took a steak out of the refrigerator and threw it into the pan that perpetually remained on the stove. Raymond sat back on his haunches, patiently waiting for his meal.

Paul picked up a fork and turned the steak. The meat sizzled, and the dog whimpered like a panhandler begging for food.

"This one's for me," he informed the dog.

Raymond didn't move a muscle.

Flame high, he turned the steak again. He liked his meat rare and his company nonexistent. Things just weren't working out to his liking.

He could feel the dog's eyes on his every move. If he dropped the steak, Paul doubted the meat would even hit the floor. The dog looked lazy, but he had a feeling the animal was fast when he wanted to be. "You know, there's a lot of your mistress in you."

Raymond chose that moment to bark.

Paul compromised and gave the dog half the steak. Raymond ate it and then watched Paul consume the other half. Paul did his best to ignore the huge brown eyes. The dog remained close by as Paul washed his dish and put it away, as if he were hoping that scraps would materialize from somewhere.

When Paul dropped into his easy chair, Raymond settled in at his feet.

For a moment, man and dog sat in harmony, listening to the fire crackle and the wind mournfully serenade a world drifting toward sleep. But within minutes, the silence was broken by whimpers.

"Now what?" Paul asked irritably.

Raymond merely looked at him, his long, pointed snout slightly raised. With a sigh, Paul remembered Judy's parting words. Reaching out, he scratched the dog under the chin, and Raymond settled back down, content.

It was going to be a hell of a long six weeks, Paul told himself.

Chapter Five

Paul bolted upright in the dark room. The sound of his own heavy breathing ricocheted around the bare walls like a muted cry of terror. The fur-lined blanket pooled at his waist. It was cold, but he was sweating profusely. His thin cotton T-shirt adhered to his body as if it had been glued on.

He was shaking.

It took Paul several moments to clear his head, to make the soothing emptiness return. And several more moments to steady his breathing. His heart was pounding against his rib cage as if he had just gone the distance in a ten-thousand-meter run.

Paul scrubbed his face with his hands and drew a long breath. It had happened again. Five years, and the dream still kept recurring. Not as frequently as before, thank God, but just as graphically. It still haunted the recesses of his mind, receding just long enough to taunt him with the hope that it was finally gone—only to reappear in horrifying colors.

The same, always the same. Just as it had happened.
Every minute detail. The traffic, the gunfire, the deflected
bullet...

And the blood.

The shudder traveled through him involuntarily. The
memory of that day was too fresh, too startlingly vivid, to
shrug away. Paul caught his breath and jumped when he saw
a pair of eyes staring at him in the doorway.

Her dog.

Paul fell back against the headboard, the air whooshing
out of him as Raymond bounced onto the bed. The dog
placed a paw on Paul's chest as if in silent comfort. Before
Paul could duck, the animal's long tongue had darted out
and christened him on his nose and both cheeks.

"Damn dog!" Paul wiped his face and moved the animal aside. It took more effort than he'd expected. Raymond remained on the bed, watching him uncertainly.

He must have been yelling in his sleep, and the animal had
heard him, Paul guessed. Judy had probably indoctrinated
the animal in an intensified course of cheerfulness.

Judy!

Today was to be their first full day together. What time
was it? He grabbed his watch on the nightstand. Vision still
blurry, he struggled to make out the numbers. Six-thirty. He
might as well get up. He was too wide-awake to try to get
back to sleep. Besides, he had to be up in half an hour, anyway.

Raymond jumped off the bed as Paul swung his legs over
the side. The floor was frigid beneath his bare feet. The
thought hardly had time to register when he heard a knock
on his front door.

"Who the hell..."

Paul looked at the dog, and then he knew. It was her. His
own private albatross. Effervescence mixed with an obses-
sion to be early. How the hell had he ever gotten so lucky?

Still closing the pants he had hastily pulled on, Paul made
his way to the door. It seemed as if Raymond were dancing

from paw to paw as he followed less than half a step behind Paul.

"Well, at least one of us is glad to see her," Paul muttered, dragging his hand through his dampened hair.

She'd accomplished one thing, he realized grudgingly. The threat of her presence had obliterated the last traces of his dream.

Paul opened the front door, and Judy rushed in, along with more than a small flurry of snow. Behind her, daylight had already gotten a firm toehold on the day, trying to spread its fingers through a stubbornly gray, cloud-filled sky.

"It's snowing," Judy announced.

She stomped twice just inside the door, getting rid of the layer of snow she had accumulated on the soles of her boots in the short walk from the four by four to his door. Lucky for her, Humphrey slept in a room at the back of his shop. She had roused him apologetically, afraid that if she waited, she might be snowed in and suffer a setback.

Judy pushed her hood from around her face. It didn't feel that much warmer in the cabin than it did outside. Snowflakes floated from her bangs and clothes with every movement she made.

There was snow on her hair and eyelashes. She looked almost eerily ethereal, Paul thought before he roused himself. "You came early just to tell me that?"

She shook her head. More snowflakes loosened their hold and drifted to the floor. "No, I was afraid that if it snowed any more, I might not be able to drive over."

God forbid.

She could tell by the look on his face that he mourned the loss of that opportunity. She purposely kept her eyes on his face, though she had to admit she found the rest of him distractingly attractive. He was brawnier than she had thought when she saw him in his uniform and heavy jacket yesterday. The man had all the qualifications to be a model, including immobility.

"Or that you might have to leave early to do whatever it is that you do in an emergency situation. So I thought I'd get here early and spare us both a hassle."

The two halves of her statement didn't agree, but he knew it was an exercise in futility to point it out. He did, however, need to have something cleared up. "What emergency?"

"Being snowed in."

She was a hopeless tenderfoot. "Snow is a way of life here. It takes a lot of it before anyone considers it an emergency."

He ran a hand over his face and realized that he hadn't shaved yet. There were more important things to be taken care of than talking to this woman, even if she did look like something from a midwinter night's fantasy.

He opened his mouth to say something about coffee, but Judy suddenly dropped to her knees right in front of him. The dog barked a zealous greeting. In return she buried her face in his coat, hugging the animal as if she had been separated from him for fourteen months instead of fourteen hours.

The woman was putting a new spin on enthusiasm, Paul thought, shaking his head as he watched. She didn't seem to mind having her face washed by a dog, he noted.

Raymond knocked Judy over in his excitement. Still holding on to the dog, she fell backward, then rocked forward on her heels.

"Yes, I missed you, too, boy." She rubbed her hands all along his fur, then looked up at Paul. "Was Raymond any trouble?"

Paul shrugged. He remembered sitting by the fire last night with the dog next to him. Though he wouldn't admit it to her, a part of him had enjoyed that. "No more than I expected."

Judy rose to her feet, brushing her hands on the thighs of her jeans. Paul tried not to notice. She looked up at him. "Is that a yes or a no?"

Things were going to have to start moving if he planned to complete his rounds. The weather threatened to be a definite hindrance today. "Want some coffee?"

He was avoiding answering her question. She tried to read between the lines and guessed that meant he had enjoyed the dog's company, but was just too stubborn to admit it.

Hattie had already forced two cups of coffee on her this morning, as well as a full breakfast, all in an attempt to keep her talking. But a little more couldn't hurt. "Well, yes, that would be nice."

He nodded. "Good." Paul turned and started toward his bedroom. "Then you can make some while I shower."

Judy unzipped her parka and tossed it onto a sagging sofa that was obviously a hand-me-down and had just as obviously seen better days.

"Do the Mounties have anything like an annual Mr. Congeniality award?" she called after him.

Paul stopped just short of the doorway and turned around to look at her, his eyes narrowing. Now what was she talking about? "No, why?"

"Just wondering," she answered innocently. Rather than ask, Judy began to poke around the small, utilitarian kitchen. There weren't that many places he could hide the coffee.

He didn't want her searching around unnecessarily. She was undoubtedly going to be doing more than her share of probing as it was.

"Coffee can's in the refrigerator. Pot's on the stove." With that, he walked into the bedroom and closed the door behind him.

Judy stood for a moment and stared at the closed door, then shook her head. "The man needs a lesson in using full sentences, not to mention finding a better disposition." Raymond yipped his agreement, and Judy laughed. "Okay, let's get coffee for two rolling."

As the coffee brewed on the stove, making its slow descent through the drip pot like prisoners dropping into an escape tunnel, Judy opened his cupboard, looking for cups.

He couldn't have handled any more company than her, she thought, looking in. There were only two coffee mugs in the cupboard. Taking one in each hand, Judy thought of her own cupboard in her apartment in Los Angeles. It was filled to overflowing with glasses and dishware. Space, though her cupboard was three times as large as his, was at a premium. Here there was nothing *but* space. The cupboard almost looked mournful. She counted three plates, two bowls, two mugs and a couple of glasses.

The dishware looked lonely, she thought as she closed the cupboard, like wallflowers at a party, waiting to be asked to dance.

The thin stream of dark brown liquid had just ceased its sporadic tap dance on the bottom of the tin pot when Paul walked into the kitchen.

She turned just as he came up behind her. "Don't do much entertaining, do you?"

Why was every other sentence out of her mouth a question? And why didn't she look out of place standing there by his stove? Why did she look as if she were meant to be there? It both annoyed and mystified him. She didn't belong here in any sense of the word, and yet she seemed to. Even her pale golden blond hair seemed to light up the room. It was like a flare sent into his dark life.

He didn't want any flares.

Paul found himself drawing closer completely against his will. "Why?" he asked her suspiciously.

She nodded toward the cupboard. "You don't have much in there. It seems so stark, as if you think you're always going to be by yourself."

"With luck," he told her meaningfully. His eyes flickered over her. Six weeks, he thought. Six endless weeks. The loneliness hadn't driven him crazy in five years. He had a feeling she was going to do it inside of the first week. "Can't you do anything without asking questions?"

She let the accusation roll off her back. "Sorry. Habit."

She lifted the coffeepot from the stove and began to pour. The liquid was dark and looked thick enough to cut with a knife. She had a feeling that was the way he took it. The light overhead skimmed along the top of the mug, unable to penetrate.

"The coffee's ready." She handed him a mug. "I couldn't find any sugar or milk."

She couldn't find very much of anything. The man didn't even have a cache of candy bars or anything sweet. She was beginning to believe that perhaps he wasn't human, after all.

He sampled the brew and discovered to his surprise that if nothing else, she knew how to make coffee. "Don't use any."

Judy wrapped her hands around the mug, appreciating the warmth that telegraphed itself through her fingertips. The kind of warmth, she mused, she'd feel touching him. Lack of snacks not withstanding, she'd bet her 600 mm telephoto lens that there was a passionate man under that supposedly dead exterior.

"That would explain the sweet disposition."

Paul set his mug down with a thump that had Raymond looking up and coffee staining the plastic tablecloth.

"Look, I think this is all a mistake." He held his hands before him as if to ward off any trace of her. "Why don't you talk to Captain Reynolds and have someone else assigned to this—this—"

He couldn't find a word that would begin to explain how stupid he thought all this was. The RCMP didn't need an updated view of their lives. They weren't cardboard good-will ambassadors, they were a peacekeeping force.

And right now, peace was the farthest thing from this room.

Unlike Paul, Judy knew very well what word he was searching for. "No matter how stupid you might think this assignment to be, I think it'll do a lot of good."

"For whom?" he challenged.

Her eyes held his, probing, perhaps even seeing things he wanted to keep hidden. "You, me, everyone. It never hurts to have people respect you."

She studied Paul closely, wondering what it was that he was hiding. Was there some dreaded secret he was harboring, or was it just that he had no tolerance for anything? In either case, she was certain she could help, at least a little. It would be easier if he let her, but there was something to be said about a challenge.

He thought of his stepfather and his own demands on himself. "No, but it might if they expect more than you can give."

Judy set down her mug. "Did someone?"

"Did someone what?"

"Expect too much of you?"

He looked away. How had that even come out? "I was speaking figuratively."

"I see."

And she did, damn her. At least a glimmer. He could tell by the way she was looking at him that she knew he wasn't speaking figuratively. That he had had a momentary slip. He waited for her to pounce, like a wolf on a fallen caribou.

When she didn't, he almost felt indebted to her. "Not bad," he said grudgingly, raising his mug slightly. The coffee was hot and, more importantly, it was strong.

"Thanks." As Paul watched, she rose from the table and crossed to the pantry. "What do you want to eat?"

Paul indicated the mug in his hands. "This'll do fine."

Judy frowned slightly, unconvinced. She remained where she was, one hand on the narrow pantry door. "I read that you need a big breakfast out here." The elements were harsh and unforgiving, the article had said. It was best to be well fortified. The coffee she'd made was good enough to see a desk jockey through to morning break, but not anywhere near substantial enough for a man who would be miles from any sort of a store when hunger finally hit.

Something akin to amusement flickered over his broad, solemn face before it sobered again. "Don't believe everything that you read."

She opened the pantry, anyway. She had already looked in there while he was getting ready, but thought perhaps she'd missed something. "Got any English muffins?"

Now she thought he was operating a restaurant. Paul set the empty mug down. "No." He tried not to watch the way her jeans strained against her rump as she bent over to search the back of the shelf. It swayed slightly as she shifted a couple of things aside. He glared down into his mug. "Didn't you eat before coming here?"

No luck. She straightened with a sigh. "Yes, but Raymond didn't."

Paul looked over his shoulder at the dog. "He eats muffins?"

As if he knew he was the subject of the discussion, Raymond trotted over to his mistress. She petted the animal affectionately. "He's crazy about them."

Somehow, it figured. "He'll have to make do with bread."

"Bread it is." Closing the pantry door, she moved toward the counter and flipped open a battered bread box that was also a gift from the captain's wife.

Judy moved about his kitchen as if she had been doing this every morning for the last five years. It stirred something vague and nebulous within him that he didn't want disturbed. Or tampered with.

And he didn't like it.

"Make yourself right at home, don't you?" He rose and put his mug in the sink.

"Occupational hazard." Judy took the mug and turned the water on, intent on rinsing it out.

Paul caught her wrist, stopping her. She was taking too many liberties here. They stood for a moment, toe-to-toe, he defending his territory, she encroaching on it.

"I travel around so much, I've learned to relax no matter where I am," Judy continued.

He released her wrist, not quite sure what had come over him, or what had just happened in that short moment of contact. "Does that include taking over?"

She shook the mug out and placed it upside down on the small counter. "No, just sharing." She took out two pieces of bread. Raymond was on his hind legs, ready. Judy glanced at Paul, waiting. "If it's all right with you."

He needed distance. But to move aside now would be declaring a victory in her favor. He stayed where he was, eyeing her as if she were a dread Chinook about to whistle through his cabin. "I think you already know the answer to that one."

She tossed one slice to Raymond, and the dog caught it in midflight, devouring it within two bites. But her attention and her eyes were on Paul. "Why do you see me as such a threat?"

To admit that would be to give her too much power over him. "Not a threat. An invader." Because looking at her right now caused longings to rise on top of annoyance, he looked at the dog instead. "To use terms you might understand, I like my own space."

She tossed a second piece of bread toward the dog. "Everyone likes their own space once in a while. Not everyone makes a religion of it."

The word rankled. "Religion has nothing to do with it." He said it so vehemently that she could almost feel the pain he was trying so hard to bury and deny.

No, religion and he no longer moved in the same circles. He saw no use in it. He had prayed five years ago, while standing in that dingy hospital corridor that smelled of disinfectant and despair. Prayed long and hard. And she'd still died. So young, and she had died. Died because of him. If he closed his eyes, Paul could still hear the cries, the accusations.

The wound was so raw, Judy retreated. She didn't know enough about Paul to help, to say the right words. She promised herself to talk to the captain the first opportunity she had. She had questions Paul wasn't going to answer. Questions she needed the answers to.

She turned toward the cupboard and tried to change the subject. "I need to give Raymond some water. Can I use this bowl?" She held it aloft.

Embarrassed at losing control over the tight rein he usually maintained over his thoughts and emotions, he waved away her question and nodded.

Judy had nothing against the sounds of silence. She liked to listen to the wind rummage through the leaves, to birds bickering over breakfast. On occasion to nothing in particular. But this silence that followed in the wake of what he had just said made her feel edgy somehow, as if words had been vacuumed out by a heavy-duty machine.

She placed the filled bowl of water in front of the dog. Maybe she wouldn't wait for the captain. "Why'd you become a Mountie?"

More questions. He busied himself by checking the safety on his service revolver. "I thought you were just supposed to take pictures."

"Yes, but there's going to be an accompanying text. Nothing extensive, just enough to fill the gaps between the photos." As she watched, Raymond made short work of the water in the bowl. She bent down to remove it. "Someone else is going to write it, but I supply the information."

She paused. Paul wasn't saying anything in response. Why didn't that surprise her? "You haven't answered my question." Judy turned on the water and let it run over the bowl. "Why did you—"

"I just did!" The words were curt, telling her to back off.

But if she hadn't been so tenacious, she'd still be lying on her back in her parents' house, unable to walk. Judy persisted.

"Everyone has a reason for doing things. Was someone you admired a Mountie?" She wiped the bowl dry and placed it back in the cupboard. "Was it the red coat? Did you fall in love with Jeanette MacDonald as a kid? Or—"

There was no way to shut her off, was there? She'd keep hammering away until he gave an answer that would satisfy her. "My father was a Mountie."

Judy's mouth dropped again. Headway! The man had feelings, after all. She scratched Raymond's head absently as she smiled. "I guess he's pretty proud of you."

Paul's expression turned rigid, as if the very bones in his face had instantly petrified right before her eyes. "I doubt it."

There was something about the way he said it, something dark and foreboding. And hurting. She studied him for a moment, waiting for him to elaborate. He didn't. She knew him well enough by now to know he didn't want her to ask. But she had to. "Why?"

"He's dead." Paul's voice was flatter than the mideastern plains.

"Oh, I'm sorry." Judy touched his arm, sympathy conveyed through her very fingertips. Paul shrugged her and her apology away as he picked up his heavy jacket. He couldn't deal with sympathy. It would tear open all the old wounds—feelings he hadn't been able to handle then, feelings he couldn't handle now.

Without a word, he opened the refrigerator and took out the provisions he had prepared last night as systematically as clockwork.

Judy grabbed her own jacket and signaled for Raymond to heel. She fell into step right behind Paul as he walked toward the front door. "Why here?"

Paul swung around so quickly, they almost collided. The woman just didn't give up, did she? "To get away from nosy, talkative women."

She let him have the shot and smiled sympathetically. "Didn't work out, did it?"

She looked far more amused than insulted. Paul wondered if she was just too stupid to understand or too kind to deal with.

Unable to deal with her, Paul walked out. The snow flurries hadn't abated, but they hadn't intensified, either. Nature was in a holding pattern. As, apparently, was she.

"Really, why here?" Judy asked, zipping up her jacket. "It's so desolate. Did you want to get back to nature? Or was it because of a woman?"

He looked at her sharply then, as if she had stumbled onto something he didn't want touched. But then the alerted look faded so quickly, she wondered if she had just imagined it. "You ask too many questions."

Judy sighed, pulling out her gloves. "So you already said."

She supposed she was pushing too hard too fast. It was all part of her "now" philosophy. Having come so close to first death and then permanent disability, she believed in living life now, this minute. She didn't hold with putting things off until tomorrow. Paul Monroe obviously did. For the time being, she'd let him. With luck, there'd be time enough to get her answers later. And what he wouldn't fill her in on, perhaps the captain would.

As they stood outside the cabin, the wind suddenly picked up. Gusting, it took the freshest layer of snow on a swirling dance along the ground in front of them, dusting their boots as it went.

Judy lifted her hood and tied the strings under her chin. "This looks like husky weather." She looked around hopefully.

She obviously had a romanticized picture of life here. "We don't use huskies anymore." He began to walk to the rear of the cabin. "That stopped in '69."

Judy felt a prick of disappointment. She shaded her eyes and looked out. White. Nothing but white. It was hard to believe that it was spring and that somewhere in Southern California, people were modeling bathing suits. "This looks pretty rough for a jeep."

He didn't bother to turn around. "I don't use a jeep in this weather."

He was being difficult on purpose. "Are you going to tell me what you do use, or do I have to go through all the types of vehicles I know?"

She would, too, he thought. "That might be time-consuming. We use snowmobiles." He unlocked the pad-lock, but left it there as her next words had him turning around to look at her.

"Built for two and a half?"

His eyes narrowed as he looked down at the dog. He didn't even want *her* along, much less the dog. "It'll be crammed."

She wondered if he always looked on the down side and what it would take to change that for him. "Think of it as cozy."

He drew himself up. There was no doubt about it, Judy thought, the man cast a formidable shadow. "I really don't think—" he began.

Time to get serious. "Sergeant, I backed away from pushing yesterday because I thought you deserved some breathing space to get used to the idea of having me along." She saw his frown. The glimmer of a smile she'd seen only once had her wondering what his face would look like when he was completely relaxed, completely happy. It became her goal to find out.

"Or as used to it as you can get. But I do have deadlines, and I do have to get started. Now," she continued pa-tiently, "like it or not, accompanying you on your rounds is a vital part of that. It'll go a lot more smoothly for both of us if you don't keep fighting me as if I were a rabbit gnawing away at your cabbage patch."

He had a sudden image of that and he almost smiled. Almost, but not quite. "I can see why you're taking pictures instead of writing the text."

"I'll work on it," she promised.

With a shrug of surrender, he took off the padlock and opened the double doors. The modern piece of machinery looked incongruous, housed within the wooden shack. The latter appeared as if it had been standing since the Mount-ies had come into the Northwest Territories more than a century ago.

He knew it was futile, but he had to try one last time. "Are you sure you don't want to wait until the weather's more receptive?"

She slowly shook her head from side to side. "That'll happen a lot sooner than *your* being receptive, but what if it snows for the next six weeks?" Out here, it was a distinct possibility.

He pushed the doors open all the way. "Then my prayers will have been answered."

"I thought you didn't believe in religion," she reminded him innocently.

She was an impossible woman, he thought, but he had known that from the moment he first saw her yesterday. "Does the dog have to come along?"

"It would be inhumane to leave him alone every day until the assignment's completed."

"It's also inhumane to torture a Royal Canadian Mounted Policeman."

She grinned. "I have no intentions of torturing you, Sergeant."

"Famous last words."

He backed the snowmobile out. Then, at the last moment, he decided to park her vehicle in the shed to forestall any sort of delay with her leaving tonight. No sense in taking any unnecessary chances.

Paul climbed into the cabin of the snowmobile, tossed his lunch in the back on the rack and turned the engine on. "Get in."

She picked Raymond up. "I thought you'd never ask."

Holding the dog in her arms, with the camera dangling at her side and more equipment housed in the case whose strap hung from her neck, Judy wedged herself in.

She was right, he thought. Even loaded down, she didn't take up much room. She seemed to fit very well in the space to his right. Perhaps a little too well.

Judy felt exhilarated. The excitement of a brand-new assignment hummed through her body. She turned her face up to his. It was framed by the fur along her hood. "Where to first?"

He turned and dug out something from the tiny space behind him—a plaid fur-lined woolen blanket. He dropped it on her lap, partially covering the dog. She raised an inquisitive brow that he found sexy even as he dismissed the thought.

"You get cold, sitting immobile and exposed," he said gruffly. He placed his hands on the wheel. "We're going to an Inuit settlement."

The blanket was entirely on her side. "How about you?" He didn't bother asking her what she was talking about. He knew he'd find out soon enough. Probably sooner than he wanted to.

"Don't you get cold?" Even as she asked, Judy slid half the blanket over his legs. "Or don't superheroes get cold?"

He looked at her sharply. He didn't want to be romanticized or glorified. He had thought of it that way once and had discovered differently. This was just a job. Until now, a satisfying one, or as satisfying as anything was for him.

"Is that your angle on this?" he demanded. "Making the Mountie out to be a superhero?"

He sounded as if he were offended. Did he think she was ridiculing him? "No, but you're acting like one, circa 1940." When he looked at her, utterly confused, she added, "Completely stony."

He put the snowmobile into Drive and looked ahead. "We all have our calling in life."

Chapter Six

He tried to ignore her.

It was like trying to ignore the weather, though. It couldn't be done. The weather wouldn't let him and neither would she.

Nestled there next to him, sharing a blanket, sharing a space, it was hard to think of anything else *but* her. With her wide-eyed appreciation of absolutely everything, she filled not only the space beside him, but she was beginning to seep in and fill the spaces within him, as well.

Or, at least, to remind him that there were spaces that needed filling.

Though he thought of her as an irritant, Paul couldn't help being aware of her as a woman, as well. A very stirring, beautiful woman. Beautiful not in the dazzling way that a sunrise was considered beautiful, but more like the quiet, warming beauty of the first hopeful signs of spring.

For a second, as Paul glanced at her, he could almost make himself believe that she could be his spring. But the next moment brought reality and his past to mind. It wiped the nonsensical thought away, erasing it like so many letters written in the sand and blown apart by the wind.

For him there would be no spring, only the harshness of winter. He had adjusted to that.

As she spoke, it became clear that they saw things from incredibly different perspectives. It hardly surprised him. For Paul, the territory that spread before them as they drove by was a giant, savage wilderness, unforgiving of any mistakes. There were no second chances to be had out here. One miscalculation and a man could easily freeze to death, become a victim of the elements or the animals that roamed here.

Judy saw it as an enormous canvas, painted with leviathan, vivid strokes. She reveled in everything she saw and told him so. More times than he wanted to hear.

To Paul, she was a hopelessly idealistic woman without a single shred of common sense or any concept of reality. And yet...

Yet there was something about her that attracted him, something he couldn't quite shake himself free of.

But he would.

Twice she had made him stop the snowmobile because she thought she saw an animal in the distance running across the barely passable road they were traveling on. It was a moose the first time. And Paul could have sworn she had all but squealed and grabbed his arm when she saw the black bear. Raymond had been sitting on her lap, lazily watching the scenery. He came to life at the sound of her squeal and began barking at the bear, protecting his mistress while safely housed against her and the warm blanket.

She was too busy framing the bear in photo after photo to notice Raymond's bravado. As Paul watched, he could see the joy that possessed her as she immersed herself in her work. It was as if she and her camera, with its bulky telephoto lens, were one, communing with her subject. Without fully realizing it, Paul envied her that feeling.

She half rose in the snowmobile, throwing her dog off-balance as she leaned forward for yet one more shot before the black bear disappeared into the brush. Raymond yipped his protest at being treated so cavalierly. Judy sank back in her seat, feeling very gratified.

She looked at Paul and saw that he was watching her. She flushed with pleasure. "He's beautiful."

Now, there was a word he'd never heard applied to a black bear. He'd been right. The woman lived in a fairy-tale world where animals performed on cue and there was no waste, no cruelty, and the creatures didn't smell.

Paul frowned at her. "He's deadly. One swipe of that paw can rip you wide open."

He was talking to her as if she were a half-wit, Judy thought. "I wanted to take his photograph, not dance with him."

Paul shook his head, but said nothing. Talking would only encourage her, and he needed some respite.

Not talking, he discovered several minutes later as they drove toward the Inuit settlement, seemed to accomplish the same thing. The woman talked to fill the silence—not incessantly, just enough to cut into it and remind him that try as he might, he couldn't shut her out or pretend he was alone.

Her words hung about him as surely as the icicles hung from the roofs of the small, modern homes that were just over the next hill.

Subscribing to the theory that if she volunteered some information about herself, it would be easier for Paul to share his own background with her, Judy decided to give him a capsule version of her life. She didn't want to spend the next six weeks traveling side by side with him and remain strangers. If nothing else, it made her feel too uncomfortable. Besides, she intended to make a friend out of him even if she had to drag him into the relationship kicking and screaming.

Paul Monroe, she had decided, desperately needed a friend, and she was volunteering for the position.

Judy shifted in her seat. Her legs were beginning to fall asleep. She moved Raymond over to the side as much as possible. "I come from a large family. I'm the oldest, and I've got two brothers and two sisters. How about you?"

He wished she'd stop wiggling around like that. Though there were several layers of clothing between them, having her move that way, brushing against his thigh, had an almost erotic effect on him. Maybe he wasn't as invulnerable to the normal foibles of man as he'd believed, Paul thought with an inward start.

He forced himself to concentrate on negotiating the road.

"How about me *what?*" He parroted the phrase, hoping that she would grow sick of having to pry things from him and stop asking questions.

The scenery whizzed by them like a colossal panorama. Judy stroked Raymond's head as she absorbed the surroundings like a thirsty ink blotter. "Do you come from a big family?" Judy asked patiently.

"No," he bit off.

Maybe that was why he was so stoic, she thought. He'd grown up an only child, completely divorced from the riotous lessons of give-and-take that were inevitably involved in growing up with loving, competitive siblings. She thought of her own, and her smile was instantaneous.

"My family thought they knew me inside out. They were absolutely speechless when I decided to give up my teaching position and try my hand at being a photojournalist. They knew I loved taking photographs, but they thought of it as just a hobby, not a way of life."

He didn't doubt they'd been speechless. She probably never gave any of them a chance to talk.

Judy paused, waiting for him to comment. When he didn't, she asked the question that had occurred to her in tandem with her own revelation. "How does your family feel about you being out here?"

He could feel a fist clenching within his stomach. "They don't."

"They don't?" Judy echoed, not comprehending. "Don't what?"

She watched in fascination as the line in his jaw became rigid. "Don't feel."

She grew silent for a moment, searching for his meaning. "You mentioned that your father passed away. Is your mother—" Judy never got a chance to finish.

"No, they just don't feel."

In any event, not about him. His stepfather was a stern martinet of a man who believed that a show of affection was a show of weakness. Frank Stockard had done his best to discipline the spirit right out of Paul. Life at home had grown worse as his mother slowly turned away from him in her need to try to garner her new husband's approval. The lines of loyalty had been drawn, and she chose her husband over her headstrong son, never realizing how she had hurt Paul. Paul couldn't really fault his mother. She had done what she needed to in order to survive. She just didn't fathom that she had sacrificed him to do it.

"My mother remarried. We don't even exchange Christmas cards, all right?"

Again, she saw the slight flicker of pain in his eyes. For the most part, he kept them dark, flat, but he wasn't completely successful at hiding his emotions. Perhaps since he hadn't dealt with them in so long, she thought, they were threatening to escape.

She hadn't slipped her gloves back on after taking the photographs of the black bear. She laid a hand over Paul's, a fingertip gliding along the exposed space between the cuff of his jacket and his glove. He could almost physically *feel* her sympathy.

"Why are you out here, Sergeant?" She wanted to call him by his first name, but they hadn't crossed that boundary yet. Maybe soon.

"Because it's what I do and what I am." He let out an impatient breath as he took a sharp curve. "You could talk the antlers off a moose, do you know that?"

If they were going to trade barbs, she had one for him. She delivered it with a smile. "With you as a conversationalist, the moose's antlers would just fall asleep."

If possible, his expression grew stonier. "Sorry if I'm boring you, but being a stunning conversationalist was not one of the prerequisites for becoming an RCMP."

She'd meant to tease, not offend. "You're putting words into my mouth."

He let out a short laugh. "That hardly seems necessary."

When she laughed, it seemed to echo from the very trees. "I'm not bored. I'm intrigued." She looked at him meaningfully. "More than a little."

Intrigued meant wanting to probe deeper. She'd already gotten more information out of him than he had wanted to give, more than he had given to his commanding officer. "You'd better mean that about the scenery."

"Or?" She was smiling, but her eyes were challenging him.

"I don't take well to probing." There was a warning in his voice.

That didn't exactly come as a news bulletin. "Well, so far, you've been dodging very well."

Judy absently looked to the left as they were driving by a lake. The snow flurries had ceased and the sun shone along a thin veneer of ice that still covered the water. But more important was what was on the banks of the lake.

"Oh, wait. Stop, stop." Judy tugged on his arm for emphasis.

"Now what?"

Paul looked around, attempting to see what had caught her attention this time. There were five small Inuit children, between the ages of five and seven, playing in the snow before the lake. He recognized two of them. Judy was out of the snowmobile before he had time to properly park it.

They were wonderful, she thought. Their bright, berry-colored faces presented a collection of innocent smiles of abandonment as they played. Children were her most prized subjects. She loved the hope she found shining in their eyes. It always managed to intensify and reinforce her own.

"Aren't they adorable?" Judy called over her shoulder to Paul without really bothering to look in his direction. She began snapping pictures as Raymond announced his presence with a bark.

The children froze, staring at the camera in her hands. At the enormous round lens attached to it.

"No, go on," she urged. "Play." She waved her hand at them, moving it around as she tried to indicate to them what she wanted.

Raymond took that as a direct command and went running into their midst. The children forgot to be shy. Giggles filled the air like bees in July.

She sensed Paul behind her as she went on capturing their play. "Are they Eskimos?"

"Inuits," Paul corrected her. "That's what they call themselves. It means 'the Only People.'" His mouth moved in a sad smile. It was a wishful description at best with the modern world crowding in, threatening to overtake them and swallow them up. But they were holding their own, trying to assimilate and fit in as best they could. "The word *Eskimo* was the Indians' name for them. It means 'eaters of raw meat.'"

It didn't conjure up a very appetizing image. She lowered her camera for a moment. "Not very flattering."

He watched the two children he recognized vie for the dog's attention. They didn't have much to be happy about, he mused. And yet, they were. He admired the resiliency that existed here, admired it even if he couldn't understand it. "Labels usually aren't."

Judy looked over her shoulder, wondering if he meant anything more by his comment than just a casual observance. A sudden, high-pitched shriek had her attention swinging around a hundred and eighty degrees to the children by the lake.

The smallest of the group, a chubby little boy in a navy parka that was at least one size too large for him, had wandered out onto the lake. Ice began cracking in a drunken, zigzag pattern beneath his feet. It radiated out like a star burst.

"Sergeant!" Judy's heart all but stopped as her lungs filled with terror.

"I see him!" Even as he said it, the ice cracked further beneath the child and a yawning gap opened under one foot. The boy screamed again.

Paul wasted no time hurrying to the snowmobile. There was a long rope packed in the vehicle along with his first-aid kit. Climbing in, Paul drove the snowmobile as close to the edge of the lake as he safely could. The remaining children scattered to either side of the oncoming machine.

As he pulled the brake up, Paul looked up and froze. Judy's camera was abandoned on the snow. She was on the ice, dashing toward the terrified child.

Paul thought he was seeing things. "Get back, you idiot!" he called after her. Didn't she realize she could go plunging through the ice at any second?

The admonishment was too late. The next moment, the child was gone, his weight breaking through the remaining ice under his feet like a rock through a window. He disappeared into the frigid waters below.

No more than five feet away, Judy hurled herself forward, making a frantic grab for the child's parka. The ice cracked in half beneath her feet and then there was nothing to stand on. Judy tumbled into the lake.

"Goddamn it!" Paul swallowed a lustier curse.

Impotent frustration raced through him. He leapt out of the vehicle. His fingers felt thick as they got in each other's way. Cursing, he tied one end of the rope to the bumper of the snowmobile.

"Judy!" he yelled, willing her out of the hole as he squinted against the hazy sun. His adrenaline was pumping through him so hard, it threatened to explode out of his veins. Of all the boneheaded, stupid things to do! Why hadn't she stayed put?

The next moment, the pale gold head bobbed up. Coughing, spitting out water, Judy held the whimpering child against her.

"I'm okay," she cried, too dazed to appreciate the entire impact of what was happening. "Just get us out of here."

"You shouldn't be there in the first place," he shouted angrily. The woman was certifiable. She shouldn't be allowed out.

Paul coiled the rope in his hand. The four other children clustered around him now, fear and excitement making them jump from foot to foot as they eagerly waited for the next part of the drama to unfold.

"I'm going to throw the rope to you!" he called. "You've got to get it securely around your shoulders and chest!"

She would have nodded in acknowledgment if she could have, but every part of her was growing oddly numb. She had the strange sensation of fire and ice playing over her body simultaneously.

"Hurry, Sergeant, hurry." With effort, she raised her hand above her head. She clutched the child to her with her other hand, struggling to hang on to him.

The oldest of the children hesitated a moment, then broke away from the others. Pockmarking the snow with her flying feet, she ran for the houses just behind the hill for help.

His eyes trained on Judy and the child, Paul formed a lasso. Telling himself to go slow, he twirled the rope several times over his head, working up what he hoped was sufficient momentum. When he threw, he missed his mark by half a foot. The rope fell limply into the water.

Cursing under his breath, Paul quickly pulled the rope in. He was competing with time. The longer she was in the water, the greater the risk of hypothermia. It didn't take long—ten, fifteen minutes at most.

When he threw a second time, the rope sailed over Judy like a huge, wavering hoop, then tightened as he pulled on it.

Paul let go of the breath he'd been holding. He actually felt it leaving his chest, as if someone had inserted a pin into it. So far, so good.

"All right, now hang on!" he commanded. Patton delivering an order to his troops couldn't have sounded sterner.

Never taking his eyes off her, Paul jumped into the snowmobile and put it into Reverse. He moved away from the lake as quickly as he dared. Any faster and Judy and the child could be lacerated by the jagged ice.

Judy's lungs felt as if they were bursting. She hung on to the rope with one hand, the other around the crying child. She was vaguely aware of the sensation of being dragged along through water that felt almost solid. Like a wall that was breaking up before her, the ice was cracking apart as soon as she hit it.

She thought she felt it cutting her skin, but she couldn't tell. She was too cold, too numb. The only thing she was acutely aware of was that she couldn't let go of the child.

It felt as if it were taking forever to reach the edge of the lake. Eternity traveling in slow motion. The whole ordeal had lasted less than five minutes. Finally she felt snow against her face. Gasping, she struggled upright.

The perimeter of the lake had filled with men and women from the community just beyond the water. Words from another language crisscrossed with English, melting and re-forming into a noisy din. Someone was prying the child from Judy's arms, and she realized that she was still clutching him against her despite the fact that they were on land. She had to mentally force her hand to release its hold.

And then there were hands, lots of hands. Touching her, patting her, removing the rope. Someone was roughly stripping away her parka and pulling off her boots. Before she could protest the loss, a heavy fur blanket was being thrown over her, then tucked around. Her limbs were being slowly massaged to restore circulation.

When she could focus, she looked up into very angry blue eyes. "Did you lose your mind?"

The voice of concern, she thought wearily, wanting nothing more than to lie down now that the boy was safe.

"No, and I hope I didn't lose my camera." She vaguely remembered dropping it just before she dashed out.

His anger radiated through his fingertips as he methodically rubbed her legs. Any faster might be dangerous.

"What possessed you to run out like that? Did you want a close-up?" She had scared him half to death when she'd disappeared beneath the ice. He'd thought she was dead.

A stiffness was setting in her body and with it, an ache in her arms. That was good, wasn't it? Judy wondered.

"I didn't know if he could swim. I thought that he'd go under at any minute and I just—reacted." She had no other words, no other defense for what she had done. There hadn't been time to think it through.

Paul said nothing. Still squatting next to Judy, he looked up at the woman closest to him. "I need dry clothes for her."

The young woman nodded. "This way," she urged, turning toward the settlement.

Paul picked Judy up into his arms. "I can walk," she told him feebly. But she wasn't completely sure if that was true at the moment. Now that the danger was over and reality had hit, all her limbs felt shaky.

He shifted her so that she rested against his chest. He wanted to pass some of his own body heat to her. She felt so cold. "I know that. The question is, can you keep quiet for a few minutes?"

Judy said nothing. Momentarily drained, she was content just to sink back in his arms.

He could have strangled her, he thought as he followed the young woman to her home. He looked down at Judy. Of all the stupid, idiotic—damn selfless things he'd ever seen, she took the prize.

She wanted to protest that she was too heavy for him, but it felt so good to just rest a moment, so good to be here like this in his arms. She had the sensation of being safe. Protected. She could almost believe that he wasn't the gruff, stern officer of the law he pretended to be.

All too soon, she realized that they had crossed a threshold and were entering a house. A regular house, she thought, looking around. It could have been a house transplanted from the town where she had grown up. She was aware of the sting of disappointment.

Paul set Judy down on the dark, floral sofa and tucked the blanket securely around her. Despite the possible gravity of the situation, Paul was acutely aware of his hands skirting the outline of her body.

He moved back, a shaft of reluctance shooting through him. She hadn't felt all that heavy in his arms. And there was something else. Something small and intangible that had been sparked by all the emotion that had just careened through him.

Something he didn't want to deal with. Something he didn't know *how* to deal with.

Pushing all feelings aside, he noted the confused expression on her face. "You were expecting igloos?" he asked.

The question wasn't harshly put, which surprised her. Maybe she had won him over, after all. Judy was trying her best not to shake, but it wasn't working. She was being affected by more than just her cold, wet clothing. Perhaps realization was setting in. It *had* been a dangerous thing to do. But standing off to the side, just watching, would have been worse.

The young woman who had led them here disappeared soundlessly into the other room.

"No," Judy answered, looking at the delicate wallpaper that surrounded her. It was a small house, but elegant in its economy. She'd expected more primitive conditions. "Just not electricity, I suppose."

"Do you feel disoriented?" Paul studied her face, looking for signs of shock, mental confusion.

"No, just wet and cold." She drew the blanket around her.

"Do you know what day it is?"

Why was he suddenly playing twenty questions? "Last day of April. Why?"

He nodded, satisfied that there was no amnesia. She hadn't been in the water long enough. But a few more minutes and she— He didn't want to think about it.

"Just making sure you're all right."

The woman returned, laden with the necessary essentials. She smiled warmly at Judy. "These should fit you."

Though what was left on her body felt stiff and clammy at the same time, Judy shook her head. "I can't take your clothes." As she said it, she burrowed just a little deeper into the blanket.

He'd had all the foolishness he could handle for one day. She had to get out of those clothes. Now. He leaned over her, one hand on either side of her, blocking out everything else.

"Does the word *hypothermïa* mean anything to you?" Paul demanded. He nearly stopped when she turned her wide, green eyes up at him. They shimmered, almost liquid in consistency, reminding him of the Pacific Ocean. "You've got to get out of those wet clothes fast. Or—" he changed his tone abruptly, what passed for a smile tracing his lips "—you could always stay here and dry out by the fire."

He took one tentative step toward the door, watching her eyes as surprise set in. "I'll be by here again in about three days." He glanced at the woman beside Judy. "I could pick her up then, Sara."

Judy was already struggling to gain her wet, stockinged feet. "I'll change."

In one swift movement, he picked up both Judy and the fresh bundle of clothing. Turning, he crossed to the bedroom. "One can only hope."

"You know—" Judy laughed softly, slowly beginning to feel like herself again "—I could really get used to this sort of treatment."

Relieved that she sounded as if she were feeling better, Paul resumed his original attitude. He deposited her unceremoniously on the bed. She bounced.

"Don't." He glanced at his watch, then pointed toward the clothing. "You've got ten minutes to get out of those things and dressed before I move on."

"My camera—" Judy suddenly remembered again. She had others, but they were back in Grateful Bend. She knew he wouldn't be open to swinging by Hattie's just to retrieve a camera.

Just then, a small, dark-eyed girl walked in, carrying the camera as if it were something capable of wondrous magic. She handed it to Sara. "It's the lady's," she said solemnly, pointing at Judy.

The woman presented it to Judy and was pleased to see the worried expression vanish. "You helped save my nephew," the woman explained. "My daughter saved your camera. It's far from an even exchange, but it is the best I can do for the moment."

"You have no idea how much that is," Judy told her. She watched Paul's retreating back as he closed the door behind him.

By the time Judy had pulled on the dry clothing and walked into the front room, more than a handful of the people in the settlement had crowded into the woman's house.

Tall, graceful, with sloe eyes and waist-long ebony hair, the woman turned as Judy entered. Her smile warmed the room as she crossed to her.

"How do you feel?" the woman asked. She pressed a cup of tea into Judy's hands. They were warming, she noted with satisfaction.

"Like a Popsicle that's thawing out." Grateful, she took a long sip. The tea wound through her, producing a comforting sensation. She still felt a bit shaky on her legs, but that would pass. What wouldn't pass was the warm glow she felt at having saved the child's life. She was going to savor that for a long time.

Judy scanned the room and realized there were only Inuits in the room. Paul wouldn't have just left her here, would he?

She looked at her hostess. "The sergeant—"

"He's next door, seeing to my nephew. He said to tell you that he would be right back." She inclined her head slightly, as if bowing after a formal introduction. "My name is Sara, and this is my family." She gestured around the room.

The room was filled with at least fifteen people, if not more. Their eyes were all focused on Judy. She shifted a little uncomfortably. "All of them?"

Sara's smile was wide and unoffended. "All of them. They wanted me to thank you. That was very brave, what you did for a child not of your own family."

Judy was used to taking photographs of center stage, not being in it. She flushed, a bit self-conscious. "It's up to everyone to look out for each other." She looked at the blank, smiling faces. "I guess in that sense, we're all one big family."

Sara translated Judy's words for some of the older people who had never learned the language of the people they now shared the land with. A sea of dark heads nodded in approval like an unsyncopated chorus line.

"Seems you said something that they agreed with," a deep voice said.

Judy turned as Paul entered the room. Though there were many other people here, he seemed to fill the room so completely with just his presence alone. Several men shuffled over to the side to give him room.

He appeared almost solicitous when he looked at her. "Want me to take you back to Grateful Bend?"

He was probably hoping for that, she mused. "Not a chance. You're not getting rid of me that easily."

Rather than answer her, he took her face between his hands. Judy held her breath as her heart suddenly moved and lodged in her throat. Was he going to kiss her here, in front of everyone? That wasn't the Sergeant Monroe she knew, but what other reason was there for—

And then he was coaxing her eyelids open wider with the tips of his fingers. He looked intently from one eye to the other, studying her pupils.

Now, that was the sergeant she knew.

"No, I guess no harm's been done." Except, perhaps, to his nervous system. "You can go on if you want." Almost as an afterthought, he dropped his hands from her face.

"I want."

She said the words in a whisper, and they curled under his skin, reminding him that, once, he had wanted, too. The light touch of her hand burrowed through layers of protective clothing, as if they didn't exist.

"I had a feeling you would." He turned and looked at the young woman next to Judy. "Sara, we'll bring back the clothes the next trip through."

Sara was waving away his words. "Don't worry about it. How's Jimmy?"

That episode had turned out a lot better than he might have hoped for. Thanks to Judy, he thought grudgingly. "Scared. I told his mother to keep him in bed for the day. If he starts running a fever, have someone bring him to Grateful Bend or call headquarters on the shortwave and I'll come by. Good thing he's not skinny. His own body helped insulate him." Paul was already out the door again. Judy grabbed her camera and hurried after him.

Sara nodded. She and the occupants of the cabin followed Judy and Paul out the door and all the way to the snowmobile.

Holding Judy's hand, Paul helped her into the vehicle. "I think you've acquired a fan club." Paul brushed her hair out of her face before he could think better of it. "They're not quite sure what to think of you." *And neither am I.*

Something in his gaze made Judy's stomach tighten and then quiver. She didn't trust the feeling yet. "You know medical procedure?" she asked, finding her voice again. She licked her lower lip. "Back in the cabin, when you mentioned looking at the boy. Jimmy."

He shrugged, climbing into the snowmobile. "Enough to get by. You have to out here. We don't have a hospital located on every ice cake."

Judy nodded, her mind not really on his words, but on the touch of his hand. And the way he'd held her face so gently.... The next moment, her thoughts were interrupted as Raymond bounced into the vehicle next to her.

"Thought we forgot you, eh, boy?" She nuzzled him. God, it felt good to be alive.

As they pulled away, Judy waved at the cluster of people, one hand resting on Raymond. A sea of mittened hands waved back.

Chapter Seven

For Paul, it had been one of the most exhausting days he had experienced in a long, long time. Judy behaved like a tireless athlete on megavitamins. He'd seen less effervescence in a cork exploding out of a champagne bottle. It was as if the plunge through the ice had revitalized her instead of drained her. By his count, she'd gone through at least three rolls of film and captured him more times than he wanted to think about.

And she talked. Continuously. As if she were afraid he'd disappear if she stopped.

He was definitely ready to part company by the time they pulled up to his cabin.

Permanently, if possible.

Paul purposely abbreviated his day. As the snowmobile slowed, Raymond leapt off Judy's lap. The animal pranced before Paul's cabin as if he recognized it as his own. He stopped the snowmobile before the shed and got out.

All things considered, it had been a great day, Judy thought as she patted the film in her pouch. She was beginning to feel a little tired, but that was to be expected. Luckily, there were no ill side effects lingering from her fleeting dip in the water. "I'll just feed Raymond and be out of your hair."

"If only it were as simple as that," Paul muttered under his breath, unlocking the padlock.

He pulled the door open and groaned. Tension had been eating away at him all day, mounting like the score of an old-fashioned melodrama nearing its climax. His whole body felt stiff. He'd forgotten that he had left her car housed within the shed, not wanting to take a chance on it not starting when they returned. But now, he was in no mood to play musical vehicles.

Judy glanced at his expression. She could almost guess at the cause. She was out of the snowmobile and beside him faster than he had thought possible. "Why don't I move that out for you and clear a path?"

It was the first sensible thing she had said to him all day. But then, the vehicle wouldn't have been in there in the first place if it hadn't been for her.

He stepped back. "Why don't you."

Judy gently deposited her camera and the case with the film and lenses in the rear of the four by four. "You would have never have made it as a Boy Scout." When he raised a brow, she clarified, "They have to be cheerful."

Next, she'd want him to sing and dance as well, he thought darkly. It was bad enough having to drive next to her all day. Was he required to smile, too?

Judy climbed into the driver's side. As Paul watched, she pulled her car out, veering its tail to the right, and narrowly missed mating the snowmobile with the four by four by less than an inch.

Any way you looked at it, he thought, the woman was a problem.

Judy looked toward him and smiled. For some reason, that annoyed him even more.

"What is there to be so damn cheerful about?" he demanded as soon as she pulled up the hand brake. He was still digesting her Boy Scout remark. "Can you tell me that?" He took her hand to help steady her as she got out. "What do you see that makes everything so wonderful?"

Judy searched his face before answering. She felt sorry for him. "Life."

That was an answer he'd have expected to find inside a greeting card, not receive from an intelligent person. "Life is a damn hard struggle, and you wind up dead at the end."

Wow. Someone had walked through his life wearing spiked boots and cut his soul to ribbons. She laid her hand gently on his arm. "It's what goes in between the beginning and the end that makes it worthwhile." She thought of the feeling that had rushed through her the first time she took an unassisted step after the accident. There'd been no triumph to equal it. "Living another day. Being able to help. You're a Mountie—a servant of the people. People depend on you. You make a difference. You help."

He'd ceased to really feel that he made a difference a long time ago. "You sound like a children's-book description of my job."

Perhaps she did, but she made no excuses for that. "Maybe you shouldn't have gotten away from that." How could she get through to him? she wondered. What was the key? "Children see things more clearly than we do. They tend to keep things uncomplicated."

He couldn't believe that she actually believed what she was saying. "They just don't know any better."

She thought of the child she helped rescue today. Of the bright, sunny faces she had seen at play. They were innocent, and yet they saw the world. They just saw it in their own terms. And they were happy. "Maybe they do," she said softly, "and we're the ones who don't."

Paul clenched his teeth together and let out a slow stream of air. It sounded like a hiss. This woman was hopeless. "Does your balloon ever land?"

She laughed, guessing what he probably thought of her. "It's been popped a couple of times," she admitted, undaunted, "but I keep a supply of patches around just in case of emergencies."

He decided there was no point in trying to show her the error of her thinking. She'd just find a way to twist it inside out somehow. It probably came from developing negatives and turning them into photographs.

"Speaking of emergencies," she began, "I never thanked you for saving my life."

He shrugged away her thanks as if it were a jacket that didn't fit. He didn't want her gratitude. He didn't want to be touched by any part of her baseless, sunny disposition. "I couldn't very well have let you go under. The paperwork I would have had to file would've been too extensive."

Judy laced her hands together and pressed them dramatically over her parka to her heart, fluttering her eyelashes. "I've always dreamed of being saved by a Mountie in lieu of paperwork." And then she laughed. The sound reminded him of crystal clear, cool mountain water running over rocks in a stream.

Impulsively, because he looked as if he needed it and because she was grateful, Judy grabbed on to his jacket, raised herself on her toes and kissed Paul's cheek. The smile on her lips faded as she lowered herself back to her heels.

They stared at one another as if they'd never seen each other before. As if they were suddenly propelled into a realm that existed away from snow and dogs and cameras. The only thing that existed was the small space where they stood. With her heart beating rapidly, Judy raised herself up again, this time almost in slow motion. Her eyes on his, her breath caught in her throat, Judy turned her mouth up to his.

What was the matter with him? he wondered. He should have just turned away and parked the damned vehicle. He was a trained professional for God's sake and recognized trouble when he saw it. Here it was, wrapped in a light blue parka. Why in the name of hell wasn't he listening to his gut instincts?

Because instincts greater than those involving training and common sense obliterated everything else within him like a bomb exploding in his body.

Suddenly he was cupping her face in his gloved hands and bringing his mouth down to hers. There was no gentle start to the kiss, no moment of exploration or wonder. There was only the immediate detonation as power and passion vibrated through him. And need. Tremendous, overwhelming, shattering need. It was as if a monster had suddenly been released, a monster that had been locked in the closet for too long. She tasted of something wonderful and pure, and he feasted on it like a man who hadn't eaten in days. Weeks.

Years.

As she wrapped her arms around his neck for support, he threw off his gloves. He wanted to feel this woman, if only through the borrowed clothes that she wore. Paul pressed her into him, his hands roaming along her back. His body was aching, beseeching. It had totally deserted the center of control he had created within himself. The control that should have had him backing away and heading down Mackenzie Highway as fast as he could.

Oh, God, she hadn't expected this. She had suspected, perhaps, but never anticipated what she'd unwittingly discovered. At best, she'd contemplated something tantalizing, romantic, mysterious. She definitely had not foreseen a solar eclipse blitzing through her brain.

Everything, absolutely everything, had completely disappeared off the face of the earth, hurling her into a vacuum.

And yet . . .

And yet it couldn't be a vacuum, not with the excitement she felt rushing through her. Not with the flashing of lights and the heating of her blood. Not with the impression of being caught on a runaway roller coaster that was set to plummet straight down off the edge of Mount McKinley.

The kiss ended as roughly as it had started, like a deep-sea diver being abruptly separated from his oxygen tank. Paul was afraid of what might follow. Afraid of the explosion within his body. Afraid of himself. He was breathing hard, just as hard as when he woke from one of his nightmares.

Judy's fingers slid down the zippered opening of Paul's jacket as she slowly lowered herself to the ground again, like a survivor of a burning building going hand over hand down a rope to safety.

Wow! The word kept echoing in her head, vibrating in her body. *Wow!*

She couldn't remember doing it a second later, but she thought she shook her head just to clear it. "I'd, um, better see to Raymond."

Paul wanted to plunge his hands into her hair and savage her mouth. He wanted to lose himself in her and never come up for air again.

But he knew he couldn't. Rigidly, he braced his shoulders, his expression stoic. "Yeah, right."

Like a man who had just nerve-rackingly picked his way through a minefield, Paul turned and walked to the snowmobile.

That was damn stupid of him, he thought, cursing his weakness, cursing his complete loss of control. Cursing her for being here to remind him that once, a long, long time ago, he'd been young enough and naive enough to have dreams and believe in them. Dreams he and his father had woven together before he had learned the meaning of reality.

Judy had opened the window to let some air in. It felt cold against her face as she drove back to Grateful Bend. The loneliness of the road hadn't bothered her before, even when she had been traveling up here, trying to find her way. Then it had been an adventure. Now, for the first time, there was a sting of desolation about it.

Paul hadn't said anything to her. Not really. She certainly hadn't expected a stunning metamorphosis to take place because they'd kissed, but she had expected *something*. This man wasn't an ice sculpture, for God's sake.

That kiss they shared had proved that. But he had acted as if nothing had happened.

Worse, he had acted as if he resented that it happened. As if he resented her for being there. It wasn't just something she could shrug off anymore.

"Too bad, Sergeant. We're onto something, and I intend to find out what," Judy said to herself.

He just needs time to sort out what has happened, she reasoned, knowing she was making excuses for him. For that matter, she needed to sort things out herself. Things had been said in that kiss, things that neither one of them had voiced or expected. She could see that he was just as stunned by it as she was. She needed a little while to come to terms with her discovery and absorb it, too.

As she drove into the small town, she glanced toward the RCMP headquarters. Making up her mind abruptly, she pulled the wheel to the left and turned in before the building. Maybe now was the time to have some of those gaps filled in, instead of later.

Pushing her hood from her head as she entered, Judy let the warmth in the room surround her for a moment. The hour was getting late, but the captain was still there, as she had hoped. He was talking to the Mountie she'd seen the day before. It took a moment before she remembered his name. Corporal Hayes.

Stripping off her gloves, Judy was prepared to wait. But the conversation evaporated as soon as the men noticed her waiting.

The captain smiled broadly, beaming like a grandfather at his grandchild's first, halting step. "Well, only one day at it and already you're a heroine."

Judy stared uncomprehendingly. She looked from the captain to Hayes. There was admiration mixed with a tinge of uncertainty in the younger man's eyes as he regarded her. "Excuse me?" she said.

"Sergeant Monroe just called in his report." Reynolds nodded toward the shortwave radio that stood in a tall, narrow table made expressly for it. "Even if he hadn't, I suspect that I would have probably heard about the incident by morning. Word travels quickly around here, even at these distances. Word of mouth is practically the only form of entertainment we have available, outside of the occasional festival." The captain leaned closer over his desk, his eyes kindly. "You really dived in after the boy?"

"I dived *for* him," she corrected. "The ice took care of the 'in' part."

Reynolds tried to envision the scene and shook his head. "What made you do something like that?"

She shrugged, wondering if she had now inadvertently plunged into *hot* water. Still, she wouldn't have done things any differently if she had the chance again. "I couldn't very well let the little boy drown."

"No, but a lot of people would have left the rescue to Monroe." She, however, wasn't like that, Reynolds judged. A very independent lady indeed.

If he wasn't about to reprimand her for her actions, she wanted to press on. She was feeling very tired now. She glanced at Hayes before addressing the captain. "Umm, could I speak to you alone, Captain?"

"Certainly." Reynolds turned toward the other man. "That'll be all, Hayes. Say hello to Rosemary for me. I'll see you in the morning."

Corporal Hayes saluted and then nodded at Judy as he left.

"Rosemary's my oldest daughter," Reynolds told Judy conversationally as Hayes closed the door behind him. "The corporal is my son-in-law. Now then." The captain sat back comfortably in his chair and gestured toward the chair in front of his desk. "What can I do for you?"

Judy sat down on the edge of the hardback chair. She was hungry and more than a little tired. But sleep wasn't going to come easily tonight. She was as keyed up inside as an overwound coil.

She took a deep breath before asking, "What can you tell me about Sergeant Monroe?"

His shaggy brow rose in an arch. "Trouble?"

"No, no," she assured him quickly, then forced herself to slow down. "I just need some background data for the notes I've got to hand over with the photographs when I'm finished. Sergeant Monroe is as silent as—well, as—" She tried to find a comparison that wasn't unflattering.

"A sphinx?" Reynolds suggested, a smile tugging at his small, mustache-fringed mouth.

Judy inclined her head. "Something like that." Actually, more like a stubborn mule, but there was no point in mentioning that.

Reynolds thought of the file he had leafed through when Monroe had initially transferred here. It was a file with more than a few commendations in it.

"Well, he's been here for five years and he's not much of a talker under any circumstances." But she was probably learning that, Reynolds mused, studying the woman before him. "Monroe doesn't join in on the festivals. Keeps to himself completely, much to the regret of the eligible ladies, my daughter Diana included." His eyes narrowed just a little. "What exactly is it that you want to know about him?"

If she leaned any farther forward, she was going to fall off the chair, she admonished herself. But after everything that had happened today, she couldn't sit back, couldn't relax. "Absolutely anything you can tell me."

Reynolds detected the eagerness in her voice and judged that it was more than just enthusiasm for her work. He rose and crossed to an open window in the rear of the office. Grasping the sash firmly, he shut it. "Corporal Hayes is a fresh-air enthusiast. Probably because he works inside a warm office," he commented.

He returned to his seat. There was something in her manner that told Reynolds his original conjecture was correct. They would make a nice couple, Monroe and Judy. And at least one of them knew that, he mused, studying her expression again.

"His father was a Mountie."

She nodded. "That much I got out of him." But not much more.

"Sgt. Mike Monroe was killed in the line of duty when Paul was—" Reynolds paused as he made the necessary calculation "—ten or eleven."

Was that the reason he was so sullen? she wondered. Ten was a very young age to lose your father, especially violently. "What sort of 'line of duty'?"

"He walked into a bank robbery. In Montreal. They tell me he was just there to cash his paycheck." Reynolds shook his head at the tricks that life played on men. "Monroe went to the Canadian Police College in Ottawa. Made the same unit as his father did in Montreal when he got out. Then, five years ago, he transferred here."

What would cause a man to leave a thriving metropolis for a place like this? It wasn't as if nature had beckoned to him. He didn't seem happy about being here. "Any particular reason?"

There was an incident written up in Monroe's file. The details in the report absolved the man of any culpability, but Reynolds suspected that one of those details was the single factor that had made Monroe abandon his life in Montreal.

Reynolds respected that a man was entitled to some privacy. This wasn't the defunct French Foreign Legion, but a man deserved to have his past kept in the past, unless he chose otherwise.

Reynolds shrugged, his expression amiable. "I'm afraid that's something only Sergeant Monroe can tell you. Why don't you ask him?"

Judy wondered if the captain didn't know the reason why Paul had transferred or if he knew more than he was saying. Was he protecting Paul for some reason? And if so, what was the big mystery? A man didn't just leave everything behind and come to a wilderness like this without a reason, unless he was a winter-sports enthusiast.

Reynolds saw the quandary in her eyes. He did what he could to ease her disquiet. "I can, however, tell you that

Sergeant Monroe is a sterling example of everything I want in a member of the RCMP.''

She heard what was said and what was missing. ''But not a sterling example of everything that you would want as a friend?''

Reynolds didn't waver in his support—as far as it stretched. ''I can depend on Monroe for whatever I need.''

She understood all too well. He was almost like a father figure, trying hard not to criticize his children. ''Except bonding.''

The silver mustache spread to a thin strip as Reynolds smiled his appreciation. ''I see that you're good at this.''

It didn't take much. Not in Paul's case, at any rate. She hadn't needed an entire day to see their differences. He was as reticent as she was outgoing. Fire and ice. But fire melted ice. Usually.

''The camera isn't the only thing that sees, Captain.''

The man wasn't going to give her any more than he already had, Judy thought, resigned. She was going to have to find the answers herself. She never doubted that she could. With a polite nod, Judy rose and extended her hand.

''Thank you for your time, Captain.'' She turned to leave. All she wanted now was a hot shower. Judy fervently hoped there was no one using the bathroom at Hattie's.

''My pleasure.'' He watched her cross to the door. ''Oh, and Judy?''

She looked over her shoulder, hope budding. Had he changed his mind? Was there something he'd forgotten to tell her? ''Yes?''

''No more imitations of the polar-bear club, all right? I'd hate to have to tell your publisher you froze to death while under my jurisdiction.''

She managed a smile, though even her facial muscles were suddenly tired. ''I'll do my best.''

Somehow Judy managed to leave the car at Humphrey's. In the midst of a one-sided argument, the burly man had taken the keys from her and parked the vehicle in the shop

himself. He'd offered to drive her back to Hattie's but she
felt foolish. After all, the boarding house was less than half
a mile away.

Besides, Humphrey was busy. There was a slight, red-
headed man challenging Humphrey's decision to keep his
Jeep at the shop overnight in order to diagnose the problem properly.

She smiled her thanks for the offer and left Humphrey to
calmly overrule the other man.

The snow hindered her progress. Her legs like lead, Judy
felt as if she were walking through angel food cake. Finally
she arrived at the boarding house.

Hattie hurried her ample form up to the front door. From
the smells following her, Judy guessed that Hattie had
scurried out of the kitchen with dinner in progress. Concern wrinkled the brow beneath the henna-rinsed bangs.
"You poor lamb, are you all right?"

These people might not have cable, but they certainly had
their own way of getting news around fast, Judy thought,
amusement temporarily winning out over weariness.

"How did you hear?" Judy didn't even bother to ask
what Hattie had heard. It was obvious.

Hattie tucked a wide arm around Judy's shoulders,
wrinkling her nose slightly at the quality of the parka the
younger woman had been lent. She clucked as she ushered
Judy into the room.

"Why, I was just at Sam's Emporium, buying some
things for tomorrow's dinner," she said, justifying her actions quickly out of habit, "when Corporal Hayes stopped
by to get some things for his wife before he went home. He's
married to the captain's daughter, you know. Has to treat
her like a princess or she'll whine to Daddy." Hattie puck-
ered her face in disapproval. "Anyway, I was just leaving
when he starts telling Sam about Sergeant Monroe's report."

Hattie stopped by the stairs, her expression that of a
mother used to putting up with foolishness from her off-
spring. She wagged a thick finger at Judy as if Judy were

five years old. "My dear, you could have caught your death of cold out there, doing that."

Cynthia walked into the room, her stomach rumbling. She was hungry and wanted to know why there was a delay. Her eyes lit up when she saw Judy. "Doing what?"

Hattie swung around, the town crier at her best. "Why, Miss Treherne here saved five children single-handedly from a black bear that was attacking them right there on the ice."

Judy rolled her eyes. News traveled fast, all right, and like a snowball let loose at the top of the hill, it seemed to have gathered speed and a lot of extra packing during its descent.

"A black bear?" Cynthia cried out in amazement. Her eyes opened so wide, it looked as if they would literally pop out of her head and roll away on the wooden floor like dark green marbles.

Judy couldn't help wondering if setting the record straight would ultimately change the story. Paul Bunyan was probably originally a man about Humphrey's size with a bluish Siberian husky named Babe. Look what he had evolved into.

But she had to try for her own peace of mind. "No, I took a picture of the bear."

Cynthia looked at Judy, confused, then smiled broadly as she figured it out to her satisfaction. "Is that how you rescued the children? You blinded the bear with the flash from the camera?"

Judy sighed and shook her head. This was going to take more effort to untangle than she thought.

"I'd like to take a hot shower and change my clothes first." Both women looked disappointed at being deprived of her company. "I promise I'll tell you all about the details at dinner." Though the sun was still out, Judy suddenly realized that it was late. "I didn't miss dinner, did I?"

Cynthia's stomach rumbled again, answering Judy's question before Hattie could. It didn't stop Hattie from talking. "No, no," she assured Judy warmly. "We held it up just for you."

Judy had a feeling that was no exaggeration. In all likelihood, *she* was probably the main course tonight.

Thanking Hattie, she turned and wearily walked up the stairs. She hoped she wouldn't fall asleep standing up in the shower. If she did, she was sure Hattie would look in on her and drag her out so that she could continue her story.

Chapter Eight

Paul couldn't get her out of his thoughts.

Like the scent of smoke clinging to a room long after the fire had been put out, Judy lingered in his mind, refusing to evaporate, refusing to release him. She represented a fissure in his control.

She reminded him of the path not taken, disturbing his set way of living. He had adopted a course that had allowed him to live with his problem. She was disrupting it by making him feel again. Along with the wonder came the old, painful feelings. Paul resented her for doing this to him with passion he had believed long depleted from his body.

More than anything else, Paul wished that she had never come to the Northwest, barging into his life, barging into his mind.

And now he wanted to see her again.

He pulled on his shirt, his hair still damp from his morning shower. Maybe all this solitude *was* making him a little crazy, he decided. Why else were ambivalent feelings ricocheting through him? No, *ambivalent* wasn't a strong

enough term to describe the depth of the feelings he was experiencing.

Muttering, wishing for the peace he'd had only a few days
ago, he walked to the kitchen. Raymond followed him, eager for food. Eager for companionship. Eager. Like her,
Paul thought.

"Hold your horses, it's coming, it's coming," he told the
prancing animal. Opening the refrigerator, he reached for a
bag he had tossed in there last night.

A knock on the door had Paul stiffening and his blood
speeding to double time.

"Doesn't waste a minute, does she?" he murmured to
himself.

He released the refrigerator door and turned, eyeing the
front door as if just concentrating could make her disappear. Another knock followed on the echoes of the first. No
such luck.

When he opened the door to admit her, Judy's face fairly
glowed. "Ready for more adventures?" she asked, crossing the threshold.

Making herself right at home. In *his* home, he thought.

She had practiced her opening line all the way over, nerves
jumping through her as if she were an adolescent on her first
date.

In a way, maybe she was. She'd never encountered anyone quite like Sgt. Paul Monroe before and she had no idea
how to react to him. Everything she did seemed to rub him
the wrong way, and she desperately didn't want to do that.
She was attracted to him. Very strongly attracted. His
brooding good looks were appealing and the hurt she detected in his eyes spoke to the perpetual do-gooder in her.
She wanted to set things right for him.

And then, of course, there was that kiss.

One kiss, and she had come as unraveled as a ball of yarn
tossed over the edge of the Grand Canyon.

There she was, Paul thought, his own personal thorn. He
raised a brow over her greeting. "Why, are you planning on

diving through another hole in the ice today?'' He closed the door behind her.

A normal woman, he thought grudgingly, would have gotten a cold and stayed home to nurse it. Or at least been frightened enough by the incident to stick close to headquarters and bother the Mounties there. But then, Judy wasn't normal.

''Only if necessary,'' she quipped, looking around. ''Did you miss me?''

''No, I—'' He turned, ready to inform her that she had been the farthest thing from his mind, ready to use any lie to save himself, when he realized that she was talking to the dog. She was down on the floor, roughhousing with the animal.

Paul let out a long breath, chagrined at his error. ''Your dog is an eating machine.''

That was no exaggeration. Raymond would have eaten her out of house and home if she'd let him. She looked up at Paul. From this vantage point, the man looked as sturdy as an oak. And as warm as one. ''You've got to learn how to say no to him.''

''The word *no* doesn't seem to work very well for me lately.'' Paul looked down at her meaningfully.

She didn't have the good manners to look embarrassed, he noted. Instead, she grinned.

''Wonder why that is.'' Judy rose, dusting herself off. She unzipped her jacket as she followed Paul into the kitchen.

Well, nothing ventured, nothing gained. ''About yesterday...'' she began.

Paul refused to turn around. He opened the refrigerator and reached inside for Raymond's breakfast. ''What part of yesterday?''

She didn't believe in games or half truths. She'd always played it straight from the shoulder. ''The part that kept me up last night.''

Paul shrugged as if he didn't know what she was talking about. She almost stopped herself from continuing. She hated looking like a fool as much as the next person. Except that there was something in his eyes, a glimpse that told her he knew *exactly* what she was referring to. And that he hadn't slept well, either.

She pressed on as he took a package of muffins from the refrigerator. She grinned to herself. He remembered. When had he had the time to pick up the muffins? "I just want you to know that I'm not going to let that get in the way here."

How noble of you. He ripped open the package and was about to place a muffin on a plate when Raymond snatched it out of his hand. The dog didn't hang back any more than his mistress did, Paul thought.

"He didn't nip you, did he?" Concerned, she took Paul's hand in hers.

He jerked it away roughly, not wanting any contact between them. It would only weaken his resolve.

"No!" He wanted to apologize for sounding like an ogre, but that, too, would work to his disadvantage. It was better if she thought of him as an ill-tempered clod. "Nothing's going to get in the way because there's nothing *to* get in the way."

That was a lie, and they both knew it. She wandered over to the coffeepot and poured half a mug, looking for the right words. She eyed him over the rising steam. "How far into denial are you?"

The last thing he wanted was some two-bit analysis. No, he amended, the last thing he wanted was for her to be standing here in his kitchen, looking like the first rose of spring. And desirable as all hell. "Ms. Treherne—"

There were icicles surrounding her name. She broke them off as she pinned him with a look that said she saw through him, at least part of the way. She placed the mug on the counter and took a step toward him, an animal trainer trying to win her subject's confidence.

"You know—" her voice was low, silky "—if you hold things back all the time, you're going to explode someday." Her eyes remained on his as the distance melted to nothing between them.

He could smell her. The scent she wore was in his head, surging into his blood and beating there like an anticipatory drumroll. Damn her for doing this to him. "You want an explosion, lady? I'll give you an explosion."

He pulled her into his arms and did what he had unwillingly fantasized about all night.

He kissed her again.

His hands dived beneath her open jacket, beneath the heavy black sweatshirt she wore, and touched the soft, cool skin at her midriff. He encompassed her waist with his palms, savoring the very feel of her. Holding her to him, absorbing her, he kissed her lips over and over again. Kissed her so hard that both her mouth and his soul felt bruised.

He could hear his own heart pounding in his ears, hear the low moan that escaped. Whether it was his or hers, he hadn't a clue. He just knew that he needed this. And she was right—holding back only made the explosion that much worse.

Her head whirled as she pressed herself against him, her hands searching for the warmth of his skin. Just as he had touched her, she needed to touch him, to know that this aching man was flesh and blood. But his uniform got in the way.

It was almost like a madness had seized her. She was unprepared for it. Unprepared for her own reaction to it. Each time he kissed her, the sensation escalated, growing more unpredictable.

As if a thunderbolt crashed over him, Paul realized what he was doing, where this would lead if he didn't regain control of his desires. He released her as if he had been holding a hot poker with his bare hands. His hands slid down her hips to his sides.

He'd lost his head again. Like a person unused to drinking and downing a glass of alcohol quickly, he had completely lost sight of himself in a blinding swirl.

Paul looked at Judy. The outline of her mouth was blurred. Her lips looked as if they were throbbing. God, what had come over him? He'd groped her like some stupid kid fumbling in the back seat of his father's car for the first time.

Paul ran a hand through his hair, taking in a ragged breath that failed to steady him. He forced himself to look into her eyes. "I'm sorry."

For what? she wondered. She fixed her sweatshirt. She could still feel the imprint of his hands on her. "Sorry you kissed me?"

She knew what he meant. Why did she have to make him sound like a fool? "Don't oversimplify everything."

Why was he ruining this? It was good. It was special. "Don't overcomplicate everything," she countered, trying to keep her voice light. "You kissed me. Twice. It can stop here or it can go ahead. One step at a time." Her eyes held his as she searched for the entrance to his soul. "But there's nothing to be sorry for." She smiled, and he felt his stomach tighten all over again. "You didn't do anything wrong."

He had no idea how to put it into words, how to tell her what she was doing to him. Creating earthquakes, tidal waves. Upheavals. Turning day into night. He settled for the obvious. "I practically flattened your mouth."

She ran a fingertip over it, as if to seal in his flavor. He found it hopelessly sexy and wished he didn't.

"Okay," she agreed. "You're a little forceful, maybe. There's something to be said for that. But we can work on it if you'd like."

He closed his eyes. He didn't want to work on anything. He wanted his peace back. He wanted the moratorium he had declared on the world. "Ms. Treherne—"

That finally got her angry. To his surprise, she hit his chest with the flat of her hand. His eyes flew open, and he stared at her.

"Dammit, *Sergeant,* we've kissed each other twice. It's time for first names, don't you think? Don't be afraid to feel something," she pleaded, her voice calming down. "Feeling just proves you're alive."

"Maybe I don't like being reminded." His expression grew dark.

He should have been in that girl's place, he thought, not the other way around. She should be the one who was alive, who was experiencing things for the first time, not him. He had no right.

Judy wasn't about to let him bury himself under that sort of mire. "If that were true, you wouldn't be putting one foot in front of the other. You wouldn't be here, wearing a uniform. You wouldn't be, period."

Enough was enough. Judy tugged on his arm, leading him toward the door.

"C'mon, Sergeant. It's a beautiful day, and I have lots of film to use up." Her eyes were coaxing him as she looked up into his face. "Take me places." She released his arm and slowly walked toward the door, the dog dancing at her side.

Take her places. Huh! If anyone was taking anyone places, she was taking him. Paul felt as if he were following the rabbit down the hole. And in all likelihood, he'd probably get stuck in the descent.

With a sigh, he followed her out.

It was so quiet once the snowmobile had been turned off, and all Judy could hear was the sound of the wind leafing through the trees. It was so mournful looking, it almost hurt her to see it.

"It looks so deserted." She whispered the words, as if saying them aloud would make her supposition a reality.

He watched her thoughts wash over her face. It amazed him that he could almost read her reactions. Why did she seem to care? The people who had lived here were long gone. Long dead. "That's because it is."

She turned to face him. "A ghost town?" It was something she associated only with the Old West, not Canada.

It was so hard to scratch out the foundations of a town, why would anyone turn their backs on it after all that effort?

Paul nodded. "The Northwest is littered with them." He looked around. For some reason, he could almost feel the ghosts here. She was probably affecting him, he thought, glancing at her. "Cities started in hope, abandoned in despair."

The man needed to see things differently, she thought. "You have a poetic, brooding soul, do you know that?"

He wondered if she meant that as a criticism or a compliment. He wanted neither. "I just see it for what it is."

She said nothing for a moment as she framed in her lens a crumbling building she guessed to be a church or meeting hall. What sort of people had been here? Did they laugh? Or were they filled with despair? Did they have dreams once? And what kind? "Do you stop here regularly?" she finally asked.

He watched her. Even in the snow, she moved with grace.

"Once in a while. Sometimes an adventurous idiot wanders out too far, takes shelter here or in any one of a number of these places. They need rescuing before too long. Once in a while an escaped criminal hides out in an abandoned town or reservation."

It sounded more and more like the Old West. Desperadoes hiding out in an old ghost town. She remembered seeing a Western like that as a child. Several of them.

Abruptly, she raised her camera. Surprising Paul, she managed to photograph him against the rundown saloon. "Are you after one of them now? Criminals," she prompted.

He wished there were some justifiable way to disable her camera. He was getting used to her snapping away at him, but he still hated it.

"No. I just thought you might like to see a ghost town." Instinctively he knew that this was the kind of place that would appeal to her. He gestured around at the snow-covered buildings.

She grinned. He'd thought of her. And bought English muffins for her dog. There was hope for the man yet. "Oh, I would, I would."

Paul stood patiently back, waiting for her to finish. Judy wandered around, filling her wide-angle lens with the tumbled-down structures. There had been pride here once. And hope. She could swear that she felt the hope, as well as the sadness when all was abandoned. It must have been hard to see it die. She hated endings almost as much as she loved beginnings.

She glanced over her shoulder and saw Paul standing near what had probably been the general store. Dressed in somber navy blue, his arms folded before his chest, he was looking off into the distance. She wondered what he was thinking.

Did he ever have any fun at all? Did he ever loosen up? It was high time to start him on that road.

Impulsively, Judy capped her lens and tucked the camera away in her case. With hands as gentle as a mother with a newborn, she set the case down. Then she quickly packed a snowball. Snowballs were her specialty. Just this last Christmas season she had survived a battle royal with her niece and nephews.

Balancing the snowball in her hand behind her back, she turned toward Paul. "Oh, Sergeant." Her voice was soft, melodic. Innocent.

Was she through? He turned in her direction, half expecting to see the camera aimed at him again. Instead, a snowball came flying at him. Taken completely by surprise, he couldn't react quickly enough to save himself. The packed snow went crashing into his face.

"What the—" He wiped snow away from his mouth and cheeks, tossing it disgustedly on the ground. "Have you gone completely crazy?"

Energized, she was balancing her weight on her toes, shifting from foot to foot like a prizefighter waiting for the bell to ring. She was ready to run at a moment's notice. "No, I just wanted to see your reaction."

Without thinking, Paul scooped up two handfuls of snow and headed toward her. "How about *your* reaction?"

Judy was already taking a step backward. Her eyes shifted from the snow in Paul's hands to his face and then back again. "Oh, you wouldn't."

"Wouldn't I?"

She looked at the unexpected glimmer in his eyes and knew that it was safer to run than debate. A lot safer. She pivoted a hundred and eighty degrees, making a mad dash for the safety of a building.

But she kept slipping. His legs were far longer and his strides were twice hers. He was on her in a moment, dumping the entire load of snow on her head as she squealed and pleaded for mercy. The snow slid down on all sides, going right into her parka. The cold made her yelp in surprise and delight.

"You don't just get mad," she said, laughing with pleasure, "you get even. And so do I," she exclaimed suddenly, just before she threw two fistfuls of snow straight at him.

When she turned to flee again, Paul, half blinded, dived for her legs and brought her down. Wiping the snow away with the back of one hand, he threw his body on top of hers. Pinning her, he could feel the laughter rippling from her body against his.

She hadn't expected this. He looked too big to move *that* fast. "Now what are you going to do with me?" she teased as she tried to wiggle out from beneath him.

Not taking a chance on getting another face drenching, he caught both of her wrists in each of his hands and held them above her head. "Boiling you in oil comes immediately to mind."

Her breath was beginning to back up in her throat again. His mouth was so close. And she could feel his warm breath gliding along her face like a seductive sea breeze. She shook her head slowly at his suggestion. "Horrible waste of a resource."

He knew he should get up, yet he remained where he was, savoring the contact, doomed to continue his mistake. "But satisfying."

"Something else might be just as satisfying." Judy's smile softened invitingly as her laughter gentled.

He had absolutely no willpower. Not at this distance. Not against her. "Damn, why'd you have to be so right?"

"Had to happen sometime," she murmured a moment before his mouth was over hers.

He kissed her. And this time, there was something more. There was a gentleness seeping through the fire, between the demands. A tenderness she had known he was capable of, even if he had forgotten it himself.

His tenderness affected Judy more than the passion had. Lost in the kiss, she gave herself up to the sensations that had been churning within her all night, that had all but broken free in his cabin this morning.

She was dragging him up over that wall again, the one that had the barbed wire strung across the top. The one with the No Trespassing sign on it. Dragging him over it until he was breathless with wonder and needs that slammed all through him.

He was lying in snow like some silly adolescent who had no sense, seeking his salvation in the ripe taste of her mouth. He knew he was tottering precariously on the edge. The other side had no net. No future. He *knew* that. So why was he doing this? Why didn't he pull back?

Because there wasn't anything more he wanted to do at this very moment than kiss her. He pulled her close to him, but he couldn't pull her close enough. His mouth was fitted over hers as if he would die if he broke contact. As if nothing could sustain him except her.

His mouth left hers for a moment, and they realized simultaneously that they needed air. He leaned his forehead against hers, wishing he didn't need this as much as he did.

There was snow in her hair, all around her, but she was oblivious to it. To everything but him. Judy touched his face gently. "Definitely better than being boiled in oil." She drew a breath to steady herself. It did no good. "But I think the same degree of heat's involved."

He looked down at her, wondering what it was about her that had penetrated through his wall so sharply, so keenly. Why her and not someone else? He didn't know. He just knew he wanted her the way he hadn't wanted anyone or anything in more years than he could remember.

For a moment, he contemplated picking her up in his arms and just going into one of the deserted buildings. To make love to her until he was completely senseless.

But stunts like that were for kids, not for grown men who knew better.

Still...

The sound of Raymond barking urgently from somewhere brought Paul to his senses. With a sigh, he shifted and then rose to his feet.

The dog was nowhere to be seen. But he was certainly being vocal. "I think your dog is jealous."

She sat up, dusting snow from her hair. Raymond's timing was miserable, she thought. Paul took her hand and raised her to her feet.

"Thanks." She brushed herself off. "Raymond's too busy being hungry to be jealous." She scanned the area. There was nothing stirring. "I hear him, but I can't see him. Where is he?"

Hastily shaking off the remaining snow from her parka and hair, she looked around. Only the buildings were visible. She cupped her mouth with her hands.

"Raymond!"

"That is one stupid name for a dog." Paul's voice was gruff as he tried to draw attention away from his momentary slip into the waters of insanity.

His voice didn't fool her. She was getting to him, and she was glad.

Judy retrieved her camera case and began to walk around. "It's better than King." Paul looked at her, knowing by now that more was to come. "That's what his original owner called him."

"Original owner?" The wind made it difficult to pinpoint the dog's barking, but he thought it was coming from the north side of the town.

Judy nodded, following Paul. "He was going to send Raymond to the pound. Said he couldn't handle him. My guess was that he didn't really want Raymond, not once he stopped being a cute puppy." She shrugged, hating her reasoning all the more because she knew it was true. There were a lot of people like Raymond's former owner. "I guess the magic had worn off."

"And you saved him."

She detected the slight sarcastic edge. Why did he have to do that with everything? "Anything wrong with that?" she asked evenly.

No, there wasn't. It just seemed to fit in with her altruistic aura, and he never trusted selflessness. Was afraid to trust it, really. There was usually a dark underside to be reckoned with.

"Not a thing. The barking's coming from here." He indicated an old building that looked as if it had once been a schoolhouse. It was tall, narrow and austere, like a thin dour-looking teacher in an old-fashioned shirtwaist dress. "Fool dog's probably got himself caught on something and can't get out."

She looked at Paul meaningfully. "There's a lot of that going around."

He said nothing. He knew when he was outmatched. "Let me go in first, just in case there's a wild animal in there." He put his hand up, already knowing Judy well enough to anticipate her charging in ahead of him without looking.

It was bleak inside the building. Though some of the tall windows were broken, the rest were so dirty, light had a difficult time struggling in. The large communal room was almost totally devoid of desks and benches, except for a couple by the wall. There were fresh tracks on the snow in front of one. Footprints. Small ones. And Raymond's tracks ran over them.

Judy looked at Paul uncertainly. The barking had stopped a moment before they entered. "Like I said, sometimes hikers get lost or—"

They heard a noise coming from the wooden closet that ran along the far wall.

"Raymond?" Judy called, taking a step forward. She felt Paul's hand clamp onto her wrist, silently telling her to stay in place.

The dog barked, emerging from the closet. But rather than run to Judy, he remained by the wooden enclosure.

Judy let out an exasperated breath. "Raymond, what are you doing?" she demanded, walking toward him. "You could have gotten—"

She stopped abruptly when she saw the scuffed toe of a boot protruding from the closet. She laid a hand on Paul's arm, calling his attention to it.

Paul placed his hand on his service revolver and eased it out, then motioned Judy behind him. "Come out of there," he ordered. Raymond barked, as if to reinforce the command.

Nothing stirred.

"This is Sergeant Monroe with the Royal Canadian Mounted Police. Come out with your hands raised. Now!"

The boot moved and then disappeared. Paul took a step forward, one hand on his gun, the other on the door. Just as he touched it, the door moved back. A young woman stepped out, her hands raised over her head.

She was a girl, really, Paul thought, looking at the haunted, frightened face. A girl with long, stringy brown hair that hung down like a faded, torn curtain about her thin face. Her eyes were huge. She couldn't have been more than about sixteen, perhaps seventeen, though a young seventeen.

And she was pregnant.

Judy looked quickly at Paul, but there was no sign of recognition in his face. Taking the initiative, she laid a hand on top of the gun barrel and gently nudged it aside.

Paul flushed, annoyed that he still had it out and trained on the girl. He holstered it. "Are you lost?" His voice was almost sympathetic.

The girl just moved her head from side to side.

"Hurt?" he pressed. What was she doing here? Who was she? In his mind, he reviewed the Missing Children posters that crossed his desk with heartbreaking regularity. Beneath the layer of dirt, she could have been any one of a number of them.

"Hungry?" Judy asked.

The girl ran the tip of her tongue over her lip and then nodded. "Maybe just a little."

Judy looked at Paul. "Why don't you get something to eat out of the snowmobile?"

He didn't particularly like Judy taking charge, but in this case, perhaps it was better if he let her handle it. Women always responded better to women, he thought. Especially pregnant women.

He left to get the food they had packed, and a blanket as well. The girl looked cold.

"What are you doing here?" Judy asked gently as soon as Paul left them alone.

The girl shrugged vaguely. Judy looked closer and saw that her expression wasn't vacant after all. On the contrary, she was alert. Apprehensive and defiant all at once. "Waiting."

What could she possibly be waiting for in a ghost town? "For what?"

The girl hesitated, as if contemplating whether or not to answer. She saw no harm. "Sara's supposed to be by this afternoon. Sara comes by every second day."

"Sara?"

"One of the Eskim—Inuit women," the girl corrected herself at the last moment, not wanting to give offense.

Judy wondered if she meant the woman she had met yesterday in the settlement. "Why don't we leave a message for her?" Judy suggested, taking the girl's hand gently and leading her toward the door. "Sergeant Monroe can take you home and—"

But the girl shook her head as she pulled her hand away from Judy's. "No, this *is* home."

Chapter Nine

Judy stared at the young girl, uncomprehending. The girl's face was partially hidden in the dusky room as she tucked her arms around herself self-consciously, crossing them over the mound that swelled before her.

"What do you mean, this is home?" Judy asked. "We're in the middle of an abandoned, dilapidated ghost town."

The girl flushed even as her chin raised stubbornly. She pushed the stringy, dirty hair away from her face with the back of her mittened hand. Judy could see two fingers peering out where the yellow mitten had begun to unravel from wear.

"The house on the end of the street's pretty comfortable. There's a bed and a fireplace." There was defiance in her brown eyes, and her voice was cold. "I've got a table and everything I need."

Judy very much doubted that, even if the girl's expectations were of the lowest order. First things first. "What's your name?" Judy prodded gently. "Mine's Judy Treherne." She offered a hand that went ignored.

The girl hunched her shoulders closer to her body, as if seeking her own warmth to give her support. "Christina. Tina. Tina Chambers." As soon as she gave her name, the girl added in a rush, "And don't start thinking of calling anyone about me, because there's no one to call."

Tina squared her shoulders now, attempting to look older than she was. As old as she felt at times. "There's nobody's looking for me, so you and Dudley Doright can just save yourself the trouble and go away."

Beneath the angry defiance was a streak of hurt as wide as a canyon river. Judy ached just hearing it. A runaway teen, fleeing home because no one seemed to care.

"Your parents—" Judy began slowly.

Something akin to a sneer curved Tina's lips. "I never had any. Not real ones, at any rate." The girl let out a breath that was closer to a sigh than anything else. "Foster ones that changed like the shape of the moon." She liked the way that sounded and curled her tongue around the description. She wanted to write poetry someday. Poetry people would read and weep over. "With regularity and the same amount of warmth."

It was a haunting thought. Judy tried again. There had to be someone. "The baby's father—"

Tina gave a short, empty laugh. Restless beneath this woman's supposed sympathy, she roamed the small room like a caged animal planning an escape.

"Gareth is long gone. We started out together. He thought it'd be a neat adventure." She turned to look at Judy over her shoulder, to see if the older woman understood. "You know, like some kind of wilderness family, living close to the land, all that stuff?" Tina shook her head. More lies she'd believed in. "Except he got tired of it all— the adventure and me—and wanted to quit." She had come full circle around the room and stood before Judy again. "I kind of liked it here, so I said I was staying." Tina shrugged, as if it hadn't hurt. As if she hadn't cried. "Then he left."

Judy knew that it took all kinds, and not everyone was basically decent. Still, she couldn't really understand how someone could be so heartless. After all, she was pregnant with his child. "He left you *alone?*"

"No, I'm not alone," Tina told her proudly. She wanted no pity. Once she had thought pity might make people treat her more kindly. But it didn't. Pity and contempt went hand in hand more often than not. "I've got the baby coming, and Sara looks in on me every couple of days." Tina's chin jutted up again as she stuck her hands in her pockets. "Gareth's more alone than I am."

That was probably truer than the girl realized, Judy thought. "That's a very mature answer." She heard the wind beginning to pick up outside. It made the town feel that much more desolate. "But you can't stay out here like this."

Threatened, Tina took a step back, away from Judy. "Why?"

"Because you have a baby due soon," Paul told her gruffly.

Both women turned toward the doorway as Paul entered. He carried a blanket and the sack of food he'd packed for himself. Judy's was still in the snowmobile.

He'd been listening for a few minutes at the door before entering. He had a feeling that Judy could get more out of the young girl than he could in his official capacity. People didn't generally regard him as a father confessor, but he could see them spilling out their innermost thoughts to Judy with ease.

Tina took the sack before he even offered it. Searching through the sack, she drew out the wrapped sandwich and held it aloft the way a miner would hold a nugget of gold after finding it in his pan. She took a bite, then closed her eyes as if savoring a piece of heaven. When she swallowed, she felt more like answering.

"Baby's not due until the summer, and I want him to be born right here, with me to love him."

Paul saw more scars on the girl than Judy did. He recognized the calluses that a lack of love formed on the soul.

Tina eyed them both warily. "Don't try to talk me out of staying here. Sara's already tried to make me come live in her town, but I don't figure I belong there any more than I belong anywhere else.'' She paused to take another bite, then carefully wrapped the remainder to save for later. She shoved it into the recesses of her coat pocket. "I'm of age," she told Paul, figuring that he was the one to stand up to, "so there's nothing you can do."

Paul looked at her dubiously. Huge belly or not, she was a child. "You're eighteen?"

Tina's head jerked up and down. "I'm eighteen. Just. Three weeks ago." The words shot out like BB pellets at a bull's-eye. "I look young for my age because I'm small." An almost wistful note entered her voice, but like a fluttering hummingbird, it was gone the next instant without a trace. "Mrs. Hilton always said that should've helped to get me adopted, but it didn't."

Tina could see that neither the blond woman with the camera nor the Mountie believed her. An edge of panic began to frame her words.

"I've got papers in my knapsack to prove who I am. A driver's license and everything." She set her mouth firmly. "Will that set your consciences at ease and make you leave me alone?"

Judy and Paul exchanged looks. Paul was the one who answered. "No, but it's a start."

Tina turned and nervously beckoned for them to follow. She placed one hand protectively over the pocket with the sandwich in it. "C'mon, I'll show you."

Raymond bounded ahead of them, fairly flying down the three steps leading from the schoolhouse to the ground.

An ingrained instinct had Paul offering his hand to Tina before she took the stairs. She pushed it away. There was no sign of gratitude, only annoyance.

"I don't depend on nobody." Tina tossed her head so that her stringy hair flew over her shoulder.

Pride or not, Judy didn't want the girl falling down the steps, which were still icy. Taking a firm hold of the girl's elbow, Judy said, "You don't have to depend in order to lean once in a while." Tina looked at her sharply, but to

Paul's surprise, the girl didn't pull away. "Everyone does it, they just don't realize it."

Tina took the stairs awkwardly. "But if you lean when there's no one there—"

"You fall down," Judy finished easily. She smiled at Tina and released her. They were on firm ground now. "But right now, someone's here."

Tina said nothing. She turned and walked ahead, leading the way.

"You get these sayings off a sampler?" Paul inclined his head toward Judy, his voice low. "Or do you make them up as you go along?" He was trying to provoke her, but it wasn't working. He could relate far more to the pregnant girl than he could to the overly optimistic woman at his side. He understood pain and bitterness. Abject happiness was a mystery to him.

"It'd do you some good to listen, too," Judy said calmly.

"I listen," he replied softly, looking straight ahead. "I just don't believe."

For the most part, the tiny house that Tina had claimed as her own was livable. Some of the shingles were missing and many more were rotted and curled, like thick wooden potato chips. There were several planks missing from the walls, too.

Inside, Judy looked around. The fireplace in the living area had fresh ashes in it. A mound of wood was next to the hearth. The house was small, but clean. Tina had done her best with what she had.

There was a small pile of books neatly stacked next to the narrow bed in the corner. It was a place for meditation, for a hermit to withdraw from the world. It wasn't a place for a young girl about to give birth.

Judy turned to look at her. "What do you do here all day?"

"Read." Tina kept an eye on the sergeant, obviously not trusting him. Her only brushes with the law had all been negative. The law was there to bully and restrict, not to understand. "Enjoy nature." She placed her hand protectively over her belly. "Think about my baby and how things'll be different for him or her than they were for me. He's gonna have lots of love."

That was the second time Tina had said that. The girl waved the lack of love like a ragged banner of war over her head. Judy glanced at Paul and wondered if it had been the same for him.

Judy picked up the top book and leafed through it, though she didn't see a word. Her mind was too full of Tina.

"I could take you back with me," Judy offered, closing the book. "I've got a room at the boarding house in Grateful Bend." She replaced the book on top of the pile. "I could put you up in another until the baby's born."

Suspicion flared in Tina's brown eyes like twin torches as she immediately closed ranks within herself. "Why would you do that?"

Paul was thinking the exact same question. What Judy proposed was expensive, and this girl was a stranger. Why would she put herself out like this for someone she didn't know?

Judy didn't see how the girl could even ask. "Because you need it."

Was it that simple for her? Paul wondered. Just need and supply? Just like that? He couldn't get himself to believe that she was for real. People weren't that selfless. His own mother...

There was no need to think about his mother. He banished the memory.

Tina's eyes narrowed. She had a strong distrust of charity. "I don't need anything." She gestured about the Spartan room. "I've got it all here." She eyed the sack that Paul still carried in his hand. "Could use another sandwich, though."

Paul shook out the sack on the table and then crumbled the bag in his hand. "I'd like to see that ID now."

Tina's eyes gleamed like Aladdin's when he stumbled into the cave full of jewels. Her hand hovered over the food; then she pulled it back when she realized that Paul and Judy were both watching her.

Forcing herself away from the table, she crossed to the bed. A sleeping bag was on top of it. On top of that was her knapsack. She retrieved her cheap, cracked plastic wallet and flipped it open and smugly handed it to Paul.

Paul glanced at Tina's driver's license. Judy laid her hand on his arm and tugged it down to satisfy her own curiosity. Paul's expression remained unchanged as he handed the wallet back to the girl. "She's eighteen, all right."

"Told you." The smug expression weakened a little around the edges. Tina lowered herself into a rickety chair at the table. Lately it had been harder and harder to stand for long periods of time.

Judy didn't care if the girl was twice eighteen. That didn't change the fact that Tina was living in a house in the middle of a ghost town all by herself. Optimistic though she was, Judy wasn't ignorant of what could happen to a young girl alone. Possibilities vied for priority in Judy's mind. She didn't like any of them.

Judy studied Tina's pale face. She had a sister close to Tina's age. Judy would have dragged her out of here kicking and screaming if the situation arose. "That still doesn't mean we should leave her here."

Tina half rose in her chair, ready to argue. Paul's next words made it unnecessary. "She's not breaking any laws."

There were things that went beyond the jurisdiction of the letter of the law. "There's got to be something—" Judy insisted.

"There is." Paul looked at her sternly and wondered if Judy was capable of it. "It's called leaving people alone."

Judy knew that he was referring to more than just Tina's situation. *Fat chance.*

Judy's eyes swept over the girl's swollen belly, and she frowned. Tina really shouldn't be alone at a time like this. Still, she could understand that, for whatever reason, Tina needed the solitude that she found here. At least for the time being. Once her time drew near, the girl would change her mind. If not, Judy would find a way to convince her.

"Do you think you might change your patrol?" Judy asked the question half an hour later as they made their way to the snowmobile.

She had taken more than a dozen photographs of Tina. Safe in her "home," the girl had eventually warmed to them somewhat—particularly, Paul noted, to Judy. Everyone, he thought, seemed to warm to her. It was like traveling with Saint Francis of Assisi. Saint Francis with a camera around his neck.

"What do you mean by change?" Paul lowered himself into the snowmobile.

Raymond yipped a protest. Paul had sat down on the dog's tail. Muttering, Paul shifted. Raymond moved his tail, his tongue doing double time on Paul's wrist.

"I mean, shift the schedule so that you can look in on her every couple of days."

He was way ahead of her. "Already done," he assured her.

He also intended to run as thorough a check as possible on Christina Chambers, faxing his questions to Ottawa on the captain's new pride and joy. Ottawa was the city listed on Tina's license. He'd made a mental note of the street address as well when he had glanced at the card. He'd have the RCMP in Ottawa research the case for him and see if Tina was really as independent of all ties as she claimed to be.

For the most part, he thought as he started up the snowmobile, Tina's story was probably true. It was an all too familiar scenario. Unloved children grew up fast and not always well.

Paul reworked his schedule to include passing by the ghost town on a more frequent basis, just as he'd promised Judy. They returned in two days. He, Judy, Raymond, Judy's camera equipment and a box large enough to house a Shetland pony.

He had resisted bringing it with them. Though he was now driving the Land Rover instead of the snowmobile, there was really no room for the box. But Judy had found a way. He was really beginning to believe that Judy always found a way, no matter what.

Tina was suspicious and uncertain when faced with the package wrapped in brown butcher paper. It took only a little encouragement from Judy before the paper went flying. Within the box were new clothes for Tina, toiletries and a few miscellaneous things for the baby. There was also a new book for Tina to add to her collection.

"I thought you might want to read something new," Judy explained when Tina looked at her in wonder.

She took photographs to commemorate it all, including Paul in them whenever she could. There was enough here, she thought, for two books. One on Mounties and one on the people they lived with and aided.

The contents of the box was spread out on the table and the bed. Tina went from one thing to another like a child at Christmas. A child who had believed that Christmas was going to pass her by, only to discover at the last moment that it wasn't.

Paul leaned over Judy. Standing behind her was the only way to evade her damn camera lens. "Why did you do all this?" he asked in a barely audible whisper.

For a moment, she retired her camera. Some things, Judy knew, were private. She half turned her face toward him. "Why not?" She tossed it off lightly. "I had fun shopping at the Emporium. I had no idea that there were so many things to choose from out here."

"Yeah, a regular Macy's department store."

As the days went by, Paul was no closer to understanding why Judy went out of her way for Tina than he had initially been. The girl was nothing to her, the same way that the child on the ice had been nothing to her. Why did she insist on getting so involved in the lives of total strangers?

And why, when he had so many other things on his mind, did she constantly keep crowding in, breaking up his train of thought, invading his work? Invading his life when she wasn't even around. And when she *was* around, she kept probing him, asking him question after question. She was clever. She mixed in just enough queries about the land and the people to throw him off guard. Then she'd sneak in a question about *him*.

She wanted to know little things. Inconsequential things. What was his favorite color? Did he prefer sunrises or sunsets? Where had he gone to school? Had he hated it? Did he like oranges? Did he ever frequent Grateful Bend's only movie theater?

Day in, day out, like water eternally dripping against a rock, she seemed determined to wear him down, to break down his walls. By the end of the third week, Paul was afraid that she would succeed. She was masterminding an invasion of his life that would put the D-day invasion of Europe to shame.

He knew damn well that he wasn't going to have a shred of peace to call his own until she left.

Paul sighed as he set down his coffee mug. He took solace in the fact that it was Saturday evening. Saturdays and Sundays Judy left him alone and aimed her camera at other people's lives. She had told him about every scrap of her life here, as if he were interested. And sometimes, despite himself, he was. She told him that she drove to see Tina for part of each Saturday. Judy usually took Cynthia, Hattie's daughter, with her. The one with the doe eyes that followed him everywhere, he thought absently, clearing away his solitary dish.

The rest of the time Judy spent trailing after Reynolds and making herself the veritable darling of the RCMP force. Hayes had let drop that he and his wife had had Judy over for dinner last Sunday night.

Paul shook his head. The woman got around faster than a dandelion seed riding a summer breeze.

Well, as long as she did it without him, he thought as he sat down by the fire, he had no complaints. Paul stretched his long legs out before him and let himself relax. As had become his habit, Raymond came and lay down at his feet, waiting to be scratched. The dog raised his head expectantly.

Paul heard something that sounded like a knock. He thought it was the wind rattling the door. Hoped it was the wind rattling the door. Leaning over, he idly began scratching the dog. But the knocking continued. With reluctance, Paul drew his long legs up, rose from the chair and answered the door.

He found Judy standing on his doorstep—the barely fading sunlight glinting in her hair—as sunny as the day was long. At times her sunny disposition grated on his nerves.

This was one of those times. How was he ever going to clear his head of her if she continued to pop up like a piece of toast?

Raymond was at her side, barking and licking her hand. "What are you doing here? It's not Monday."

She patted Raymond's head. "Good evening to you, too, Sergeant."

He disliked her addressing him by his title as if it amused her. The rank was supposed to garner respect, not mirth.

She pretended to peer longingly into the cabin. "Are you going to ask me in?"

His hand remained on the doorknob as he looked at her archly. "If I don't, will you go away?" He already knew the answer to that one, but he thought he'd give it a shot, anyway.

"No."

He shrugged indifferently. "Then come in."

Paul turned and let her close the door herself. She wasn't going to interrupt one of the few moments of comfort he allowed himself. He settled before the fire, hoping to be soothed by the flames. He stared straight into them. Agitation remained. "To what do I owe this sudden pleasure?"

He could certainly be sarcastic when he wanted to. "I brought you this."

He turned in time to see her taking a thin volume out of the deep pocket of her parka. She had already unzipped it and was making herself at home. As usual.

"What is it?"

"Most people call it a book." She grinned as she handed it to him. "See, you're not the only one who can be sarcastic."

She wanted to be near him. Hesitating only a moment, she sat on the arm of his chair instead of the sofa. Her thigh brushed his arm ever so lightly.

She was far too close for his liking. He turned his attention to the gift.

It was a book of verses, leather-bound with small, gilt letters. He raised his brow. "Poetry?"

Judy tapped the spine with the tip of her finger. *"Don Juan in Hell."*

He turned it over slowly in his hand. It had a nice feel to it. "You found this in the Emporium?" Paul couldn't recall seeing something of this quality in the store. He would have remembered.

She wanted to run her fingers through his hair. She wanted to just sit back and be with him, with no parrying, no hammering at walls that wouldn't give. "No, it's mine."

He started to give it back to her, but she pressed it into his hand. He eyed her warily, accepting nothing at face value. "Why?"

Judy smiled. "You don't go to the movies. You don't have a television set or a radio or even a cassette player." She looked around the small cabin. The only light came from the fireplace. There was a lonely aura to it. "There's nothing but silence for you in here."

He eyed her. Tonight, the dim cabin seemed unusually intimate. "Maybe I like the silence."

She looked at him as if he were saying the lie for her benefit. She disallowed it completely. "I thought that you could fill the silence with written words." Her fingers glided

over the volume's cover. "Besides, you remind me of Byron."

Paul snorted at the comparison. "Byron was slight and
dark, with a clubfoot."

Judy looked at him in pleased amazement. "You *did*
study poetry."

He shrugged. He knew the danger of giving her an inch.
"I went to school, if that's what you mean. This—" he
flicked a finger at the book "—was part of it."

"So was geometry, but I don't remember any of it. To
remember, you had to like it, at least a little. I love poetry."
It gave them something in common, and that delighted her.

She tried to get comfortable. It was impossible. But she
stayed where she was because she wanted to be near him.
"To answer your previous question, you're tall, fair and, as
far as I can see, have everything in the right proportions."
Humor highlighted her eyes. "But you both have brooding
souls. From what I read, he wasn't happy, either."

Just what was she getting at? "And reading his poetry is
going to make me happy?" He flipped open the book. He
was more than passingly familiar with the titles that floated
by him.

She thought again about leading a horse to water. "No,
but it'll let you see a kindred spirit. If you do, maybe you
won't feel so all alone."

There was no way to hint at this delicately. "Judy, alone
is the way I'd like to feel and can't right now." He saw the
smile slide into place and widen. He tried not to notice how
much it affected him. "What are you grinning at?"

He hadn't realized his slip.

"That's the first time you called me by my name."

He thought a moment. "No, it's not." Her brows drew
together, questioning his words. He wanted to gather her
into his arms and kiss her. Paul gripped the armrest to keep
his hand away from her. "I called you Judy when you were
on the ice, saving the Inuit boy."

She eased herself onto his lap. Her smile warmed, enticing him. "Maybe I should go out on the ice again."

He tried not to think how good she felt against him. How much he wanted to touch her. How much, he thought with growing alarm, he wanted to make love with her. "There isn't any ice here."

She snapped her fingers. "Foiled again." His hands were lax, away from her. Was he just hanging back, or was she making a fool of herself?

He was trying his damnedest to distance himself from her, and it wasn't working. Not at this proximity. "Maybe you should stop trying to orchestrate things."

She was in so far, she couldn't back down now. "I would if you made a few moves of your own, Paul."

He didn't want the closeness to go further than it already had. His mouth sobered. "I like *Sergeant* a lot better."

She was going to crack that shell around him if she had to take a sledgehammer to it. "Funny—I don't."

Without meaning to, he let his hands drift to her waist. Judy made herself more comfortable. And him less so. The golden light from the fire bathed her skin in amber waves. His mouth felt dry, and she was the water to cool him. "Why do you like to barge in so much?"

"Maybe I like a challenge." She resisted gliding her hand over his face, though she was sorely tempted. "Maybe I'm a walking greeting card." She could see that went completely over his head. It made her want to laugh. "You know, if you see a man without a smile, give him one of yours."

The woman was hopeless. Paul just shook his head. "I'm glad I ate dinner early."

This time, she did touch him, her fingers lightly tracing his lips. They twitched slightly as she caressed him. "It only takes a few muscles to smile and three times as many to frown."

He wished she'd stop. It was creating that same yearning within him he'd felt before. The one that could have no release. He was who he was and had no right to enjoy the fruits of life. Not after what he had allowed to happen.

"Maybe I like getting a workout."

Determined, she wound her arms around his neck. "Then maybe you're in luck."

He should have moved away. Instead, his arms tightened around her waist. "I don't think luck has anything to do with it."

She inclined her head, her eyes searching his. *Let me in, Paul. Let me try to make it better.* "Wrong. Luck has everything to do with it. They wanted to send me to the Yukon originally." Things always happened for a reason. The car accident she had suffered had changed her life completely. It had given her the impetus to seek a career she had always dreamed of. Choosing to come to the Northwest had brought her here, to his doorstep. Because he needed her. "I decided to come here, instead."

"Lucky me." Paul barely mouthed the words as he drew Judy closer to him, relying on pure instinct instead of common sense.

"Yeah." Her breath skimmed his mouth. "That makes two of us."

The last word was swallowed up as he kissed her.

Chapter Ten

Uncertainty gnawed at him like rats attacking a wheel of cheese, taking huge chunks out of it. He was spinning madly down into a deep hole, an abyss.

But it wasn't really an abyss. He knew what lay at the end, knew what he would feel if he permitted himself to open up to this woman the way he yearned to. He had to be strong and push her away, had to send her away.

Judy sensed his inner turmoil, sensed that he needed help. She touched his face. Her lips parted to speak, but for the first time in her life, she wasn't quite sure what to say.

His eyes skimmed along her parted lips, her soulful eyes. His concentration broke. Paul grabbed her to him. His mouth was hot on hers as he drew sustenance and salvation from it. From her.

This wasn't right. She had no idea what kind of man she was getting involved with. No idea at all. For her own good, Paul couldn't let this go any further than it already had—he had to stop before things got out of control.

No matter how much he needed her.

He placed his hands firmly on her shoulders and gently pushed her away.

A cold chill passed through her as if someone had suddenly opened the door. Judy felt like a cartoon character who had suddenly looked down to discover that there was no ground beneath her feet and began plummeting into the emptiness. There was no bottom, and he had let her fall. Willingly. Why?

Judy swallowed. She tried not to look as bereft—as confused—as she felt. Instead, she cupped his cheek with her hand. A nerve in his jaw visibly tightened and jumped. "What's wrong?"

He wished she didn't feel so good on his lap. He wished she didn't feel as if she belonged there. "We shouldn't be doing this."

Could she really have expected him to say anything else? But after three weeks, she could hope. Oh, God, she could hope.

Summoning patience, she asked, "Why not?"

Perhaps he owed her an explanation. He didn't know. But even so, he couldn't form the words, couldn't open up. "Because you don't know."

"Don't know?" she echoed. She bent her head toward him. Her hair fell forward. The soft blond curtain shielded him from the light of the fireplace. Somehow, that made her words that much more intimate. They seemed to float on his skin. "Don't know what?"

"The kind of man I am." If she had known, she wouldn't be here, offering books, offering comfort. She'd be asking Reynolds for a different subject. Someone who could arouse faith and empathy within her, not scorn.

The look in his eyes had her hesitating. There was a wall between them. She picked her words carefully.

"That's true," she agreed. "At least, I don't know what happened to you before you came to Grateful Bend." She thought of the captain's words: Why don't you ask him yourself. *As if he'd tell me, Captain. As if he'd tell me.*

She had to try. "So tell me."

She had the most beautiful eyes he'd ever seen. Like the first shoots of grass in a long anticipated, overdue spring. He didn't want to see loathing in them. It was better to back away. "Long story."

She shrugged casually, giving no indication of the impatience she felt. "It's a long night. I listen well." She grinned at the skeptical look that slipped over his face. "No, really. Just try me."

He almost did. For one brief moment, he almost told her. The words rose to his throat. And then stuck there, immobilized. It was his cross to bear, not anyone else's. He thought of how his father would have felt about him if he had been alive to learn of the incident. He'd joined the RCMP to emulate his father and had brought only shame to his memory.

There was no corner of the universe where Paul could hide from what had happened in that alley in Montreal. But she didn't have to know any of it.

Paul shook his head. He didn't want to taint her, and just listening would do that. "It won't work, Judy."

She saw his torment, saw the anguish in his eyes and fervently wished there was some way she could discover what cross he had hung himself on. It couldn't have been anything as bad as he felt it was. Had he taken a bribe? Betrayed someone? No, she refused to believe that he was capable of something like that. It went against everything she felt she had learned about him.

But even if he had done any of those things, it wouldn't have mattered, not to her. She cared for him for what he was, not what he had been.

But whatever he believed he had done, it was getting in the way of their finding each other. "No, you're right, it won't work. Not if you don't even try. Things are always doomed to failure if you don't even try."

He didn't need one of her sampler philosophies now, not when his blood raged to take her to his bed. Not when he was fighting to do the only decent thing he could in a situation like this.

Paul drew her arms away from his neck. "Don't push it."

Reluctantly she let her hands drop, but she remained on his lap. "I wouldn't if you'd just tell me—if you think it matters. If it didn't matter to you, then I wouldn't care." She could put up with not knowing, as long as it didn't affect him like this. But it did, and someday it would have to come out in the open.

He looked at her, vacillating. Damn, she was turning him inside out.

"Why?" he demanded, summoning anger as his only defense. "Why do you care? About the Inuits, about Tina, about that girl at Hattie's."

Her eyes filled, but she forced herself to will the tears away. "Cynthia," she supplied.

"Cynthia," he repeated. "Why do you care about any of us? We're all strangers."

She lifted a shoulder and then let it drop. "It's the way I am, I guess. I like people. I like to see them happy." *What would it take to make you happy, Paul? Could I do it?* "I like happy endings."

His mouth curved, but his eyes remained flat as he saw the girl lying there in the street. "Endings are never happy."

She let out a breath. "No, I suppose you're right. But we can try to make them that way." Her smile faded. "Talk to me, Sergeant. Tell me what you're carrying around inside of you that's making you so miserable."

He eased her off his lap until she had to stand, then rose himself. He needed distance between them before he could forget himself and give in—to her and to himself. The log in the fire finally broke, sending sparks shooting everywhere. He couldn't let his resolve break that way. "What difference could it possibly make to you?"

The question cut through her the way a razor-sharp knife cut through rotting cloth.

"I think," she said quietly, "if you have to ask, you haven't been paying attention." She circled so that she could place herself in front of him. "Maybe I can help." She saw the denial rise to his eyes like a meteor. "Sometimes, just letting whatever's bothering you come out helps."

She was almost pleading now. Whatever he kept within himself was eating him up a bit at a time, like a slow-acting poison.

"I'm not here to make judgments, Paul." She laid a hand on his arm. "I'm here to be a friend."

He shrugged off her hand. If he let her touch him, he'd forget all his noble intentions and take her now. "I don't need a friend."

She refused to believe that. She didn't think he believed it, either. He wasn't just hiding something, he was protecting someone. Was it her? Did he think that whatever he had done would change her mind about him? "Everyone needs a friend, Paul. Life's a lonely business without one."

He turned on her. Maybe if he attacked, she'd back off. "And what do you get out of this?" His eyes were dark, challenging.

"A good feeling." She licked her lips. "I suppose I need to be needed. And you need me," she said slowly, firmly. "Or someone like me, but I'd like to think that it's me."

At this moment, he needed her almost more than he needed to breathe. But he also needed to maintain a shred of self-respect, and sending her away would do that for him. Giving in and taking her, accepting what she offered, would be selfish. And wrong. And he would wind up hating himself for it.

Because she would.

She wanted more than he could give. He believed that at this moment, she had the power to make him do something that no one else could have tempted him to do. But he knew her well enough now to know that he would only hurt her in the end.

He needed to be alone. His emotions were pulling him apart. "Assume a lot, don't you?"

The grin wasn't nearly as confident as she tried to make it seem. "Yeah."

He stared off into the fire for a long time. So long that she thought he'd forgotten she was even in the room. Finally, he spoke. "I'll let you know when I need to talk."

She sighed, wondering if he would. Probably not. But she couldn't press the subject any further tonight. "Sounds fair enough." A smile blossomed again as she took off on another subject. "Speaking of fair..."

The woman was relentless. He raised a brow. He had a feeling he knew what was coming.

"Cynthia tells me that Grateful Bend is holding their annual carnival tomorrow."

Actually, *everyone* had told her that. The town had been talking nothing but carnival preparations for the last week.

"Is it?" He had been oblivious to the preparations. Things like that held no interest for him, and he dismissed them completely.

She hooked her thumbs into the belt loops of her jeans. "Yes. I'm going."

She had made the declaration with too much innocence. He was on to her now and he looked away. "Good for you."

Rather than circle him again, she tugged on his arm. When he looked at her, she coaxed, "Come with me."

"I don't—"

"Have anything to do," she finished his sentence. "Captain Reynolds said so. Yes, I asked him," she answered before he had a chance to form the question. She wanted to see Paul there, eating cotton candy and talking about nothing in particular. Just talking. And, perhaps, holding her hand. "C'mon, what are you afraid of?"

"You" was on the tip of his tongue. He was afraid of her. Afraid that she would burrow in and stir things inside him that had no business being stirred. Afraid that she already had. He had come to terms with life as it was and he made the best of it. He didn't want to be reminded of what he felt he couldn't have, what he shouldn't have.

Because he had deprived that girl of her life. He was alive because she wasn't.

Paul had almost forgotten what it was like to feel, and now Judy was reminding him. Reminding him in vivid terms that there could be life outside his netherworld, at least for a little while.

But he couldn't tell her that.

It would be difficult to control emotions once they were released. They could go anywhere. If he opened up to Judy, there was no telling what would happen. And they would both pay the consequences.

"Nothing," he finally answered. "I'm afraid of nothing."

She took that as agreement on his part. "Great, then I'll come by and pick you up." Her eyes sparkled in the firelight as she reversed her position on the subject. "Unless, of course, you'd like to pick me up instead."

She left him dazed and breathless without having moved a muscle. "Are you always this brazen?"

Judy laughed. "Only with reticent Mounties. Ten o'clock sound good?" She didn't wait for his answer. "That'll give us the whole day."

He held his hands up before him to ward her off. He felt as if he were snow on a mountain and she was the toboggan running over him. Continually.

"I don't want a whole day. I don't want any part of the day. I am—"

"Being a complete grouch about this." She pulled out the big guns. He gave her no choice. "In case you've forgotten, Captain Reynolds assigned you to me. I want photographs of my Mountie subject against the local carnival backdrop."

She had outmaneuvered him. It was beginning to come as no surprise. "Pulling rank?"

She was completely unembarrassed by her ploy. "Pulling anything I have to." Her mouth softened and she tilted her head beguilingly. "It'll be fun, Sergeant."

Fun again. She acted as if the entire world was one big carnival, instead of three-quarters cesspool. "How do you know it'll be fun? You've never seen Grateful Bend's carnival."

She pretended to brush away some lint from his shirt, her face turned up to his appealingly. "I just know these things."

It was time to leave. She would have been content to stay here all night, even if it meant just trading barbs with him. But she had made enough headway for now. As eager as she was to go even further, she knew it would be a mistake to push. The man wasn't ready to let her in yet.

But he would be—she promised herself that. He would be.

"All right," he conceded, having no choice. "I'll meet you in town."

"I'll see you at ten. Don't bother walking me to the door." The door was all of fifteen feet away. "I'll see myself out." As she slipped on her parka, she nodded toward the chair. The book she had brought was still on the seat. "Don't forget to read."

With a toss of her head, she eased the door closed behind her and was gone.

The cabin was as silent as the plains in the aftermath of a tornado.

Paul dropped into the chair, exhausted. Raymond came trotting over to him now that his mistress had gone. Automatically, Paul dropped a hand to the golden head and scratched the dog behind the ears. "What just happened here, dog?"

Raymond barked once. Paul had a feeling that the animal probably had a much better handle on the situation than he did.

With a sigh, Paul opened the book of poetry. Judy had written something to him on the flyleaf.

"We all make our own heaven and our own hell. The choice is up to us. Love, Judy."

He shook his head. If only it was that easy.

* * *

As summer solstice hovered less than a month away, sunlight was in abundant supply from a very early hour every morning. The people of Grateful Bend took advantage of it, beginning their day at five in the morning. Half the town was involved, in one way or another, with something that had to do with the carnival. Armed with hammers, nails, bunting, cups, punch bowls and enthusiasm, they were setting up stands, organizing decorating teams, gossiping and generally feeling good about themselves and each other.

There was nothing like a carnival to bring out the best in everyone, Judy mused. She was everywhere, helping where she could, taking photographs when she couldn't. The air fairly sang of goodwill and anticipation.

Cynthia gave her a brief rundown of some of the day's events. The girl ticked them off without a thought, but Judy stopped Cynthia when she got to the fourth event.

"Blanket tossing?" Judy stared at her, waiting for Cynthia to correct her mistake.

The girl was busy tacking up bunting around the beverage stand. It was filled with soft drinks. Like a lot of towns in the Territories, Grateful Bend was considered a dry town, but there was always someone who tried to sneak alcohol into the festivities. It was up to the Mounties to keep a tight rein and see that the only spirits at the carnival were natural ones.

Cynthia glanced up from her work. "Inuit men, women and children hold a large blanket and toss each other up in the air. We've got greased-pole climbing," she continued, the staple gun punctuating her words, "and tugs-of-war over the mud and a wrestling contest." Cynthia caught herself and realized that she sounded enthused. She shrugged nonchalantly. "I mean, if you like that kind of small-town thing."

Judy held up the other end of the bunting until Cynthia reached her with the staple gun. "I love that kind of small-town thing." Her lips quirked in a smile. "Except I've never wrestled."

"You don't." One last staple and the stand was completed. Cynthia stood back to survey her work and smiled. "You just watch and take sides." She lowered her voice as she inclined her head toward Judy. "We bet, but Captain Reynolds isn't supposed to know."

Judy was certain that Captain Reynolds knew everything, but turned a blind eye to it for diplomatic reasons.

All morning people arrived from the reservation and from the Inuit settlement, as well as from the sprinkling of homes that existed outside of Grateful Bend, solitary structures bravely standing up to the elements. Everyone wanted to take a part in the setup, a part in the feeling of well-being.

Sara brought Tina with her, though the girl looked physically uncomfortable to be in public. Judy wondered if Tina had made a miscalculation and if her time was due sooner than she had thought. Though Judy had tried to convince her, Tina staunchly refused to see either the midwife in the Inuit community or a doctor in Yellowknife, even when Paul offered to run her over there.

The investigation that Paul had conducted on Tina had led to a blank wall. Tina was not a runaway. No one had reported her missing. No one, Judy thought with pity, seemed to care where she was. Or *if* she was.

Judy and Sara sat Tina in a wide, high-backed chair that Cynthia snuck out of her mother's boarding house. Soon the other women from Grateful Bend were converging around Tina to offer suggestions about the approaching "blessed event" and reliving their own children's infancies.

And all the while, Judy continued to keep one eye out for Paul.

It was already past ten o'clock, and he hadn't arrived. The carnival had begun at nine-forty, only ten minutes later than Hattie had decreed it would start. The booths with refreshments were already doing a respectable business. Children and their parents were taking an equal interest in the ringtoss booth and the sharp-shooting contests. The latter involved blasting plastic rabbits to smithereens. The more exotic events, as Judy regarded greased-pole climbing and wrestling, were to take place later in the afternoon.

On the south side of the center of the town, a place had been cleared for the band. Hattie had put together a seven-piece band that was to start up at five and play for the remainder of the day into the well-lit evening.

Judy wondered if Paul would dance with her.

She couldn't deny the pull she felt between them, didn't really want to deny it. Unlike Paul, she wasn't afraid of a relationship, although she had to admit that there was an intensity here that left her nervous. But it was a good nervous. It was the kind of feeling one had before jumping headlong into something breathtaking and wondrous. There was always a little anxiety, a little fear involved, but it only served to heighten the experience, not detract from it.

In the back of her mind, she knew that in three more weeks her assignment would have her moving on to Montreal. And Paul would remain here. But she didn't want to think about that. She only wanted to think about the moment. And she wanted him in it with her.

Tall order, she sighed, turning her camera toward the huge totem pole that had been erected in the center of town yesterday afternoon. Originally, Grateful Bend had been built around the pole for luck. The pole had been taken down some fifteen years ago in an attempt to march into the future, but the locals resurrected it each year for the carnival. It was as if they wanted the faded, grimacing creatures depicted on the totem pole to bless the event for luck.

"Careful around that one. It's the god of fertility."

She turned, the smile on her face reflected in her eyes and in every fiber of her being. "You came."

Paul was dressed in a casual blue turtleneck shirt, jeans and a Windbreaker, but he still had the bearing of a Mountie, she thought. Raymond jumped up and licked her face, his tail wagging madly.

"Looks that way." Paul shrugged. "I figured if I didn't, you'd come and drag me here. I thought it would be undignified and make the locals lose their confidence to see one of the Mounties being pulled around town by a slip of a thing like you."

He could use any excuse he wanted to. He was here, that's all that mattered. And he was here with Raymond. The fact that he had brought the dog with him made her smile broader. He might be kicking all the way, but Sgt. Paul Monroe was definitely coming along nicely.

Paul realized she thought he had brought the dog along because he was getting soft. Well, he wasn't. Not exactly. "I had to bring him." He glanced accusingly at Raymond. "That dog of yours would probably eat what little furniture I have if I left him alone for the day."

Judy nodded solemnly, as if she bought into the exaggeration. "Smart move."

He folded his arms before his chest. Maybe he should have waited her out at the cabin. She was getting too smug.

"A smarter move would have been if I had never ticketed your car that day. You would have picked someone else as your guinea pig." And he would have continued with his life without having to fend off her damn questions and scratch her damn dog every night.

He didn't understand, did he? "Don't you believe in fate, Paul?" It was apparent to him that she did. "I would have chosen you anyway."

He saw the captain hoist his granddaughter onto his shoulders for a better view of the carnival. The little girl had an ice-cream cone in her hand. He had a feeling the captain was going to regret what he had just done, and soon.

"You would have been coupled with Muldoon," he told Judy. "And the two of you would have talked each other to death."

She'd met Muldoon on three occasions. "Possibly," she allowed. "But Muldoon is a little too perfect, or so he believes." She picked the Mountie out in the crowd. He was in the center of a ring of young women, flirting for all he was worth.

"And I'm not?" Paul had no idea why he was asking that. The question just seemed to rise up of its own accord.

She couldn't help teasing. "So imperfect it hurts." Judy caught her tongue between her teeth, but her eyes were laughing at him.

Broad daylight didn't help Paul. He still felt like kissing her. Luckily, there were too many people watching for him to give in. He stuck his hands into his back pockets. "Well, I'm here, imperfections and all. What do you want to do now?"

She laced her arms around his. He could feel the brush of her small breasts against his arm and mentally he began counting backward from a hundred. Raymond moved to her other side. "Everything."

Paul sighed. "I was afraid of that."

She meant it.

Judy wanted to try everything. With her camera strap slung over her shoulder, she was set to indulge in every sight, sound, taste and event the carnival had to offer. The enthusiasm around her was infectious, not that she needed any outside input. But it was almost awe inspiring to be around people who celebrated every shred of spring with a frenzied joy that rivaled sheer rapture.

She sampled the native dishes as well as the tried and true. To her delight, Sam from the Emporium manned a stand that sold cotton candy. The color arrangement matched the Canadian flag. She chose red and forced Paul to share some with her over his protests. He got more pleasure out of watching her eat it than eating the tuft she had given him.

When she licked the red remnants from her fingers, his stomach tightened so hard, he thought he would rupture something vital. He wanted to glide his tongue along her fingers, sampling the taste of cotton candy mixed with the flavor of her skin.

Dragging Paul over to the games being played, Judy discovered that she had a better eye for getting rings over the long neck of a glass milk bottle than she imagined. But the newfound aptitude completely vanished when she picked up a BB rifle. After watching her fire two shots at the plastic rabbits, Paul made Judy solemnly swear never to pick up a weapon within fifty miles of another living creature.

She wasn't content to do things on her own. Judy cajoled and coerced Paul to join her. He had absolutely no intentions of competing in any of the events, but Judy had other ideas. Devouring a hot dog in short order, she placed two hands against his back and all but shoved him toward the three-legged race.

He hung back as others were busy lashing themselves to their partners. Judy had registered them and dangled the long blue cord in front of him. He let out a hiss between his teeth as he took it from her.

"This has to be the stupidest suggestion you've made so far." Muttering, he tied his right leg to her left. "You're a foot shorter than I am."

She had to struggle not to fall over when he took a step. "Fourteen inches," she corrected, "but who's counting."

She tottered dangerously as they approached the starting line.

"We can't possibly maneuver like this," he complained as he looked around at some of the other contestants.

Undaunted, Judy positioned herself as best she could. "We'll find a way," she told him as the gun went off.

And they did. In a manner of speaking.

Amid cheers and shouts of encouragement from the sidelines, Paul and Judy came in fourth. It was due entirely to her sheer grit and refusal to be held back. Judy hobbled beside him with the determination of a one-legged, wounded bird trying to outrace a cat.

Her spirit, even in something so simple as this, astounded him. They crossed the finish line and then fell because she was laughing so hard. He was quick to shift away from her body.

"See?" she crowed. "Never give up!"

He didn't know whether to throttle her or to kiss her. There were too many witnesses around for either.

"C'mon, I'll help you get untangled," he volunteered, sitting up.

"I sincerely doubt that," she muttered, though audible enough for him to hear. Making herself comfortable, she sat back and watched him as he undid the knot.

Now if he could only do something about the knot in his gut, Paul thought, helping Judy to her feet, he'd be fine.

Chapter Eleven

The tug-of-war contest was centered around the large, oval mud puddle that had been eagerly created through the combined efforts of the children of Grateful Bend and the Inuit settlement. There was no way on earth that Paul figured he was going to join the ridiculous test of strength that would pit him, along with various other members of the crowd, against the opposing side. Absolutely no way.

At least, that's what he thought.

So he was still rather unclear how it happened that he came to be standing right behind Judy, his hands wrapped around a thick piece of scratchy hemp when he would rather have had them wrapped around her. Just as tightly if not more so.

"We can't lose," Judy assured him just before the event started. She pointed with confidence to the hulking giant at the front of their team. "Humphrey's on our side." Humphrey, she had already noted, was the brawniest man in Grateful Bend.

Paul supposed that there was a certain logic to that. There was also a certain logic to avoiding the whole damn event altogether. He knew there was. But he couldn't seem to tap into it, not when she was so near him. She was able to talk around any excuse he attempted to offer, speaking so fast that his thoughts were prevented from entering his head. They weren't able to penetrate the incessant buzz she generated.

He made the best of it.

Paul had positioned himself as the last man on the line. He had a feeling that it was better to be as far away from the middle as possible. Just in case.

He was right.

Humphrey's effort not withstanding, the other team, with several Inuit men and women who looked as if they would weigh in at well over the two-hundred-pound mark, managed to pull them over to their side. Heels digging into the softened ground, muscles strained to capacity, combatant after struggling combatant was pulled across, unceremoniously dragged through the puddle and muddied beyond recognition. All to the hoots and cheers of the crowd.

Making a split-second decision, Paul grabbed Judy's waist and yanked her to him, forcing her to let go of the rope. A whoosh of air left her lungs as she was lifted off her feet. He dragged her away and saved her at the last moment from joining the fate shared by the rest of their team members.

Judy was laughing so hard that Paul could barely hold on to her. Annoyed at having been somehow talked into this in the first place, and embarrassed by his instinctive action, he released his hold on Judy. She slid almost bonelessly down the hard slope of his body until her feet touched the ground.

Her body throbbing from the close contact with his, Judy turned slowly and looked up at him in surprise. "Why'd you do that?"

He shrugged. He was asking himself the same question. "I didn't think you wanted to get mud all over you. I know I didn't."

"Thanks."

The word hung awkwardly in the air between them. She dragged a hand through her hair. It was tangling and curling like a corkscrew in the damp air. Judy looked up at the sky. It was past seven, but the sun was as bright as it had been at noon. There was something to be said for the intimate, soothing power of nightfall. "I miss it getting dark."

Because he wanted to hold her, he shoved his hands into his pockets.

"So do I." The darkness brought with it a solitude that he craved. A solitude that had been denied him lately. Because of her.

Judy looked around for an event she hadn't tried yet. She decided that she had pretty well covered the entire carnival.

As they moved away from the crowd that was congratulating the tug-of-war winners, she heard the strains of music. She looked toward the stand that Humphrey and Corporal Hayes had helped to set up. Five men and two women, dressed in what had to be their Sunday best, were just returning from taking a break. Instruments were being tuned and tested again, as if they hadn't just filled two hours with music.

Judy's eyes darted toward Paul. "Looks like the band's getting ready to play again."

If there was a blatant hint in her words, he acted as if he missed it completely. He was watching two lovers walk off hand in hand behind the Emporium. Just before they disappeared, the girl glanced over her shoulder furtively. Paul wondered if he should interfere or leave them alone. He decided they both had looked of age and opted for the latter.

"Looks like it," he echoed.

The man certainly took being the strong, silent type to heart, Judy thought. Also to extremes. Being blunt was the only way she was going to get a reaction from him. "Would you like to dance?"

He finally glanced in her direction. His expression was completely impassive. "No."

She could feel the rhythm of the music seeping into her body, making her sway in time. Determined, she tried again. "Would you dance if I asked you to?"

Paul raised a brow as he stopped walking and looked at her. "I thought that was what you just did."

She saw no harm in pushing. So far, it had gotten her everything she wanted today. Almost. "Sergeant—"

"There are plenty of men available here who would love to dance with you." Paul gestured, vaguely indicating the entire area. There was no way he was going to make a fool of himself in front of everyone again. She had had her pound of flesh. He'd done his duty by her and then some. Even Reynolds couldn't fault him.

But she didn't want plenty of men. She wanted him. But his answer intrigued her. He had noticed other men's reactions to her. "How do you know?"

"I just do," he answered irritably. Why did she always insist on picking everything apart?

He could tell by the way Muldoon and some of the others had looked at her as she passed by today that they would like to do more than dance with Judy. A lot more. But that was none of his concern. Just as long as she stayed out of his hair.

Okay. Maybe a little reverse psychology would work this time instead of bashing him over the head with a two-by-four, Judy thought. Although the two-by-four was the more appealing way to go at the moment.

She raised her brows innocently and looked around. Then smiled. He tried to discern what or who it was that had caught her attention, though he told himself that as long as he was off the hook, he didn't care.

"Okay." Judy was already edging away from him. "Why don't you get yourself something to drink and relax? I'll see if I can find myself a partner."

"Fair enough." He spit the words out as if they were rusty nails.

Turning his back on her, Paul walked toward the beverage booth. He had all but physically thrown her into the arms of someone else. It was his own doing. So why did the fact that she was going to do just what he told her to—for probably the first time since they had met—annoy him so much?

Maybe being around so many people for such a long stretch of time irritated him, he reasoned. He tried to rein his exasperation as he crossed the last five feet to the booth.

Captain Reynolds smiled broadly at Paul as he stopped next to him at the beverage stand. Off and on all afternoon, the captain had been observing Paul with Judy. And he had liked what he saw.

The boy in the booth handed Reynolds his cola. "Quite a little lady, isn't she?" Reynolds nodded toward Judy before taking a swig from the bottle.

Paul looked. It figured. Muldoon had become her willing partner.

He looked closer. Maybe too willing. The man seemed to be trying to absorb Judy right through his clothing. If he held her any tighter, she would be behind him, not in front of him.

"Yeah, quite." Paul tamped down his temper and shrugged in response to Reynolds's question. "Orange," he told the boy at the counter.

The tall, lanky youth reached into a cooler and produced a bottle of orange soda pop. Handing Paul the bottle with one hand, he held his other out, palm up. Paul paid him. The money clinked into an old cigar box with multicolored birds on the lid.

Reynolds was eyeing Paul while pretending to watch Judy. "If I wasn't as happily married as I am, I think I might give her a spin or two around the floor myself. But I wouldn't want to make Mrs. Reynolds jealous."

Paul glanced at the captain and saw that he was serious. There was no end to her admirers, he thought darkly. Paul looked toward Judy once more and saw that she had changed partners already. The lumberman who had won the greased-pole climbing contest, now dressed in a fresh set of clothes, looked as if he had another climbing event in mind. Paul exhaled rather loudly.

Reynolds's thin mustache spread as he smiled into his soda pop. "You know, we Mounties have always had the reputation of rescuing people." He used the bottle as a pointer and indicated Judy. "I'd say that girl needs rescuing."

"She can handle herself," Paul said grudgingly.

He tried to turn away, but his eyes followed Judy, anyway. Now Sam from the Emporium was taking his turn with her, slipping a beefy hand against her back. Paul's hand tightened around the neck of the slender bottle.

The reaction didn't go unnoticed. Reynolds wondered how much longer Paul would hang back on the sidelines while everyone else had a turn with the woman he cared about.

"Of course, there's also that one about Mounties always getting their person," Reynolds murmured philosophically as he tilted the bottle back.

"Man," Paul corrected absently. "Mounties always get their man."

Damn her, why didn't she say no to any of them? Was she trying to set some kind of record? How many men could paw her during the course of one song?

"In these politically correct times, Sergeant, we have to broaden our definitions," Reynolds pointed out. He set his bottle down on the counter and moved closer to Paul. His tone lowered, father to son. "Why don't you go get your *person,* Monroe, and stop scowling?" He nodded toward the pole in the center of the town. "You look like one of those totem figures meant to frighten away evil spirits."

Paul's frown deepened. He didn't need to listen to a lecture, no matter how well-meaning. And he sure as hell didn't need to watch men paw Judy.

Rapping the bottle on the counter, Paul abandoned his drink and strode out onto the floor. Couples stepped aside to give him room.

Simpson from the boarding house was approaching Judy from the other side, ready to claim his turn with her when Paul moved in to block his way. Ignoring him, Paul poked Sam on the shoulder. Hard.

"I'm cutting in." It wasn't a request, it was a command. He didn't wait for Sam to say anything or even to so much as step back. Paul took Judy's hand and pulled her to him.

If he was a Norse god, his brows could have shot thunderbolts, she thought. "I thought you didn't like to dance." She made no attempt to hide the amusement she knew was in her eyes.

"I don't." He fairly barked the words out at her.

He never gave an inch, did he? Or let her enjoy a small triumph. She tried to remove her hand from his. "I wouldn't want to make you do anything you didn't want to do."

He felt her backing away. "The hell you wouldn't," he growled.

He tightened his hold around her waist and pulled her closer to him. The song the band was playing wasn't nearly as slow as his movements were, but Judy wasn't complaining. She liked the way it felt to have him hold her.

It was a moment before he trusted himself to look down into her face. He tried not to think about the fact that his pulse was racing. Or how soft she felt against him, soft and sweet like new-mowed hay. "Why did you let them pour themselves all over you like that?"

She felt as if she were being interrogated. But there was something in his eyes that kept her from taking offense. Did he actually care, after all?

"We were dancing, not pouring," she pointed out. "And as you so eloquently mentioned in the three-legged race, I'm a runt." She grinned, her anger cooling. "When a man's taller, he tends to hunch."

She was right, but he couldn't stop himself. Something small and intangible had gotten ahold of him. If he didn't know any better, he would have said it was jealousy. But that was impossible. "Hunch, not grope."

The anger returned, flaring white-hot in a way Judy had never felt it before.

She turned her eyes toward his, and the look Paul saw there surprised him. It was the kind he imagined was mirrored in his own most of the time.

"No one groped, Paul." Her voice was low, incensed. "You know better than that."

Yeah, he did. And he was behaving like a horse's rear. "Maybe," he mumbled.

Her brow rose and disappeared beneath the fringe of blond hair. "Maybe?"

It wasn't in him to apologize in the middle of a dance floor. It wasn't in him to apologize at all. He didn't know how to wrap his tongue around the words. But right now, he wished he did.

"Shut up and dance," he said softly. His fingers threaded through hers and he pressed her hand to his chest. He let the music do the rest. "It's what you wanted, isn't it? To dance?"

"Not quite like this," she began, then decided there was no point in arguing. It wouldn't lead anywhere, and he was right—she had wanted to dance with him and now she was. "But I'll settle," she added quickly. "I'll settle."

And she did settle, right up against him, he noted, his body tightening like the strings of a guitar being tuned too hard, too fast.

How could he feel so soothed and yet so alert at the same time? She made him feel strong and weak in the exact same moment and completely, utterly confused.

He shut his eyes and danced. And absorbed. Maybe that was enough.

Someone tapped him on the shoulder. Paul opened his eyes and saw that it was Muldoon, trying to cut in again. Paul gave him a dark look and said in a low, quiet voice, "The lady's with me."

No one attempted to cut in any more.

It wasn't until several dances later that Paul realized he had succeeded in drawing a fair amount of attention to himself. People were watching them move in time with the music.

As he glanced around the perimeter of the dance area, Paul caught Reynolds's eye. The other man said nothing, but he didn't need to. The amused look was enough. Paul abruptly released Judy and stepped away.

Just when she had begun to entertain hopes that things were progressing well. Complacency never lasted long around Paul. Judy sighed and followed him away from the band. "What's the matter?"

Paul continued walking. She realized that he was going toward where the cars were parked along the roadside.

"I think I've had enough carnival to last a long time. You can stay and enjoy it." In fact, he preferred it that way. "But I'm going home."

It had occurred to Paul when he saw the expression on the captain's face that he had let his guard slip. And in doing so, he was allowing feelings to creep in. The old man had seen that. It was obvious by the look on his face.

Paul stopped and looked around for Raymond. He'd seen that damn animal here somewhere. He whistled, a loud, two-note call. Within a few moments, Raymond came trotting over as if he had been responding to Paul's signal all his life.

He motioned the animal to follow. "Let's go, dog."

Judy felt as if she were on one of those amusement-park rides that suddenly inverted a hundred and eighty degrees. One minute, Paul was dancing with her, holding her so close that every fiber in her being was scrambling madly, almost to the point of desperation. The next, he was leaving. Just like that. With only the flimsiest of explanations left in his wake.

With an exasperated sigh, she hurried after him.

He didn't want her coming with him. That would only lead to an even greater mistake than he had already made. He turned on his heel just as he reached the Land Rover.

"Where are you going?" he demanded. "I thought you liked the carnival." He gestured toward the booths as if to wave her back toward them. Turning his back on her, he got into his Land Rover. Raymond looked undecided, then leapt in beside him.

She didn't want to discuss carnivals. "We've got some unfinished business, you and I."

He wasn't about to get into a discussion with her. He knew enough to know he'd lose any argument they had. He was no match for her tongue. "It's Sunday. My day off. Whatever business we have is finished."

With that, he gunned the Land Rover and pulled out.

Paul slammed the front door to his cabin, narrowly missing Raymond's tail as the animal darted in behind him. The door vibrated violently in Paul's wake as he muttered a stinging curse that encompassed the carnival, the town, Reynolds and nosy, petite blondes with cameras. He didn't need this in his life. He didn't need to be unsettled, to have desire creating itches within him that he couldn't scratch.

He glared at the door when he heard the knock. Damn, would he ever have any peace from her? He tried to ignore it, but knew before he started that it was futile. Another oath crackled in the air like thunder during a summer storm as he crossed to the door.

He threw it open.

If looks could kill, she'd have been dead on the spot.

"Whatever business we have is *not* finished!" she declared in the same tone he had used.

She stormed into the cabin like the first blizzard of winter. Mimicking him, she slammed the door behind her, and it rattled dangerously against the jamb. She didn't care if she knocked it off its hinges.

She whirled on him with all the impotent fury she felt. "What's between us is not just about photography or a book or the captain's orders."

He turned from her wordlessly. Judy refused to let him walk away. She moved in front of him again, planting her feet squarely on the wooden floor. "It goes a whole lot deeper than that, and you know it."

"I might know it," he allowed evenly, trying to hold on to his temper, trying to hold on to the emotions that were churning within him, "but I'm trying my damnedest to ignore it, and you're not helping."

Didn't he understand? That was the whole point. She laid a hand on his arm. "I don't want to help, not in that way. One minute you're warm and sweet, the next minute you're backing off as if I were a grenade about to go off."

Her face was turned up to his, and temptation raged through him. He remained immobile, but it wasn't easy. "It's not you, it's me."

"I know it's you. You're the one putting up all the obstacles in our way." His arm was rigid beneath her fingers. Judy dropped her hand.

Frustrated, she shoved both hands into her back pockets and began to pace about the small room. Raymond shadowed her steps, his paws padding along the floor in time to the click of the heels of her boots.

Pressing her lips together, she turned to face him again. "Paul, I don't generally throw myself at a man. No—" she held up her hand as if to erase the last words "—I *never* throw myself at a man." The look on her face was almost fierce in her desire to make him understand. To make him open up. With a sigh, she tried again. "But I think there's something here between us, something that could be good, and you're not even giving it a chance to grow."

She didn't understand, and he couldn't tell her. Wouldn't tell her. "It doesn't have a chance to grow—" He couldn't let it.

He'd probably sat down and written out the pros and cons on a sheet of paper. "Will you stop reasoning things out for a minute," she pleaded, "and just feel?"

She knew he could. She knew he did. Each time he kissed her, she could feel the passion, the desire, could feel that they would be good together if only he would let go of his demons.

Paul shook his head. "I can't, it's all dead inside. I—"

She whirled away from him so sharply, he was unprepared. He caught her wrist and jerked her toward him, thinking that she was tripping. It was then that he saw the tears shining in her eyes. Tears, damn it. He didn't want her to cry. Not over him.

"Don't do that." Paul barked the words out like an order, though he meant them as a plea.

Judy raised her head stubbornly, wishing the tears could just slide back into her eyes. "I'm not doing anything." She sniffed, hating the fact that she was crying. She wanted to throw things, not cry.

He grabbed her by the shoulders, as if to shake some sense into her, as if to shake away the tears. "Yes, you are. I— Oh, hell!"

Unable to resist both his own feelings and her any longer, he pulled Judy into his arms. His mouth molded over hers as if another moment's separation would mean total extinction.

Maybe it did, anyway.

Surrendering, kissing her, was the end of his resistance. It was the beginning of something else, something overwhelming. Something he had thought he'd shut himself away from five years ago. Something he felt completely unworthy of experiencing.

She had stirred passion within him, passion from the very first time he had seen her green eyes innocently looking up at him. He had tried to avoid it, tried to ignore it. Tried to tell himself that it wasn't there, pounding against the walls of his frail dam. But the dam had just broken, and the churning waters behind it had come pouring out to drench him.

His mouth almost savaged hers as he took and took, yet struggled to somehow give a measure back. He didn't realize that he was doing so just by being.

With a cry of joy throbbing in her throat, Judy threw her arms around Paul's neck and clung to him. It had come again, just like before. That rush, that mindless whirling in her brain, that wild frenzy in her soul at the slightest touch of his mouth to hers. It was as if she were a powder keg and he a match.

She felt his hands roaming over her back, felt him urgently pressing her body into his. The rush intensified. Judy moaned as she felt the hard contours of his body. He wanted her.

He finally wanted her.

It was a quantum step in the right direction, and they made it together.

Fear vibrated through him, shaking like the ground during an avalanche. Paul was afraid that he would break Judy in two with his hands. His needs were so strong, pulsating through him, demanding release. He had to struggle to maintain the barest shred of control over himself. He had to try, however difficult it was, to be gentle with her.

He knew she'd have regrets, but he didn't want her to hate him. He had to find a way to force himself to slow down.

But it was hard to pace himself when every shred of his being cried out for liberation.

He wanted to drive himself into her, to somehow lose himself in her, in the scent, the taste, the essence of her, and never, ever surface again.

Most of all, he wanted these feelings she generated within him to blot out his thoughts.

Chapter Twelve

It was more than she had ever expected.

So much more that Judy knew there was no way she could have possibly been prepared for what she was experiencing. Even from the very beginning, it was different. She expected thunder and lightning, she received tenderness instead. The way his mouth curved over hers, so soft, so gentle, it almost brought tears to her eyes.

Even the way he held her was different, not roughly, not tightly, the way he had before. He was barely touching her, as if there were an aura between them and he was absorbing it through his fingertips.

She looked up at him, her eyes half-closed from the drugging effects of his kiss. "I won't break, Paul," she promised.

He knew she wouldn't. She was tough, resilient. She had already proven that.

"No, but I might." And if he gave in completely, if he permitted himself to be swept away by the storm that was raging within him, he knew he would shatter, like a plate taken from the freezer to the oven. He was afraid that after years of repressing all his feelings, he would come on too strongly.

Paul had struggled so hard to function automatically, almost like an android, that he actually feared he may have lost the ability to behave toward a woman in the right manner. Just as someone who had been seriously injured might have to relearn how to use a limb—slowly, by degrees.

Like the whisper of a butterfly's wing, his touch was soft, reverent, as his very fingertips worshiped her. They skimmed lightly along her face, her throat, making the rest of her tremble in anticipation. Muscles within her tightened into knots, waiting.

Her limbs felt almost too heavy now, and he hadn't even done anything yet. She dropped her head back to savor the sensations his mouth was igniting. He pressed his lips to her throat. The moan that escaped sounded almost like the purr of a cat. Her fingers grasped at his shirt, bunching it as she tried to anchor herself to something. He was making her feel boneless and fluid.

And hungry.

Oh, so hungry. She had never felt like this before, never wanted like this before. This was agony wrapped in sweetness.

He cupped the back of her head, his eyes on hers. His were haunted, she thought. And yet kind, so kind. She knew she could trust him with anything.

"Last chance," he murmured.

There was still a single strand of restraint left within him. He'd cling to it, hoist himself up out of the burning pit he was in if she suddenly changed her mind. If she suddenly wanted to bolt and run. Somehow he'd managed, though he wasn't certain just how. She was the important one, not he.

"I hope not." The words seemed to throb on her tongue, echoing the drumming pattern she felt within her body.

Judy wound her arms around his neck. She stretched her body so that she could feel more of him against her. Like molten silver being poured into a cast, she molded herself to him.

And then there were no more last chances, no more turning back.

No more anything. Just her.

Paul buried his face in her hair. Its scent swirled through his senses, exciting him. He absorbed the heat radiating from her body. He was ravenous for what only she could give him, his soul hungry for what only she could provide.

Like a man only vaguely aware of his surroundings, Paul slipped his hands beneath her shirt. Fingers outstretched, he slid them up the slim column of her torso and cupped the palms of his hands about her small, firm breasts.

She shuddered. Her eyes grew smoky. On her toes, reaching, she brought her mouth up to his, aching, wanting. Needing. Her fingers dived into his hair as she took in and savored every feeling, every sensation he had to offer her. She was insatiable for it all.

Demands drummed through Paul with the intensity of a building earthquake, yet he held back. He had to. He could only think of pleasure, the pleasure he wanted to give her. The pleasure he received by watching her respond to him. To *him*. More than anything else, he wanted her to remember this night with something more than just regret when it was over.

And there would be regrets. Hers. And his. But for different reasons.

Paul slowly worked her pullover from her body. Judy raised her arms overhead as he tugged the material from them. The bra she wore was scarcely more than a bit of white lace. It tempted him to touch, to take, to possess what was just beneath. He fought off the temptation to tear it away. Instead, he glided his outstretched hands over it, like a seer trying to divine a hidden answer.

Though Judy tried to control it, anticipation caused her trembling to increase. It threatened to overpower her as his hands cupped her again, as his fingertips teased the flimsy lace down.

Gently, his thumbs brushed against her nipples. Instantly, they were rigid, as rigid as his desire for her. Paul lowered his mouth, his breath hot on her breasts. He peeled the rest of the material away from her. With a trail of open-mouthed kisses that had her knees buckling, he suckled first one nipple, then the other.

The throbbing within her core grew.

Demands slammed into one another inside her, pleading for release.

She half tugged, half tore his shirt from him. The sleeves tangled together as she pulled them off his arms. She needed to touch him, to feel his skin beneath her palms. To find a way to make him feel as frenzied as she did this very moment.

She splayed her hands over his chest and felt him tremble ever so slightly.

He looked almost calm, but his eyes gave him away. Intense and dark, the desire within them seemed to burn right into her flesh, branding her as his own. His breath was ragged.

His skin was hot. Judy felt it quiver as she touched him. Saw his need for her plain upon his face. Joy surged within her like water gushing from a fire hydrant.

The muscles of her stomach involuntarily tightened and quavered as he pulled open the snap on her jeans. Long fingers slipped beneath the material on either side of her hips and began to ease her jeans down. Heat rose, moisture formed.

He covered her mouth again, needing to take his fill of her once more. Her mouth was magical. Kissing Judy made him forget everything else. Everything. For a brief, timeless moment, she was his salvation, and he gave up a prayer of thanksgiving.

She could feel his hands cupping her buttocks as the jeans went lower. And then she remembered.

He felt her grin forming against his mouth. Paul drew his head back. "What?"

"Boots." She indicated them with only a minute movement of her eyes.

Paul looked down at her feet. "Yeah, that's what they are, all right."

Judy grasped the sides of her jeans in order to tug them back up to somehow, as gracefully as possible, pull off her boots. The next moment, Paul was sweeping her off her feet. He turned and crossed to his bedroom, still holding her.

She settled back in his arms. It amazed her how calm she could sound with her heart racing away in her throat. "Is this a new way to remove boots?"

He didn't want to be questioned; he just wanted to hold her. "The floor's probably cold. I don't want you walking on it."

It was a poor excuse at best, and she loved him for it. "I knew you were a thoughtful man the minute I set eyes on you."

He placed her down on the bed. Propped up, she watched him as he worked off one boot and then let it drop. "The hell you did." The second boot went the way of the first. He tossed it to the side without looking.

She nodded, languidly leaning back on her elbows, her eyes inviting him.

"The hell I did," she murmured, her voice low, incredibly sexy, incredibly arousing.

He lay down beside her. His heart was pounding so hard, it felt as if a herd of caribou were thundering over his chest. But he gave her no indication of the inner torment that was driving him.

Slow, slow, he schooled himself over and over again. *Go slow.*

He slipped his hands under her jeans, beneath her panties. He glided the back of his hand along her stomach, gently, flirtatiously, barely touching her. The muscles in her stomach quivered.

An eternity later, he began to ease her jeans down again, moving the material along inch after torturous inch at a time, until she thought she'd go crazy with desire.

His breathing was echoed by hers. His blood roared in his ears. And all he could think of was how desperately he wanted her.

Judy lay there in just her panties. He started kissing her knees and slowly worked his way up along her upper thighs. She sucked in her breath in surprise and anticipation, then bit her lip as he wove his way to her stomach and breasts.

With trembling, eager hands, Judy dragged his jeans from him. Still lying beside her, he used the toe of one boot to pull off the other. Jeans and boots were meshed together and thrown in a heap to the floor.

And then there were no more barriers, no more prisons. No more walls between them.

Only *them.*

He cradled her against him. Judy expected Paul to take what she so fully offered. Yet he didn't. He stroked and stoked, soothed and aroused, tasting, touching and driving her completely wild.

When she thought she couldn't take any more, couldn't support any more, he linked his fingers with hers. But he didn't fill her, didn't take her the way she anticipated, the way she wanted.

Instead, his mouth covered hers, and he slowly, methodically made love to her with only his lips. When his tongue dipped into the hollow of her throat, she could feel sensations crashing into one another like an aviary of birds suddenly set free.

She arched her body, desperately wanting to feel him covering her. Desperately wanting to feel him within her.

He couldn't hold back any longer. To do so was asking his body for more than he was capable of giving. Their hands still linked, he held her hands over her head and arched over her.

Her eyes had fluttered shut as she felt the sensations mounting.

"Look at me," he coaxed. Judy opened her eyes, a little dazed. "I want you to look at me." His voice was almost hypnotic. "When you remember this, I want you to remember looking at me."

Her eyes mesmerized by his, Judy felt him come to her. With a cry, she arched to meet him, to sheath him. As he filled her, she began to slowly rock her hips.

He whispered to her, words she didn't hear, endearments she couldn't understand.

But her heart did. Her heart understood everything and had long before she did.

The sensations built, rising and flaring as Judy and Paul became part of each other.

Harder and harder he drove them, until they went up and over the cliff together. The explosion, when it came, rocked her, and she sighed, letting herself go completely limp like a contented cat.

And there *was* contentment, contentment washing over her like soft, gentle rainwater in spring. Judy clung to Paul long after the shudders had left her body, long after the fireworks had settled into a warm, comforting glow that encompassed all of her.

Slowly her eyes drifted open. Only then did she realize that she had squeezed them shut. Against orders, she thought with a smile.

He was still lying over her, his breath not yet steady, his head resting against her shoulder. Love brimmed, strong and warm, through her veins. She locked it away like a treasured secret.

Not yet, she thought. *Not yet.* He wouldn't be ready to hear that yet.

She flicked her tongue along the outline of his ear and felt him stiffen slightly. He stirred against her, reluctant to move. She smiled, and the smile grew like a sunbeam stretching out along the ground.

"I had my eyes shut," she confessed. "At the end. Is there a penalty for that?" Languidly she ran her hand along the hard ridges of his back, as if she were softly strumming a lute.

He wished she wouldn't do that. She was stirring him up all over again, and he hadn't even recovered from the first time.

"You're forgiven."

His own regret was already setting in. He should have known better. He shouldn't have given in—but, oh, it had been wondrous. And he was only a man, only able to resist so much.

"So." Judy struggled for enough breath to form words and tried her best to look as if she were serious. "What do you want to talk about?" She didn't want this moment to end. Most of all, she didn't want Paul to draw away from her.

Paul raised his head then to look at her and realized that she was kidding. Pivoting on his elbows, he framed Judy's face between his hands. A moment longer, just a moment longer, he thought, he wanted to savor this. For it would have to last a long, long time.

"Anything you want." The words were out of his mouth before he realized his mistake. It was like giving a gambler a blank check.

"Would I be asking too much if I asked for something personal?"

Paul glanced down. Their bodies were still joined. The sheen of perspiration on her skin was a combination of his own and hers. An amused smile curved his mouth as he looked at her again.

"I think this is as personal as I get." Reluctantly, Paul rolled off Judy. Tugging the sheet over both of them, he cradled her against him.

She smiled. This had been more personal than he thought. This wasn't just sex with him. A man who looked the way Paul did wouldn't lack for women if that was all he wanted. She had seen the way the women in town looked at him. And the way he remained oblivious to their attention. No, what had happened between them was about more than sex.

But she wanted more. Eventually, she wanted it all. It was time for the next step. "Tell me about your childhood."

He settled back, one arm thrown over his head. He stared at the ceiling, trying to distance himself from the words, from the memories that hurt.

"Nothing much to tell. My dad died when I was ten. My mother remarried. I left home as soon as I could."

She turned toward him, her hair brushing against his cheek, sensitizing him. "That's just three sentences. There had to be more."

He let out a long breath. It didn't help. He had come to terms with it, but it still hurt. After all these years, it still hurt. "There should have been, but there wasn't."

She heard everything in his voice. The loneliness, the hurt. She just didn't know the particulars. Her eyes strayed around the room, and she saw the small framed photograph on the wall. A Mountie in full dress uniform. There was some resemblance.

Judy placed a comforting hand on his chest. "Tell me about your father."

Paul closed his eyes. He could almost see him. Beyond the haze that time imposed, he could see Mike Monroe. Tall, strong. A man to model himself after. A man he had failed to model himself after.

"He was great." Judy heard the fondness in his voice instantly. "A big man with a booming laugh. Everyone liked my father. He always found time to spend with me, even when he was busy. He found time for everyone. That's the kind of man he was."

Paul thought of his parents together, of the photograph he still had buried deep in the bottom drawer of his bureau. A photograph of the three of them that last Christmas. The Christmas his father had given him Windwalker.

"When he was alive, my mother used to laugh all the time. After my father was killed, though, she stopped laughing." The words slipped into the darkness that was enshrouding the room.

The silence in the room was dividing them, not bringing them together, and she didn't want to be shut out. Not again. "And when she remarried?" Judy prompted.

He didn't realize that his jaw had become rigid, or that bitterness had entered his eyes. But Judy saw it all. "She didn't smile then, either."

Paul had begged his mother not to marry Frank. Frank Stockard had been a stern man with small, cold eyes. Eyes that frightened a child. She didn't listen. And they both paid the price.

"She remarried because it was rough for a woman alone with a kid. She didn't have anyone to help her but me." And he had tried, tried so hard to help her, but what did a ten-year-old know about the things that frightened a woman in the middle of the night, alone in bed?

"She wasn't much good at making decisions without having someone tell her what to do, what to think." He didn't bother to hide his bitterness. "My stepfather was very good at that."

Judy's heart ached for the ten-year-old he had been and the love he had lost. "And the two of you didn't get along." It wasn't a question.

He had already said too much, but he couldn't seem to stop himself. Just this once, it seemed to be all right. "I don't take orders very well."

She smiled fondly. "You're a Mountie."

He shrugged. There was a world of difference between obeying a stern disciplinarian who hit first and talked later and taking orders from his commanding officer. "That's different."

Yes, she could see how it would be. He was an honorable man, a man who wouldn't be broken by the whims of another. "And you became a Mountie because your father was one."

He turned to look at her, tucked in next to him as if she belonged there. As if she had always been there. Maybe if she had, things would have been different. But she hadn't and they weren't. There was nothing he could do about that. "You already know that."

Like a child who wanted the reassurance of hearing the same story over and over, she smiled. "Tell me again," she coaxed.

He stared straight ahead again. He didn't want to see the sympathy in her eyes. It only intensified the failure that he felt. He hadn't measured up to Mike Monroe.

"I did it because I thought that somehow it would bring me closer to him, even though he was gone. Becoming a Mountie would make me like him. He was everything I ever wanted to be. Kind, loving. Loved." It hadn't turned out the way he wanted it. None of it. "I thought that if I went to the same academy, joined the same force, that I could—I don't know—carry on a tradition. Pay him back for what he had given me. That becoming a Mountie would somehow fill in the gaps."

Shadows were playing on the wall, shadows cast by the moon filtering through the trees outside his cabin. It seemed eerie. "But it didn't turn out that way."

What had gone wrong for him? What was there that Reynolds had said she'd have to ask him about herself? And why wouldn't he tell her? "How *did* it turn out?" she whispered.

They were on the edge, tottering, but he couldn't go over. He couldn't let go. "I think your twenty questions are up, Judy."

The door that had opened was closed again. But it had opened once and it would open again. She was sure of it. And she wasn't greedy. Yet.

Her eyes teased him. "Will I get another chance?"

The wariness was returning. He had shared as much as he was able to share. The rest he couldn't tell her. Couldn't burden her with. That cross was his alone. "At the questions?"

She played it safe and chose the sweeter path. "At being here beside you."

He raised himself on one elbow and looked down into her face. Moonlight bathed her skin, giving it a pale, ethereal hue. She'd probably like that description. "You really are brazen, aren't you?"

She rolled that over in her head, amused. She'd be more than that to be here with him. "I guess that fifty years ago, Hattie would have labeled me a hussy."

He laughed at that. "Hattie would probably label you that now."

She couldn't help wondering if, deep down inside, he might be harboring the same kind of thoughts. She cupped his cheek. "Hey, Sergeant, I want you to know that this was unique for me. I don't hop into bed with every six-foot-three-inch Mountie I meet."

He grinned. "Neither do I."

She laughed then, picturing the scene in her head. She laughed so hard, her sides ached. Watching her, he laughed as well. The tension between them broke. For tonight, no matter what tomorrow brought, they were two lovers. "I don't think you're Muldoon's type."

He sniffed, remembering the way the man had been all over her at the carnival. "Muldoon again, is it?"

She feigned innocence, loving the spark of jealousy she saw flicker in his eyes. "First tall Mountie who comes to mind."

"Well, get him out of your mind. I don't want him there." Paul traced a pattern over her breast that felt very much like a heart. "Or here."

She squirmed under his touch. Small tongues of fire were beginning to ignite again. "Figure you've got squatter's rights?"

He kept his hand where it was. He liked feeling her breast rise and fall beneath his fingers. "Something like that."

She prodded a little, to see him react. "Squatters have to stay on the property they're claiming for more than just a day."

He raised a brow. She moved, and he could feel himself being aroused. "What are you proposing?"

Judy linked her arms around his neck and brought him closer to her. Brought his mouth closer to hers. "I dunno. Why don't you surprise me?"

Her warm breath, sweet smelling and enticing, washed over his face. And he found himself wanting her all over again, more fiercely than the first time. "So far, I've managed to surprise *me.*"

It was her turn to arch a brow in curiosity. "You didn't want to make love with me?"

She knew the answer to that, but he humored her. "I've made love with you a dozen different ways in my mind almost every night—"

She laid a hand dramatically to her breast. "Why, Sergeant Monroe, I'm shocked."

The hell she was. Nothing could shock her. Except for what he had done, what he was guilty of and would always be guilty of.

But he let that go for now. All he wanted was this small island of time, this small reprieve to hold on to when the nights were longer than the days and time fed into itself and made no headway.

"But I never thought I'd actually do it," he concluded.

That did surprise her. "Did you actually believe that I'd say no?"

Her feelings had nothing to do with it. She couldn't judge wisely if she didn't know, didn't have all the facts. "I said it for you." He looked down into eyes that held him prisoner. Eyes he could so easily become lost in. "Except, I guess I didn't say it loud enough."

"Lucky for me you're hard of hearing." Judy grinned as she raised her head and nipped at his lower lip. Her appetite whetted, she pressed her mouth to his and kissed him soundly.

He could stir her to heights she'd never been to with just a kiss, just a touch of his mouth. She was his, completely and willingly. He didn't even have to ask. As long as he didn't try to send her away. She didn't think she could bear that after this.

Paul watched Judy lie back against the pillow they had bunched beyond recognition only a few minutes before. Her face was now half-hidden in shadow, but he could hear her smile in the way she breathed, in the way she moved invitingly against him.

"So, you never told me, what exactly did you have in mind for me right now?"

He loomed over her. "Exactly?"

She lifted her arms to him, her body ready, her eyes teasing. "Exactly."

"I'll have to show you."

"I was counting on it."

Chapter Thirteen

He was wide-awake.

Paul had spent nearly half the night watching Judy sleep beside him. Half the night wondering how he could have lost so much control over himself and gone so far from the reclusive path he normally trod. The only way he had managed to survive and cope with both his austere childhood and the guilt that rose up to seize him by the throat in that alley in Montreal was to completely cut himself off from all feelings, to become empty.

And now Judy had changed everything. He couldn't just open up to her and leave everything else untouched. Half measures weren't in him. The old guilts and the pain they generated were threatening to resurface. He had to rebuild his walls of defense quickly. But the major crack Judy represented made it almost impossible.

He wanted to give and yet he couldn't give. It was an emotional catch-22 situation.

Dawn was tapping impatient fingers outside the window. Judy stirred, and Paul resisted the urge to kiss her again, to lightly run his hand along her body and feel its heat mingle with his own.

It wasn't fair to her. Making love with her, making her believe that something might work out, none of it was fair to her. Nothing would come of it. Nothing *could* come of it. She was sweet and pure and she deserved the best.

At the very least, she deserved someone to make her happy, to make her laugh. Someone whose conscience was clear and who could comfortably deal with his emotions.

That wasn't him.

Paul had lain there for hours, not wanting to move, not wanting to wake her. His body ached for more reasons than one. He let out a long, slow breath. He wasn't doing either one of them any good by staying here like this, absorbing the warmth of her body. Steeping himself in it. With an inward sigh, he slipped out of bed.

As quietly as possible, he reached for his jeans and slipped them on.

"I thought Mounties never ran."

He might have known. Paul closed the snap on his jeans and turned to look at her. "You're awake." He made it sound as if it were an accusation.

He watched her body move beneath the sheet as she stretched, fascinated despite his attempt not to be.

Judy looked up at him. "Long enough to know you've been watching me for a while."

He tried to remember what he had done with his boots. He couldn't seem to think straight with her lying there, hair tousled, a light fragrance of warm sex still in the air. "Why didn't you say anything?"

She shrugged and tugged the sheet up a little as it slipped. "Lazy, I guess. I like having you next to me and I was afraid if I said anything, you'd leave."

He could imagine what she was thinking. She didn't realize that this was for her own good. How could she? "I've got work to do." He found his boots and quickly pulled them on.

He wasn't just leaving the room, he was leaving her, she realized. She sat up, wide-awake. "So do I."

He didn't want her with him today. He couldn't begin to rebuild what had to be rebuilt if she was with him, talking, laughing. Being. He couldn't do it if her scent filled his senses, clouding them. Making him want her almost as fiercely as he wanted to protect her.

He needed to sort things out, to put them back into perspective. Judy had turned everything completely upside down within him. How could he hope to reconstruct his walls if she was right there?

A chill came over Judy's heart as she watched Paul's expression harden. Against her.

"I'd rather you didn't come along today," Paul said softly.

It was happening already. Judy hadn't expected him to be completely the same after they'd made love, but she had hoped that he wouldn't revert back to the way he had behaved before last night.

She pretended to take it as a joke, hoping he would let the matter drop. "That's what you've been saying to me all along, remember?"

Judy rose, dragging the sheet off the bed with her. She kept it wrapped around her. She suddenly felt cold and naked down to the bone. Not nude—naked. There was a world of difference. An ugly world.

He saw the embarrassment rise in her eyes, coloring her cheeks, and felt guilty because he knew he had done that to her. But he had to. "This time I mean it."

There was only so far she could push, so far she could close her eyes and say that it was "just his way." So far she could forgive him. Hurt made her angry, but she held both emotions down. Maybe he did needed his space. For that matter, maybe she did, too.

"All right," she said gamely. "I've got some things I could do."

But right now, she couldn't think of a single one of them. She dragged a hand through her hair, attempting to still the turmoil she felt inside. And the terrible sense of betrayal.

She made him feel reprehensible as hell, standing there like an injured bird struggling with its last shred of pride. He started to move toward her, wanting to take her in his arms, to soothe her wounded feelings.

But he couldn't. Something wouldn't let him. It was better for her this way in the long run. He had to hang on to that. There was nothing he could do for her, nothing he could give her.

He nodded toward the back. "Do you want the shower first?"

She had watched his lips move, but she hadn't heard anything. How could he retreat from her like this? "What?"

"The shower," he repeated. "Do you want to use it first?"

He realized that he'd never asked a woman that question before. There had never been anyone in his life to share these kinds of things with—a bed, a shower, a tender moment.

And there wouldn't be again.

When she just stood there, not answering, he made the decision for her. "You go ahead. I'll go make the coffee."

She didn't even nod as she left the room. The sheet trailed behind her like a wilted train.

Judy felt like someone in a trance. No, more like someone in a bad dream. How could he be so wonderful one minute, she thought, dropping the sheet to the floor, and so cold the next? Had she misjudged him? No, she had seen things in his eyes, real things. She had observed him these last weeks. He was a good man, a man in pain, and he was backing away because he was afraid. Well, in a way, that made two of them, she thought, closing the shower-stall door behind her. But she wasn't about to run off anywhere.

Judy let the hot water hit her like a thousand small, hot needles. She was hoping that it would wash away the pain she felt inside. It didn't even begin to mask it, much less ease it.

Well, it wasn't as if she didn't know what she was letting herself in for, she thought as she dried herself off five minutes later. But it would work itself out in time.

She set her mouth firmly. It had to.

Their individual showers didn't wash away the awkwardness that existed between them. If anything, the wariness intensified. Taking a shower had put Paul in a worse mood. He could smell her scent on the towel, smell her in the tiny bathroom. Desire had his stomach knotting so hard, it felt as if he had a huge muscle cramp.

Like the opposite poles of a magnet, they pushed one another farther and farther away with every guarded word, with every silence.

Judy left the cabin before Paul did, taking Raymond with her. Paul watched her go, unable to stop her, even though he wanted to. The way her back looked as she walked away and closed the door would stay with him for a long time.

He sat, uncustomarily nursing a cup of coffee. The cabin had never been so quiet.

The only thing to do was lose herself in her work. Having grown familiar with the area, she knew that there were a lot of things she could be doing, a lot of places she could be going.

She only wanted to be with him, though.

Judy shook herself free of her melancholy mood. Brooding had never been her style, except for that one short period of time after her accident, and her uncle had shown her the futility of that. Feeling sorry for herself didn't solve anything; it only made things worse.

"Brooding's Sergeant Monroe's long suit," she said aloud to Raymond, "not mine."

The dog's insistent bark reminded Judy that she had left the cabin without stopping to eat. Worse, she had neglected Raymond.

One hand on the wheel, Judy scratched the animal behind the ears.

"Sorry, boy. I didn't mean to make you suffer just because Mr. Mountie needs to be hit over the head with a two-by-four to realize what he's tossing away." She replaced her hand on the wheel as she took a curve and pointed the vehicle toward Grateful Bend. "I'll see if we can convince Hattie, just this once, to let you have a bite to eat at the boarding house."

Raymond looked like he had his doubts about that. He barked, then turned around in his space. His golden head rested on the back of the seat as he turned his huge brown eyes to something behind them. Judy glanced over her shoulder to see what had caught the dog's attention. There was nothing but the cabin in the distance. It was growing smaller by the second. Raymond sounded as if he were whimpering.

"He's busy." Judy faced forward again, pressing down on the accelerator. "He's a pigheaded mule and he's busy. You're going to have to eat somewhere else." She looked at the animal. "Better get used to it."

And it would do her a hell of a lot of good if she got used to it as well. But she doubted very much if either one of them would. In that respect, Raymond was very much like her.

Hattie looked absolutely overjoyed to see Judy. So overjoyed, she only gave one distracted "harumph" aimed in the dog's direction when Judy made her request about allowing Raymond in the dining room. Knowing she had to give a little to get a little, Hattie agreed and all but hustled Judy into the other room. The other boarders were just beginning to straggle in for breakfast. The hour was early, but Hattie, in her aqua duster, was ready for it—and Judy.

Chattering like a well-trained mynah bird with an extensive vocabulary, Hattie loaded Judy's plate down with enough food to feed three. Once seated, Judy tactfully sneaked food to an impatient Raymond, who hovered at her feet under the table.

Hattie planted herself in the chair opposite Judy and tacitly ignored the other two boarders, who seated themselves at the second table. Hattie's attention was clearly focused only on Judy. Pouring a cup of coffee for herself, she sipped and studied Judy with an eye as sharp as a circling vulture's, waiting for the last breath of life to leave its expiring prey.

"I noticed that your bed didn't need to be made this morning."

Judy almost choked on her toast. Subtlety, obviously, was something Hattie had never learned. Judy reached for her coffee. "No, I don't imagine that it did."

Hattie pressed her thin lips together, wondering if she should come right out and ask it, or try to draw Judy out. Eagerness had her going the direct route. "Now, what you do with your own time is, of course, your own business."

Right, Judy thought, hiding a smile behind her napkin as she wiped her mouth. "I most definitely agree."

Hattie looked flustered for a moment as the conversation appeared to have reached a dead end without giving her what she wanted—confirmation. Taking a deep breath, she pressed on. "And I know that Sergeant Monroe has a certain charm."

Judy had seen the way Hattie had eyed Paul at the carnival when she thought no one else was looking. Like a fox drooling over a chick it saw across a river that couldn't be traversed.

Enjoying herself, Judy leaned back in her chair and cradled her cup in both hands. "Does he?"

"Oh, my, yes." Hattie fluffed the edges of the tightly permed hair that she forced Cynthia to work on every six months. "He has, oh, *je ne sais quoi*—" Her tongue wrapped lovingly around one of the few French phrases she knew.

She didn't know, Judy translated silently. Well, neither did Judy. All she knew was that she was attracted to the man—severely, utterly, passionately attracted. "That makes two of us."

Hattie's face fell. "You speak French?" Knowing snatches of that language, she felt, had put her above the other citizens in the town.

Four years' worth, accumulated in high school and college, but Judy sensed that it was important to the other woman's ego not to mention the fact. Judy shrugged casually. "Just a touch."

Hattie drowned an English muffin beneath a mound of raspberry jam, then took a bite. She noted that Judy was hardly eating anything. Had to be love. Still, there were standards to maintain. "Well, anyway, I just don't want any of whatever happened between you two at his cabin—" she waved the remainder of the muffin, making her round-about point "—and I'm not saying anything did, mind you—" She leaned forward, her eyes bright. "Did it?"

Judy merely raised her brow and quietly sipped her coffee.

Disappointed, Hattie withdrew. "At any rate, I wouldn't want it to happen here."

Judy thought of this morning. Paul couldn't have put more distance between them if she had smallpox. "You have nothing to worry about," she said quietly. She set the cup down on the flower-edged saucer.

Hattie frowned, wishing she could get more out of Judy. She was a lot more successful deducing things from her neighbors than from this woman. So much for Americans not being able to hold their tongues.

She tried another approach. "Why isn't he with you?"

Because he's afraid. "He had some work to do—official business, he called it." Judy saw that Raymond was finished and ready to go. And so was she. She moved the chair away from the table. "Something he felt I shouldn't be around to witness." *Like the shoring up of his beaches.*

Hattie looked unconvinced as Judy took her leave. The woman watched Judy drive away and worked her lower lip, wondering who she could pump in order to find out the truth of the matter.

* * *

Wanting to fill the empty, gnawing feeling that was widening within her stomach like an ever-growing pit, Judy decided to visit Tina. She stopped at the Emporium first, to pick up a few things.

Sam Newton was behind the counter, sorting out the latest mail shipment from Yellowknife that the pilot had just dropped off. He looked up and beamed when he saw Judy enter.

"Some carnival yesterday, eh?" He thought about the dance they had had, or the fragment of a dance, and smiled. He glanced toward his wife, who was busy with her weekly inventory of the notions they sold, and thought it best not to mention it. Etta had already taken him to task about it. "Hey, where's your shadow?" When Judy looked at him blankly, Sam added, "The sergeant."

Judy wandered over to the revolving rack of books Sam kept next to the counter. "I gave him the day off for good behavior." She turned the rack slowly, glancing at titles, and wondered which one Tina might like.

"He's a good one, he is." Sam picked up the last handful of mail out of the sack and began filing the letters into the pigeonholes on the wall behind him. "Can't recall ever seeing him at one of our get-togethers, though. Say—" he held up a blue airmail envelope "—you saved me a trip. Here's one for you." He handed it to her.

It was from her sister, she thought, glancing at the return address. "I can take the sergeant's mail to him if you'd like," she offered.

Sam looked at her as if she had just said she'd seen a flying sled with eight reindeer. Then he shook his head. "He doesn't get mail."

Everybody got mail, even if it was only junk mail. "At all?"

Sam scratched the tiny bald spot on his head. "Not in the five years he's been here. You recall him getting any mail, Etta?" He cranked his neck to catch a glimpse of his wife bending behind the counter at the other end of the store.

The woman, all angles and bones stretched over a near-six-foot frame, rose and shook her head. "Not a scrap. I remember these kinds of things," she told Judy with pride. "Never sends nothing out, either. Gotta write to get written back," she said solemnly, as if she were reciting chapter and verse, then continued to arrange spools of thread to form what she felt was a pleasing color scheme.

Judy made her purchases and left. As she walked out, she wondered what it would be like never to have anyone write, never to have anyone to write to. Her family's letters followed her no matter where she went. They represented a bit of home to her while she wandered.

The letters, like the one she scanned outside the Emporium, were usually brief, but it was enough that they were sent. Her sister had included a scrawled note from her seven-year-old nephew.

Judy smiled as she folded both letters and tucked them back into the envelope. Andy wanted a photograph of "Bigfoot," by Friday if possible. That was when he had show-and-tell, and he wanted to show off the photograph to his class and impress them.

"Sorry, Andy, you're going to have to settle for photographs of caribou," she said to the letter.

And Paul didn't receive touches from home, she thought, remembering what he had said about leaving home as soon as he was old enough. He really was alone.

But not if she had anything to say about it.

Tucking the letter away, she went to see Tina.

The ghost town never failed to elicit the same sad, melancholy feelings each time Judy approached it. The snow was gone now. Weeds were pushing through the muddied, lonely street and the sky was a crystal blue, hanging like a huge canvas behind the empty, rotting buildings. The contrast between the beauty of life and the abandoned town made it seem even lonelier than it had all the other times.

She wished there were a way to get Tina to stay in Grateful Bend. She'd feel considerably easier about Tina's condition if Tina was near other people instead of miles away.

Raymond was out of the car window before she had a chance to open the door on her side. He knew exactly where he was going. The dog stood patiently at the door, waiting for Judy to catch up. Judy knocked once and then tried the doorknob. The door wasn't locked.

"Tina?" she called.

"Over here." The girl was lying on her bed, staring out the window. She turned toward Judy, trying to muster a smile.

"I feel like a whale," she complained, and the smile faded before it was ever completely formed.

"My sister used to say that." Judy laughed. "I think it's an obligatory phase of being pregnant."

Tina frowned. "I hate it. I hate feeling fat and clumsy and tired. I hate this whole thing!" She stared at the mound before her, and the real reason for her distress surfaced. "What if I mess up, Judy? What if I'm a rotten mother?"

Judy patted her hand. "Seventy-five percent of being a good mother is love. The rest of it works itself out along the way."

Tina sighed. "Yeah, well, I'll love him—or her—but I don't know *anything* about raising a baby."

"No first-time mother feels that she does." Judy dug into her pocket. "That's why I brought you this." She handed Tina one of the two books she purchased, then unzipped her jacket.

Tina's face lit up at the photograph of a newborn baby on the cover. She swung her legs over the side of the cot and struggled upright, holding the book in one hand.

Judy helped the girl sit up. "My sister swears by this book." She tapped the cover. "It should help answer any questions you have in the beginning." Judy looked at her sternly. "The doctor in Yellowknife will take care of the rest."

"I don't want to go to Yellowknife until I'm due, and I'm not due for another month and a half," Tina insisted. "God, another month and a half of looking like a house." She shuddered.

Judy sat down beside her and placed her arm around the girl's thin shoulders.

"Just think yourself past it," Judy advised her. "Six weeks isn't much time." And she herself was already more than halfway through that time, she realized with a sudden pang, thinking of Paul. She pushed him from her mind. "Here, I also brought you this." She took out the other book. It was a romance novel.

Tina took it from her, her fingers curving around the novel lovingly. She smiled at the title. "I like to read everything, but I like these best. They make me feel good." Tina pressed the book against her chest, as if she could absorb the sentiment by osmosis. "They make me think that everything'll be all right in the long run."

Judy gave her an affectionate hug. "It will be," she promised fiercely.

Maybe she could come back after her assignment was over and take Tina and the baby with her, Judy thought. Tina was going to need a lot of things, a lot of support. Judy looked at her thoughtfully. One step at a time. Tina was not the type to be rushed.

"You know, I'd feel a lot better if you moved into Grateful Bend until the baby's born." Judy began cataloging arguments in her head. "You like Cynthia and the other women—"

The captain's wife had taken a mothering interest in Tina the moment she had seen the girl at the carnival. Perhaps—

But Tina wouldn't let her continue. She could tell what was coming. "I will. Soon. I promise."

She looked around the small cabin. She had cleaned and scrubbed it as best she could and gathered whatever treasures she had found in the other buildings to make the small cottage as cozy as possible.

"But I kind of like it here." Tina's hands dug into the sides of the mattress as she dangled her legs over it, as if to anchor herself. "It's the first place I've called my own. Ever. That's important to me." She looked at Judy, searching the woman's face. "Can you understand?"

The trouble was that she *did* understand. She understood very well what it had to be like to never have anything to call your own. The cottage had no electricity, but it was warm and secure and there was a pump in the back that Tina used for water. Basics. But the baby needed basics, too.

Judy brushed the hair back from the girl's face. "Yes. But taking unnecessary chances—"

Tina struggled to her feet. The point was better made standing up. "I'm not. I've always been as healthy as a horse." A small, ironic smile twisted her lips. "I guess I've always had to be. There was never anyone to take care of me." Not anyone who cared, at any rate.

She placed her hands on the mound and felt movement. "It'll be different for him. Or her."

Judy knew that it was impossible to move Tina on the subject, at least for now. She could only make Tina as comfortable as possible. "Can I get you anything?"

Tina shook her head. She looked around her home and was content. "Got everything that I need. Sara came by and brought more food just before you came. She visits every day now." Tina smiled as she dragged her hand through her hair. "She fusses as bad as you do in her own way."

Tina glanced at the new book Judy had brought her. The one with the man and woman embracing on the cover. A small sigh of longing escaped.

"Do you believe in love, Judy?"

Judy thought of Paul, of what lack of love could do to a person. Of herself and how the love of her family had seen her through the blackest period of her life. And she thought of how she felt about Paul, how even though he tried to make her back away from him, what she felt for him made her overlook the words, the anger, and cleave to what she felt. He needed her.

"Yes," she told the girl softly. "Yes, I do."

Something in Judy's expression held Tina captive. "Does it last?" The question was wistful.

That's the million-dollar question. Judy nodded. "If we're lucky."

Tina straightened a chair against the table and brushed away an imaginary speck of dust. "It didn't last with me and Gareth."

Judy came up behind her and gave Tina's shoulders a squeeze. "You're very young yet."

God, she felt as if she were emulating the voice of experience. What the devil did she really know about it? She was skating on thin ice herself. Still, Tina didn't need to hear about her insecurities, she needed something to soothe her.

Judy turned the girl around to face her. "I think you might have mistaken need for love. It happens."

Maybe a lot more than she thought, Judy mused. Was *she* mistaking need for love? Did her own need to be needed color her perspective? No, she loved him, and she was damned if she really understood why at bottom.

The light-colored eyebrows drew together as Tina looked at Judy, perplexed. "Don't they go together?"

"Sometimes. C'mon," Judy coaxed. "I want to take a few more photographs of you."

Tina frowned at her belly. "I don't think that I'd look good in your book."

"You'll look fantastic," Judy assured. "But I was thinking of putting together an album for you and little what's-its-name. When the baby is older, you can show off your pioneering instincts."

Tina sighed impatiently, but Judy could see that she liked the idea. "Okay, where do you want me?"

"That's my girl." Judy laughed, picking up her camera.

She had stayed with Tina longer than she had anticipated, but it felt good just to kick back and talk, and Tina welcomed the company. Once her initial wariness had been shed, Tina was a warm, giving person.

They shared some of the hot chocolate Judy had brought with her from the Emporium and talked about a great many things. Once the baby was born, Tina had decided, she was going to help Sara take care of children while their parents worked. A mini day-care center, Judy thought with a smile. Progress was inching its way along, even out here in the wilderness.

On the trip back into town, Judy had nothing to divert her mind. There was only static on the radio. Even Raymond was quiet. That left Judy with only her own thoughts for company. Despite the full day she'd had, all her thoughts were of Paul. And last night.

She took the pieces he had given her about his life and tried to fit them together with things he hadn't said but she had detected. He hadn't told her about the emptiness he had felt when his father died, hadn't mentioned how he had felt when his mother emotionally abandoned him by marrying another man and siding with that man against her own son. But it was there in his eyes, plain as snow on the ground after a blizzard.

She ached for him. No one should feel abandoned like that, not at any age. She wanted to make him feel whole again.

She thought she could.

In town, Judy paid a visit to the captain and took a few more photographs of the headquarters. But rather than stay for dinner the way Reynolds had urged, she made her excuses, packed up her equipment and drove off to Paul's cabin.

She hadn't seen him all day. She knew that the territory he patrolled was large, but she had nursed the hope of running into him in the crisscross path she had taken today. No matter, she was here, she thought, stopping in front of the cabin.

The cabin was dark, and there was no sign to indicate that he was inside. She glanced at her watch. It was later than it usually was when they returned from his tour. Shutting off the engine, she sat for a momen*, wondering if he was coming back at all or if some sort of "business" had him staying away.

Or was it her?

Was he going to stay away on some pretext until her time was up and she had to move on to Montreal? She honestly didn't know. There was no second-guessing Paul, not in this matter.

She tried the door and found it unlocked. The man set a bad example, she mused. But then, there really wasn't anything of value to take in the cabin.

Inside it was dark and somber. Though far more dilapidated, Tina's cabin had been a good deal cozier. Rubbing her hands along her arms, Judy decided on her first order of business. She crossed to the fireplace and began making a fire. It was only in part for practical reasons. True, the night was growing chilly despite the fact that it was the latter half of May. But she really lit the fire because she needed its warm glow to keep her company.

After a few minutes of prodding, the long, yellowish flames seized the logs. Satisfied, Judy rose.

"Time to get you fed," she told Raymond. She'd picked up some supplies of her own at the Emporium.

With nothing but time on her hands, Judy began to prepare dinner for Paul, not knowing if he would return or not.

It definitely hadn't been one of his better days. There had been no incidents, no children falling through the ice, no arguments to resolve. No emergencies.

Nothing tangible.

It was just that he couldn't seem to shake her. Even if he could have managed to purge her from his mind, and he couldn't, Paul found that he couldn't rid himself of Judy's presence. She was all around him. Everywhere he went today, it seemed that she had been there just before him.

He stopped at the Inuit village. Judy had been there, looking in on Jimmy, talking to Sara. He went to the ghost town to check on Tina. Judy had been there an hour before him. When he walked into headquarters, he didn't even have to be told that she had been there, too. The fragrance that she wore still skimmed the air, sweetening it. Making him crazy. When he made his stop at the Emporium just before heading home, he'd been told that she had been there to buy supplies.

"Looks like you've got a nice home-cooked meal comin'." Sam had winked.

It was as if he were chasing after her when the exact opposite was true.

Wasn't it?

Or was he just trying to fool himself?

God, he didn't know anything anymore. Paul reminded himself that she was leaving in less than three weeks. No matter what mind games he was playing now, it wouldn't matter in three weeks. Judy would be gone.

As he approached the cabin, Paul saw smoke curling from the chimney. Had he— No, he hadn't left a fire going, he remembered. He hadn't started a fire this morning, preferring to let the cold envelop him and make him numb.

As if it could have.

He saw her four by four as he pulled up in front of his cabin. *Damn you, woman, why can't you leave me alone?*

Yet his step was hurried as he approached the front door. He heard her laughter first as he stepped in. It brought a smile to his face even though he fought it. She was here, and he was glad of it. He had to be losing his mind.

Judy was sitting on the floor before the fireplace, playing with Raymond. He couldn't help thinking that it looked like a scene out of a Christmas movie. She belonged in *It's a Wonderful Life,* and he belonged in the book of verses she had given him. *Don Juan in Hell.*

She heard him come in and swung around, but didn't rise. "Hi."

He stood where he was, feeling oddly wooden. "Hi."

She wasn't sure what to say, what to do. She'd been prepared with an army of words just a few seconds before. But now that he was here, she was at a loss. Nervous. It felt so adolescent, and yet there it was. Her palms were damp.

Paul stripped off his jacket and then unbuckled his service revolver. He took his time with both and placed each on the chair near her. God, she looked good. "I, um, missed you today."

Judy almost sprang up to her feet. "You did?"

It had been a mistake to admit that. "Yeah, there was no one to annoy me." He sniffed the air. There was a wonderful aroma wafting from the stove, mingling with the scent of her perfume.

Judy grinned. "That's the most left-handed compliment I ever got, but with you, I'll take whatever I can get." She wiped her hands on the backs of her jeans. "I made you dinner," she said unnecessarily.

He didn't want her cooking for him. He didn't want to fall into a comfortable groove. He wished she had stayed at the boarding house.

But he was glad she was here.

"You didn't have to."

She expected nothing less from him. "Now, don't go overboard thanking me. I wanted to do it."

Her smile faded as she looked at him. They had to get something straight. "Paul, there are no strings attached to any of this. I just want to be your friend. What happened last night between us doesn't tie you down."

"I know."

The words sounded so brittle, so hard, she felt like a fool for even trying. Maybe she was. She clung to her pride. "You might want to forget about it, but I don't. Because it was very special to me. I meant what I said last night. I don't do that sort of thing casually." Her eyes held his, knowing. Sensing. "And neither do you, I think. Don't spoil it."

Judy picked up her jacket from the arm of the chair where she had left it. She shrugged into it without looking at him. If she did, she knew she would make an even bigger fool of herself and cry.

"I'll be here in the morning." Taking her things, she began to cross to the door.

Paul caught her wrist. When she turned to look at him, he said nothing for a moment. Judy looked up into his eyes, trying to read signs, attempting to understand.

"Yes," Paul told Judy quietly, "you will be."

Chapter Fourteen

Judy looked up at him, not certain that she understood. Afraid to make assumptions and suffer the pain of disappointment. Once was enough. "What?"

Hesitantly, he drew her closer to him, knowing it was a mistake. Knowing he had no choice. "I can't watch you walk away from me twice in one day."

She nestled against him, stretching in order to reach her arms around his neck. She smiled up at this strong, stern man who was having such trouble unlocking his emotions. "Tell me more."

Paul could feel her soft breasts rising and falling against him as she breathed. His body tensed. "I've already said too much as it is." He couldn't say more. It wasn't in him.

Judy laughed softly. It was seductive, like the summer breeze that passed through the frozen land all too infrequently, all too quickly. "Sergeant Monroe," she teased, "no one will ever accuse you of saying too much."

He lowered his head and delicately kissed her hair, her forehead, her cheeks. Sampling, absorbing, knowing there was more, so much more, and all he had to do was ask. It gave him too much power and made him want to back away.

It still wasn't right, but he wasn't strong enough to do it. He wasn't strong enough to take the right path and leave her be. He wanted to be with her. He could satisfy her physically, but not emotionally. She wanted more of him, and he couldn't give it, wasn't even sure if he knew how to anymore.

Perhaps one more night together could be forgiven. Just once more, to last forever. For tonight he was stripped of the past. It didn't exist. And the future wasn't here yet. There was only now.

There was only her.

He looked at Judy. Her eyes were growing smoky. "This doesn't change anything, you know."

If ever a man had to be dragged into the light, kicking and screaming, it was him. Judy nodded solemnly, her eyes never leaving his. "Whatever you say."

"You're being too damn agreeable." His hands lowered to her waist and cinched it to him.

Her hips fit so perfectly against his, she thought. All she had to do was stand on her toes. A little effort. A little time. "I try."

He felt the first flare of heat as her body rubbed against his. "And too damn attractive."

She certainly wasn't going to talk him out of that. Instead, she lifted her mouth to his. "Then do something about it."

Her arms still around his neck, Judy molded herself against him.

She felt like pure melted silver in his hands—liquid, fluid and precious. He meant to go slow, like the last time. He wanted to memorize every single moment, every single movement.

But the neediness within him, the loneliness that raged like a winter blizzard, pushed his better intentions from his mind. He pulled her jacket roughly from her so that he could touch her. Just touch her.

Her softness made him groan, converting him into both captor and captive at the same moment. And hopelessly lost, without a prayer of finding his way out again.

His mouth was over hers—hot, quick, clever. And hungry. So very, very hungry. Over and over, he slanted his mouth over hers, feasting on every tiny morsel she had to throw him.

Falling ever deeper into trouble and taking her with him.

She hadn't known he could be capable of this, of making her head reel and her body set to explode into a million pieces by doing nothing more than holding her. By doing nothing more than kissing her. She didn't think that so much could be done with just a kiss. That she could be unraveled so quickly, so surely, with just the press of his mouth against hers.

Within seconds, she had been pitched into darkness. They went spinning off into the universe together by themselves, leaving the cabin far behind.

She could feel his energy, his desire, surging through him. Spontaneously, it unleashed all the longings she was harboring, cut away all her fears. They became nothing more than tiny black dots floating somewhere in space far away from her.

Judy clung to him, her hands roaming his back, frantically pressing him to her, feeling a rush that threatened to disintegrate her as his mouth made love to her over and over again. She felt helpless and divinely empowered at the same instance.

And lucky. Very, very lucky.

Her body throbbing, aching for release, Judy didn't think she could stand this sweet agony much longer.

"Paul, please, I—"

Her words vibrated in his chest like a primal call. He grazed her chin with his mouth, teasing her skin with the tip of his tongue. Judy shivered in his arms, and he felt deep satisfaction rooting within him like a tenacious seedling, growing against all odds.

He had to hold back. He'd almost gone all the way that time, grabbing quickly what he should have relished slowly. For he would never have this again.

"Shh," he murmured.

The sound rippled along her skin and made her knees dissolve. With careful, precise movements, Paul tugged her shirt out of her jeans. His fingers slid down between her breasts.

"Buttons this time," he realized aloud. He let his fingers glide along the planes of her breasts as if he were a concert violinist and she the Stradivarius he was allowed to play.

"I thought you might like variety." The words were pushed out of her throat one at a time like beads being strung on a necklace.

He felt her heart beating wildly beneath his fingers. His own matched the frantic pulse, and his breathing quickened. The silky material parted beneath his palms as he moved them to her shoulders and then down along her arms. The blouse fell to the floor.

She was on fire.

Maybe a spark had shot out of the fireplace and landed on her, she thought, almost giddy with the frenzied sensations he was creating within her. She was the canvas and he the artist. Anticipation did a war dance within her, the rhythm beating more and more frantically as it neared a crest.

Hardly aware of what she was doing, Judy began to toe off her boots. Through the steamy haze that his touch generated, she thought she saw him smiling at her.

"What?"

"You're stepping on my feet."

She looked down and she was. Somehow she had been trying to work his boot free. A pink glow rose to her cheeks.

He felt a strange tug at his heart. She looked adorable embarrassed, and it stirred something vaguely protective within him.

"Here." Before she could utter a sound, Paul lifted her and then deposited her on the chair. "Let me."

One at a time, he pulled off her long black boots. He ran his hands along the length of her leg as he did so and burned away the denim that separated his hand from her skin. She squirmed in the chair, gripping the armrests as his fingers lightly glided along her bare soles.

Were feet erotic? She'd never thought about that before, but it seemed like that now. Every part of her had turned erotic at his mere touch.

No, there was nothing *mere* about it. His touch made her body sing, her mind reel and all of her ache to have him within her.

Rather than rising to his feet, Paul remained where he was and toyed with the snap at her jeans, moving it back and forth. His eyes held hers, making love to her with a smoldering gaze. Silently, gripping the armrests harder, she lifted her hips and pressed her lips together as he slowly drew the material, jeans and panties tangled together, away from her.

Tossing them aside without a glance, he slowly moved his hands up her legs, toward her thighs, and then rested them on the swell of her hips. His thumbs gently played along her quivering belly, creating small circles that were inducing ever-widening auras of desire within her very core.

She *was* on fire.

"You're still dressed," she protested, her voice low, raspy. "Hasn't equality come to the Northwest Territories yet?"

"It has." His eyes washed over her, reverent in the desire that shone there. "Oh, it has. Women share in the work."

He rose, bringing her to her feet slowly along with him, holding her body to his. If he hadn't held her, she wasn't completely certain she could have stood. Everything felt like quaking jelly inside of her.

Judy could hardly bear the wait. Frantically, she tugged off his shirt first, then his trousers, casting them heedlessly aside.

He tried not to think what those swiftly moving fingers were doing to him, to his frayed control. "No respect for the uniform?"

"I'll salute it later," she breathed.

Her hands were hot on his bare chest, sliding down along the long, sinewy muscles. They curved around his taut waist and moved up his muscular back, then down. Her eyes fluttered shut for a split second as her fingers gripped his buttocks.

Like a mirror, he mimicked her actions. Their bodies came together hot, pulsating, sending shock waves through them.

Whispering her name like a prayer, he lost himself in her, just as he had wanted.

There was nothing but her, no other sound, no other scent, no other world. Just Judy.

He felt her hot flesh against his, moving urgently, aching for him, and he knew he had no strength to take her into the bedroom, no more willpower left. His bedroom might as well have been in the next province. In the next universe.

Mouths tightly pressed against one another, bodies sealed, they sank to their knees before the hearth in a sea of passion that threatened to drown them both.

She'd never experienced anything like this before, not even the first time, not even with him. The land he took her to was filled with rushing stars and whirling lights. Yet the air was thick and heavy, and she couldn't gulp in enough to sustain her.

He was her air, her source of life. Her everything.

Her limbs felt as if molasses had been poured through them. They were heavy, so heavy, and yet desire strummed an urgent melody through every fiber. She was all things, felt all things. Because she was with him.

His hands were everywhere, arousing her, then gentling just enough to give her a moment's respite before he sent her spiraling up to new heights.

He explored, claimed, excited. As his hands dipped between her thighs, Judy clutched at his arms. She was afraid of leaving marks on him with her nails, but he was doing that to her, making her want to scratch, to somehow hold on.

Tensing, she scrambled up the summit and then shuddered as he brought her up to yet another new plateau. Panting, perspiring, she regained a little of her orientation. But he allowed her to remain lax for only a heartbeat before he began again. Before his mouth wove a spell that she couldn't begin to comprehend, driving her relentlessly on.

Breathless, she ran to every new place he showed her, to every new sensation he offered.

She was all things to him. She was all he ever wanted, all he ever needed and within the recesses of his soul, he almost cried with the wonder of it. It was as if the other part of him, the part that was right and good, the part that *might* have been, were here, embodied within her.

And she was his. For the moment.

She was his.

Judy was gasping. He had brought her up and over the edge once more, and every shred of her being was damp and exhausted. Yet she still wanted him, still needed him. She wanted to be joined to him, the way a man and woman should be joined.

She reached down, and her fingers curved lightly around him.

Paul groaned. ''Judy—''

''Come to me,'' she whispered. No legendary siren on the seven seas had ever sounded more seductive.

He vaguely remembered that sirens called sailors to their deaths, dashing them against the hidden rocks. But it didn't matter. If she represented his demise, he'd gladly go there, just for one more taste, one more surge. One more memory.

He couldn't hold back any longer.

His arms bracketing her body, Paul balanced his weight. He hovered over her a moment, wanting to remember her just as she was, half wild with wanting, half dreamy with what had already been.

She guided him in, her eyes on his just as he had asked her to do the first time. As he entered, her hands shot up to encompass his neck, to hold him to her.

To hold on.

To anchor herself before she completely disappeared into the fiery pit. Her hips began to move urgently, echoing the movement of his. The ride was swift and heated, and it took them to the finish line together. The cry that echoed through the cabin was one that mingled their voices together.

Spent, he let his body dissolve over hers for a moment, too tired to move, too sated to want to.

He shifted slightly after what felt like an eternity. "Am I hurting you?"

She wanted to keep him with her. Instinctively, she threaded her arms around him. "Not like this." Her breath rippled over his chest making his muscles tighten. "Never like this."

Nonetheless, he moved his body away from hers until he was lying next to her. Tongues of fire snapped and crackled in the hearth, casting a light that played over her body. It gave her an amber glow, making her seem somehow not quite real.

And maybe she wasn't, he mused. Like an arrow, she had shot into his life from nowhere and, like an arrow, she would disappear again shortly, going to places he could not follow.

But for now, for this moment, she was here. And in that small microcosm of time, he had all he could possibly ever want.

Paul gathered her to him, absorbing her warmth and taking comfort in it. He caressed her cheek with the back of his hand. "We never made it to the bed."

It was a small gesture, but it meant so much to her. She wove her fingers through his and pressed his hand to her lips. "I guess your cabin's just too large."

Tiny earthquakes were going off within him. Drawing his hand away, he raised himself up on his elbow. The floor was meant for walking—not lying—on. There wasn't so much as a scatter rug beneath her. "Uncomfortable?"

She hardly felt the floor. She hardly felt anything except the emotion that filled her every pore. She loved him. She was dying to tell him, to share it with him, but she knew it was too soon.

She shook her head. "A cloud couldn't be more satisfactory."

Completely unconvinced, he reached over Judy to pull down his jacket from the chair. Using the same hand, he wadded the jacket up, then eased it under her head. "You realize that you're crazy."

She grinned as she settled back. His arm was still under her head, and that was the best pillow of all. "There's been talk." Her eyes danced as she looked at him. "But I don't pay any attention to it."

As their lovemaking became a warm, distant glow, reality was pouring in its harsh waters. They needed to get dressed. "You'll catch cold."

Judy turned on her side. She seemed to flow into his arms. With an inviting smile, she looked at him meaningfully. "Then keep me warm."

She seemed insatiable. Almost as insatiable as he felt. "You require a lot."

She shook her head. "No, not a lot." She raised her head and kissed him lightly, then leaned back again. "Just everything." Her mouth teased his as it curved. "Are you up to it, Sergeant?"

Lightly, she glided her fingers along the hard muscles of his stomach. She felt his muscles quiver and dipped her hand lower. Paul's shoulders tensed slightly, and she laughed in triumph. "I guess maybe you are at that."

He covered her hand with his own. "Put that way..." he began, a smile forming on his lips.

He made her feel delicious all over. "A Mountie, I read, has to put out a hundred and ten percent just to do his job."

"I'll give you a hundred and ten percent," he mocked.

"I certainly hope so." Her laughter turned to a fit of giggles as he pulled her to him.

"C'mere, you." Cupping his hand at the back of her head, he brushed his lips over hers before settling her on top of him.

Obviously, he didn't have any problem with the woman being on top. She liked that. She liked what that said about him.

Judy wiggled, as if trying to find a comfortable spot for herself. She watched desire color his complexion. "I always like to obey the law."

She was making his blood pump double time and she knew it. "Like hell you do."

"Okay." She gave a sigh of surrender. "Place me under house arrest." She bent her head, lightly touching his lips with her own. "I'm all yours." She began to move back, but he combed his hands through her hair, framing her face on either side.

He studied her for a moment in silence. "You don't know what you're asking for."

"Then show me, Sergeant." Judy's words danced seductively over his lips, her mouth an inch away from his. "Show me."

He pretended to groan. "I might have to send out for vitamins."

She laughed softly. It sounded like rainwater sliding into a stream. "Steak and liver help, too. Also oysters." He made a face. "I'll pick some up tomorrow." She settled against him, stirring him. "Tonight, you're going to have to wing it alone."

"No." He caressed her cheeks with just the tips of his thumbs as he continued to frame her face, making love to it slowly, sensuously. "Not alone. Not tonight."

He brought her mouth down to his, prepared to take another ride on the merry-go-round. Maybe this time he'd snatch the brass ring.

And if he didn't, the ride was still worth everything.

She was worth everything.

Judy murmured his name as she moved her head back, then brought it to his throat. He tasted of dark, manly things that had her blood surging, questing for more. It drummed in her head and rushed in her ears.

Would she never stop wanting him like this?

She hoped not.

As she circled his throat with warm, openmouthed kisses that grew in passion, Paul groaned. He cupped her buttocks, his hands curving over her.

Judy began to move slowly, deliberately, stoking fires that had only been smoldering, waiting to be ignited again.

With movements governed by timeless instincts, she opened for him. Sheathing him once again, they were off, riding toward midnight. Toward the known and the unknown at the same time.

And at the end, neither one of them was capable of moving a muscle.

She poured fluidly over him, content to remain with him like this forever. She wished for a snowstorm, for a timeless bubble that could seal them in until eternity was over.

Most of all, she wished that he was hers.

"You said something about dinner."

"Maybe," she was willing to concede. "In another lifetime."

"Will it burn?"

She concentrated and finally remembered shutting off the stove. "No."

He let out a sigh that she felt echoed in her chest. "Good." He wrapped his arm around her, and they drifted off to sleep. Together.

Chapter Fifteen

They didn't discuss it.

No mention was made of the nights they spent with each other or what those nights meant, what they represented. Paul had set the pace.

He found the newly unleashed emotions emerging within him impossible to deal with. He didn't know where to begin, how to sort them out, how to live with them in light of his past. Somehow, since these newfound emotions were so raw, so tenuous, so frail, it seemed better not to talk about them. He actually didn't think he knew how to.

There was no past, no future, just the moment they were living in. It was enough for him. Or so he told himself.

Judy wanted to talk about what was happening between them, what was happening to her. She wanted to explore each layer as if it were a treasure dropped unsuspectingly in their laps by a whimsical fate. But she knew with the timeless instinct of a woman in love that if she veered from the course, the glass skiff she was in would shatter. She had to wait until it was stronger, until what Paul felt was strong enough to withstand the light of day.

But there wasn't much time, and though they were together each day, it felt as if time were dribbling through her fingers like water.

For the next week and a half there was tension in the air between them, but for an entirely different reason than before.

Before, Paul had felt the prickling tension of apprehension, the feeling that there was something imminent pending. Something he wanted to stave off for his own preservation.

Now the tension that rode roughshod over him, like a relentless broncobuster trying to impose his will on a mustang, was because of the future, the future he was trying to hold at bay.

Though he said nothing, tomorrow was coming. They both knew that. But he didn't want to think about it, just as surely as he didn't want to remember the details of that long-ago yesterday.

He'd taken his first hesitant step forward, like a baby learning to walk. He had made love with her. To her. He was only beginning to learn how to be comfortable with his feelings, his emotions. It wasn't easy, since in feeling, he opened himself up to an avalanche of guilt. Guilt only added to the impetus to retreat to the shelter of the solitude he had nurtured, the solitude that had become second nature to him. With her deadline approaching, he knew he had to make a decision. A decision he wasn't ready to make.

He'd changed in the last week and a half, Judy noted. He was more gentle with her now, and more thoughtful. In his own gruff way, there was a tenderness to him. It made her heart sing. She had come in direct contact with the man she had known existed all along, the man she had fallen in love with.

And each day they came a little closer to the end.

Judy tried as hard as she could to ignore her schedule. She continued her work, taking scads of photographs. When time permitted, she developed them in the tiny lab she had set up in her room. And all the while, she refused to think of where it would all end.

Within her was a fear, even when Paul held her in his arms, even when he kissed her. A fear that when it was over, it would be over forever. Paul had given her no verbal indication that anything was going to change within the following week, though she had left every path open to him. She desperately wanted to hear that he didn't want her to leave or that he meant to go with her if she did.

Of course, she wouldn't let him do that, but he could have at least offered. Her heart felt heavy.

No plans were made, no words were spoken. He seemed comfortable with the relationship as it was. There was no progress, no movement forward. It was as if there were a timelessness surrounding them and tomorrow would never come.

But it would.

Judy kept her mind on the assignment and was grateful for what she had now. Grateful, she thought with a smile. Grateful in Grateful Bend. So many people never experienced anything close to what she had.

But, damn, she wanted more, she thought, looking at Paul beside her in the Land Rover. She wanted more.

She searched for something to take her mind off next Friday, the day she was to leave for Montreal. The countryside that whizzed by was all familiar now, like an old friend who had been taken for granted.

Judy realized that they were on their way to the ghost town. And Tina.

"You know," she began as she idly ran her hand along Raymond's fur, "I'm really worried about Tina."

Paul glanced at her, one brow raised quizzically. Judy hurried on, trying to keep her thoughts from getting tangled up in her emotions.

"She says she's not due for another month and she absolutely refuses to go into town to stay with anyone." Judy had tried several more times to talk her into it, as, she knew, had Sara. Tina had stubbornly declined. "Isn't there something you could do to make her go?"

Paul could physically carry the pregnant girl to Grateful Bend. It was a notion he'd talked himself out of several times, arguing that everyone had a right to live the way they chose. Outside of that, there wasn't anything else he could do.

"I already told you that she's not breaking any laws."

Judy let out a little huff between her teeth. Sometimes he could be so maddening. "This goes beyond the letter of the law and you know it." Judy balled her hands into fists.

Paul glanced at her fists and wondered idly if she was intending to use them on him. He wouldn't doubt it, he thought, amused. If nothing else, she was a scrapper, he'd give her that.

"There's such a thing as the spirit of the law, isn't there?" she continued when he said nothing.

She wanted him to agree with her, not remain there rigid, like a cigar-store Indian. Didn't he care?

Judy waved her hands around impotently, frustrated. "The law's supposed to be merciful and all those kinds of things."

Paul shook his head, mystified. There were times he wondered what went through her mind. Lots of times. "What planet do you live on?"

She crossed her arms stubbornly before her chest. "A good one."

He sighed. Maybe it was, at that. Too bad it wasn't real. Still, she had a valid point, though he wasn't going to say as much. "I'll see what I can do."

Judy worked her lower lip, contemplating the problem. "Maybe vagrancy," she announced suddenly, thinking out loud.

Paul glanced in her direction before taking a turn. "What?"

The idea rushed to her tongue at the same time that it formed in her mind. She talked fast. "Tell her she's breaking some sort of local ordinance by not having a source of income. Tell her she has to be within two hundred yards of RCMP headquarters if she's a vagrant." Judy's face lit up like a sunset as she spoke. "That'll keep her at Hattie's boarding house."

Paul couldn't help smiling. "You are devious, aren't you?"

Judy leaned against the cushion, satisfied with herself. "When my back's against the wall," she agreed. Content with her solution, she grinned. "I can have her stay with me until—"

She stopped, not wanting to say "until I leave." That sounded so final, it brought a frost to her heart. "Until I can make arrangements for her to stay with Sara."

Paul said nothing for a moment, and she thought that perhaps he was thinking through the silent meaning of her words.

"That sounds like a good idea," he finally told her without looking in her direction.

Judy only sighed and continued to stroke Raymond's head.

When they approached the ghost town, there was nothing unusual about it—nothing to make Paul feel there was something different from a dozen other trips here.

Yet the back of Paul's neck seemed to prickle, telling him that something was wrong.

He just didn't know what.

Paul scanned the long, lonely street, trying to ascertain what it was that made him feel so uneasy.

But there was no one and nothing lurking in the shadows, nothing out of the ordinary. Nothing to differentiate it from all the other trips they had taken here. He was just being edgy.

Displaced feelings, he thought. He was just having difficulty dealing with the fact that she would be leaving soon. He didn't know what to do or how to handle it. He didn't want her to go, but he had no right to ask her to stay, either. No right to be in her life at all.

He turned off the ignition and pocketed the key. Judy scrambled out of the Land Rover ahead of him. Instead of her camera, she was carrying another package for Tina. He wondered if there was anything left in the Emporium that Tina didn't have. He couldn't quite understand the joy Judy received from spoiling Tina, but he reasoned that it seemed good for both of them, so there was no harm in it.

Raymond raced ahead of Judy and stopped at Tina's door. He began to bark loudly.

"Down, boy," Judy chided him. "Don't scare her half to death."

But Raymond scratched at the door's splintering wood and barked again. Above the noise, Judy heard an unearthly sound, like keening. She looked over her shoulder at Paul, her eyes wide.

"Open it," he ordered. Paul was half a step behind her as Judy pushed the door open.

Judy's eyes filled with horror. "Tina!"

The girl was writhing in agony on the floor. The pain was etched into deep creases about her mouth and eyes. She was too exhausted to even lift her head when she heard them entering. She'd been like that since late last night when the horrible, stabbing pains had begun.

A pool of blood surrounded her, a macabre circle soaking into her clothes, encroaching on her like a silent stalker.

Paul quickly moved Judy out of his way. As gently as possible, he slipped his arms beneath Tina and started to lift her.

"No, no," Tina whimpered as fresh sweat washed over her face. "It hurts, hurts so bad. Please." She forced the word out through parched lips. Tears that had long since dried and turned to dust had left dirty, grimy tracks on her face.

"Honey, we have to get you to a doctor." Judy's voice was low, soothing, and she struggled against her own strangling fears. There was blood, so much blood on the floor. What if—

Fear pricked Judy's scalp, making it tingle.

They were too far away from help. There wasn't much time. Perhaps none.

"We can't move her," Paul told Judy, wishing now that he had forced the girl to stay in Grateful Bend the way he had wanted to. Damn, why hadn't he? He wished for a phone to summon help, but there wasn't any, not for miles and miles.

It was up to him.

Tina didn't seem to hear him. Her eyes had glazed over, and she was staring at the ceiling when he placed her on the bed.

Judy was beside her, holding the girl's hand in both of hers. Tina looked at her, as if slowly realizing that she wasn't alone.

"I'm dying," she whispered. There were tears in her throat. "My baby's dying."

"No, you are not," Judy said fiercely, dropping to her knees beside the girl. She continued to clutch Tina's hand in hers. "You're going to be fine, just fine." She fought back her own tears as she brought every shred of conviction she had into her voice, willing her strength into Tina. "Both of you are."

Judy looked mutely over her shoulder at Paul, wanting him to tell her she was right. Wanting him to *make* it right.

He was stripping off his jacket as he looked around the small cabin for something he could use. He didn't know how much time he had. Tina looked as if she were near the end of her labor. He needed towels, a basin, thread—simple, everyday things that seemed to elude him.

"She's in labor," he told Judy needlessly, his take-charge voice rising above Tina's cries. "We're going to have to deliver the baby."

Still on her knees, Judy pressed her lips together and nodded. Another strangled scream tore from Tina's cracked lips. Judy blamed herself.

"I should've listened," Tina babbled, reality and dreams mingling with the pain. "I should have listened to you. You were right. Judy? Judy, are you here?"

Judy squeezed her hand tighter around the cold, wet fingers. "I'm here, honey, I'm right here."

With her free hand, Judy stroked the girl's damp forehead, brushing aside the wet bangs. Judy felt miserably powerless.

Paul stood behind Judy. "Tina." The girl turned her head toward him, her eyes blank. "Tina, how far apart are the contractions?"

Thinking was so hard. Everything hurt. She couldn't think, couldn't breathe. It was all so painful.

"I don't know. I don't know anything." The words dripped from her like her perspiration. "All the time. They hardly stop now." She tried to take in a deep breath, but it didn't help. Nothing helped. "I am going to die, aren't I?" Her voice quavered, and she sounded like a little girl.

"Every woman feels that way when she's about to deliver," Paul said gruffly, hoping his voice wouldn't crack.

He looked at the floor by the entrance. It looked as if she'd been trying to go for help when she fell. The blood reminded him. Reminded him of another girl, younger than Tina, another girl lying on the ground, surrounded with a red ring that was the calling card of death.

He shook himself free. If he let it get to him, if he froze, he wouldn't be of any use, and *this* girl needed him now, not the other. The other was long past needing anything.

Paul turned and started for the door.

Judy's head jerked up. "Where are you going?" She tried to keep the panic out of her voice, but he had heard it.

Paul picked up an old bucket Tina had found during one of her treasure hunts through the abandoned buildings. She used it to carry her daily supply of water from the pump in the back.

"I need water." *And a hell of a lot of other things I don't have, like a doctor.*

Judy nodded, her throat dry. She was letting her nerves get the better of her. As Tina strained and arched again, Judy threaded her fingers harder through Tina's. "What do I do?" Judy asked him helplessly.

"Stay with her. And pray, if it helps either of you any."
Paul closed the door behind him.

He was distancing himself, Judy thought. Why? Tina
desperately needed help, and he was shutting down right
before her eyes. How could he do that?

Judy forced herself to calm down for Tina's sake. Maybe
he had to do it this way. Maybe he operated better when he
was removed, she thought.

Tina was thrashing again, arching and screaming, when
Paul returned. He quickly set down the pail and the old
blanket he had found. Judy was attempting to hold Tina
down with the weight of her own body, but the girl's
strength was almost unnatural in her pain.

Paul tried to empty his mind of all extraneous thoughts.
He'd never delivered a baby before. But he had been trained.
And he had seen life. And death. If he could just pull himself together and concentrate on the training film, he could
get them through this, he told himself.

He fervently wished he didn't have to.

"It's too big," Tina sobbed after another contraction had
threatened to tear her apart. "Too big. I can't do this." She
was almost scrambling up Judy's arm with her hands, her
nails, leaving scratches in her wake. "Kill me, please kill
me," she first begged Judy, then Paul. "I can't take it. I
can't take it."

In her agitation, Judy realized that she was breathing almost as hard as Tina was. She looked at Paul. "Is the baby
breech?"

Slowly, he probed around Tina's abdomen. Everything
felt the way it was supposed to. At least, he couldn't detect
anything out of the ordinary. But then, why was she bleed-
ing?

"I don't think so." He began to perspire, wishing he could
remember the training film more clearly. Wishing the sight
of the blood wasn't making him recall another time, another place where fate had taken circumstances out of his
hands.

He looked at Judy. "Help me get her legs up. I don't think she has the strength to raise her knees."

Tina didn't. She seemed almost beyond hearing them. Her screams were blocking out everything. Paul braced a shoulder against each shin to keep the girl's thin legs from sliding down onto the bed again.

Perspiration beading on his lip, Paul pushed away the bloodied nightgown. "I see the crown. The baby's almost here."

He looked at Tina, his eyes dark, stern, trying to will strength into her. "I want you to push, Tina."

He ordered her the way he would a raw recruit. The way he had ordered his partner to follow when the man had been too afraid to enter the alley with him. The alley in Montreal.

"Push!"

"I can't, I can't!" Tina was panting, crying and moaning all at once.

Judy got behind the girl's shoulders and lifted her into a sitting position.

"You can do it, Tina. Love, remember love?" Judy's voice was coaxing, urgent, cutting through the haze of pain. "You said you were going to love this baby. He needs help, Tina, your help. Now. You've got to find the strength from somewhere, honey," Judy begged her. "Push. Please push." Judy's eyes met Paul's over the girl's head. Fear shimmered between them.

Tina swallowed her tears and hiccuped. Drawing in a huge breath, she screwed her face up. Every ounce of her body concentrated exclusively on Judy's voice. On Judy's commands.

The shriek that escaped Tina's lips sounded like something being torn from the bowels of the earth.

Tina slumped against Judy's supportive hands, exhausted beyond words. "I can't. I . . ." Tina was too weak to even form the words.

"Just one more time, Tina," Paul instructed. "With the next contraction." His voice was devoid of any feeling. He couldn't afford to feel anything. Couldn't afford to be distracted. "You've got to push. I can't help you if you don't help yourself."

Tina's head lolled back. She thought she could see Judy through her tears. Her eyes widened, terrified. The pain was too much for her.

"It's happening. Again." Tina groped for Judy's hand, then shrieked as Judy firmly pushed her into an upright position once more.

Tina's baby was born on the cusp of a shriek.

"You did it," Judy cried, tears spilling freely, running down her cheeks. "You did it!" Like a burned-out sparkler, the joy stopped when she looked at Paul's face. It was ashen. "Sergeant?"

Tina heard the hushed question and frantically tried to prop herself up to see. "My baby. What's wrong with my baby?"

The tiny baby girl he held in his cupped hands was blue. The umbilical cord was wrapped around the infant's neck.

Tina had fallen back onto the bed, a pool of exhaustion and despair.

Judy could hardly draw in a breath herself as she looked from the baby to Paul. "Paul, it's not—" She couldn't bring herself to say it.

Paul didn't answer her. He set the baby down on the blanket on the floor. Frantically, he released the cord from the baby's neck and wiped away the mucus from the mouth and nose. His hand looked large enough to completely cover the baby's chest. Massaging it, he then covered the infant's nose and mouth with his mouth. He blew gently, trying to restrain the sense of urgency that was drumming through his veins. CPR was something he had practiced, but never on someone so tiny, so frail. He was afraid of hurting her, of breaking the little body in half.

God, please God, she's got to live. The words throbbed through his mind like an endless chant as he continued massaging, continued struggling with death for the life of the tiny baby.

Judy held her breath, afraid to move, afraid to talk. Every prayer she knew flashed through her mind as she held tightly on to Tina's limp hand. The baby had to live. She *had* to.

A whimper was followed by a wail. Indignation at being pulled from a warm, secure home swelled the tiny child's lungs.

Paul sank back on his heels and let out a long sigh, completely drained. But there was no time to pull himself together. There was too much to do.

Paul checked to see if the umbilical cord had stopped pulsating. Satisfied that it had, he cut it with the knife he sterilized over a flame. Quickly he tore his handkerchief into strips and then tied a strip around the edge of the cord.

Feeling almost light-headed, he wrapped the baby securely in the blanket and handed her to Judy.

"It's a girl. And she's breathing." There was so much emotion in his voice, it threatened to choke him. He wiped his forehead with the back of his wrist.

She had never seen anything so beautiful in her life. Her heart swelled with love for the miracle of birth, for Paul, for life itself. Blinking back tears, Judy placed the baby into Tina's arms.

Tina's smile was wan and far too weak. Judy decided to stay here tonight with her. In the morning, when Tina was stronger, Paul could bring back an ambulance. They'd take her straight to the hospital in Yellowknife.

"A girl," Tina murmured, trying to absorb the information.

Her limbs felt oddly numb, as if they no longer belonged to her. As if none of her belonged to her anymore. The pain had stopped, almost floating away from her, and she was struggling for just a few more minutes.

Judy didn't like the way Tina's eyes looked, as if the light in them was fading. As if her very soul was fading away.

"She'll look like you when she grows up," Judy promised, looking for words to push away the hollow feeling that was growing in the pit of her stomach where contentment had been only a second before. She reached behind her for Paul's hand as he joined her.

"I won't be there to see it." The words were becoming harder to form. Tears were sprinkling down her cheeks again as she looked from her daughter to Judy. The effort to turn her head was almost too much for Tina. "Take care of her for me."

Judy's heart began to hammer hard, as if she had been running a long way. Running from the truth.

"Sure. Until you're better." She swallowed, trying to dislodge the lump she felt in her throat. It wouldn't leave.

With her last ounce of strength, Tina reached for Judy's hand.

"Swear. Swear you'll take care of her for me." Her eyes fluttered shut for a moment, but the girl struggled back to the surface one last time. "And love her. Please love her. Swear." The last was a whisper, a fierce whisper echoing in a room where only silence reigned.

Judy could hardly see for the tears in her way. "I swear. But—"

Tina's hand dropped from hers, limp. Her eyes stared, unseeing, at Judy.

"Tina?" Judy cried. "Tina, wake up. Please wake up!" Her voice cracked as she tried to shake the girl into consciousness.

Paul was on his knees beside the young girl, feeling her wrist for a pulse. There was none. There was none to be found at her throat. For the second time in the space of fifteen minutes, Paul used CPR and wrestled with death for the life that hung in the balance.

This time, death won. The score was even.

"Paul, she can't be dead, she just can't be." Judy's throat was clogged with tears.

Paul said nothing. He took the infant he had just brought back into the world and placed her in Judy's arms.

Tears fell on the baby's head as Judy held her close and cried. "I should have forced Tina to stay in town. That day she came to the carnival, I should have—"

Paul slid the sheet over Tina's body and turned to look at Judy. His eyes were warm and compassionate. They shone with moisture he wouldn't allow himself to shed. "*Should have* doesn't change anything. You did what you could. It's all that anyone can do."

And then he placed his arm around Judy's shoulders and held her while she cried.

Chapter Sixteen

The territorial coroner from Yellowknife examined Tina's body. He determined the cause of death to be excessive internal hemorrhaging and released her to Judy. It was no surprise to Paul that Judy had declared herself the responsible party. It was what he had come to expect of her now.

Tina was buried in the ghost town behind the little house that had been so important to her. Judy insisted on it. No one had the heart to attempt to talk her into burying the girl in Grateful Bend's cemetery.

It was a small funeral service. Captain Reynolds and his wife attended, along with Hattie, Cynthia, Sara and a few of the men and women from the Inuit village. And Paul. The women all took turns holding Tina's baby as the service was being read.

Emotion vibrating through her, Judy looked around at the people who had come to pay their last respects to a girl who felt she had never had any. Slowly, Judy raised her camera, aimed it and began doing what she had been doing since she arrived in Grateful Bend. She took photographs of everything. Someday, Tina's daughter would ask questions about her mother. There would be a great deal Judy wouldn't be able to answer. But she wanted the girl to be able to see, as much as possible, how greatly people had been affected by her mother's death.

Maybe it would be beneficial somehow.

And maybe it would help Judy work through her own pain now, she thought.

The clicking of the shutter was a soft underscoring of the old minister's words.

Paul glared at the camera as if it had a life of its own. As if it were an obtrusive voyeur. "Why are you taking pictures?" Paul demanded under his breath. "Can't you put that thing aside even now?"

What was the matter with her? This was a funeral, not a three-ring circus. He remembered Sally's funeral, a cameraman angling to take videos of the grieving parents for the local evening news. Funerals were private. Cameras had no place there.

Judy looked at him. Her eyes were hard, to keep the tears from breaking through again. "I'm doing this for Tina's daughter." *Because if I don't, I'm going to break down.* "She'll want to know when the time comes. I want to have something to show her."

Rather than hear what Judy was saying, Paul read all her reasons in her eyes. Read and understood. He'd worn the same look when he had attended his partner's funeral. And stood in the background at the cemetery as they had buried the girl who took the bullet intended for him. Sometimes you had to stay hard to keep from cracking.

Paul nodded. In that moment, he felt for Judy. He empathized with her pain and was closer to her than he ever had been before. His expression softened as the minister said the final blessings over the small casket in the ground. Judy's hands tightened around the camera as she took the last photographs.

Paul took her elbow and guided her toward the car. It was over, and Tina was now a memory. "Let's go."

* * *

Judy returned with Paul to Tina's grave the next day. She wanted to leave flowers on top of the newly turned earth. Seeing the gay colors seemed comforting somehow. Judy knew Tina would have appreciated them. Tina loved flowers.

There was a temporary marker on the grave. Judy had given Humphrey a sizable check, and he was fashioning a marble headstone to put in the marker's stead. His big, chunky hands were capable of very delicate work. She smiled sadly to herself. There was no end to the hidden talents to be found in this small town.

Paul waited beside the Land Rover with Raymond, allowing Judy to have her privacy as she mourned. He didn't understand death, but he respected it and the long fingers it spread, touching everyone as it grasped its victims. As for himself, he had never had much to say to a mound of packed dirt. He'd stood beside his father's grave several times and words had never formed—not on his lips, not in his mind. There was always something blocking the outpouring of emotion. Maybe he was afraid that once he started, he wouldn't be able to stop.

"I'll take care of her," Judy whispered to the spirit she was certain would hear her. "I promise." With a last look at the grave, Judy retreated.

Paul waited until Judy reached him. Now was as good a time as any to broach the subject. He knew she wasn't going to like it.

"We're going to have to contact the social services at Yellowknife." He waited until she sat down and then got in behind the wheel.

We. Judy wondered if Paul realized that he used the word. He never had before. Were they a *we* now? In *her* mind they were. They had been for some time. Had he just accepted the fact without question, the way one did the changing of seasons? She hoped so.

But he sounded so solemn, she had to question his statement. "Why?"

Paul started the car. "Someone has to take the baby."

For the moment, the infant was staying with the captain's wife, Esther. She was lavishing all the love and attention on the baby that beat in the breast of a doting grandmother of five.

Judy looked at him in total disbelief. He was talking as if he hadn't been right there, standing beside her when Tina had begged her to take care of her baby. Begged her with her dying breath.

"I'm going to take care of the baby."

Paul looked at Judy sharply. He veered slightly to the left, but it didn't matter. The road was empty. "What?"

Digging for patience, Judy explained. "I've already spoken to Captain Reynolds about it. He's putting me in touch with all the proper authorities. They'll pass on reams of paperwork, I'm sure, but I think in the end there shouldn't be any problem, not with the captain vouching for me. The baby's going to be mine."

The second day he had known her, Judy had risked her life to save a child. What was it with this woman? People just weren't that selfless, that kind. His own mother hadn't gone out of her way for him.

A stab of bitterness from the past rose to his lips and misdirected itself at her. "Another good deed?"

Judy wasn't quite sure just how he meant that. It sounded harsh, but she struggled not to take offense. "I promised Tina I would."

He stared straight ahead, his hands tight on the wheel. He couldn't understand. "Tina's gone. She won't know."

How could he say that? She'd seen how he had fought to save first the baby and then Tina. He wasn't cold, he wasn't disinterested. Why did he act that way now? How could he question her?

"But I'm still here, and I'd know. I saw that baby come into the world, and I love her as if she were my own." Judy realized that he didn't understand. Had his own mother been so distant from him that he couldn't understand a maternal instinct? Judy searched his face, trying to touch him somehow. "You were there. You gave her life."

He shrugged off her words. "Her mother gave her life. So did that worthless jerk who deserted them both." He couldn't begin to understand or excuse abandoning Tina like that. If he'd had Gareth before him now, he would have strangled him.

Rage, Paul thought. The only emotion he was capable of was rage. He glanced at Judy and thought that she deserved so much more.

Judy caught his look and wondered about it. It didn't seem to fit in. It felt too personal, but she knew she couldn't question him.

"You brought her back," she reminded him. "You saved her life." Did he fathom the depth of the act? He seemed to shrug off the good he accomplished so easily that she wondered if he really didn't see the significance.

An innate instinct prompted her next words. "Your father would have been proud of you."

The nerve in his jaw tightened. He had disgraced his father's memory a long time ago. He hadn't been worthy of it. "Yeah, well, he wouldn't have had a hell of a whole lot to work with up to now if he were alive."

A gaggle of geese flew overhead. Their cries pierced her words as she placed her hand on his arm. "How can you say that?" She knew the kind of man he was. She had seen the way he was with people in the area. Quiet, stoic, but dependable. Any man would have been proud to call Paul his son.

He wouldn't look at her. He couldn't. Her eyes would have him saying things that were still best left unsaid. "Because I know things you don't."

"Then tell me."

Her plea was almost seductively coaxing. It wasn't easy to resist her, or the need he suddenly had to purge himself. But he held out. The Inuit village was up ahead. She'd have other people to talk to. And she'd stop chipping away at his soul. "Not now."

Judy felt as if she were hitting her head against a brick wall. The wall wasn't suffering, but she was.

"When? When will you tell me, Sergeant?" Her voice was so sharp, he hardly recognized it. "I'm leaving in a few days." *Ask me to stay, damn you. Ask me to stay. We can find a way if you tell me you want me.*

"Before you go," he said stoically. *Because once you know, you'll go even if you wouldn't have before.*

Judy leaned back in her seat, staring straight ahead. The village was beginning to take shape. She didn't see it. All she could see was her own pain.

So, he intended on letting her walk out of his life. Just like that, without a word to stop her. Tears stung, but pride kept her from allowing them to fall.

The next few days were a jumble of activity. Nothing seemed real to Judy. She increased her pace, cramming as many things as she could into a day. Trying to keep her thoughts as far away as possible.

Though Mrs. Reynolds had been more than willing to keep the baby, Judy had taken Tina's daughter to stay with her. She wanted to get in as much time as possible with the infant while she could still rely on outside help. Judy named the infant after her mother, so that the little girl would always remember who had given her life.

Chemicals and makeshift darkrooms were abandoned for the remainder of her stay in Grateful Bend. The development of the rest of the photographs she took would have to be entrusted to her publisher's laboratory. Judy had more important things to do.

Between the hours of six at night and six in the morning, Judy was taking a crash course in instant motherhood.

And trying to forget just how much her heart was aching.

As the oldest of five, babies were nothing new to Judy. But there had always been her mother or her aunt around to fall back on. This time it was up to her. She was first-string now, not the backup, and it was scary. But she only had to look down the hall for help.

Cynthia was all thumbs and elbows, but her spirit was indomitable. It more than made up for her lack of experience. She was there for Judy at every turn, offering to walk the baby, to feed her, change her and do whatever was necessary. Both her affection for the infant and her near hero-worship of Judy spurred her on.

"I'm going to miss you when I leave," Judy whispered to Cynthia late one evening after they had gotten Tina washed and fed. The baby lay sleeping in a crib Hattie had unearthed from the attic. Nineteen years ago, it had held Cynthia.

Cynthia slanted a look and twisted her fingers together nervously, like a child about to recite a poem before an intimidating audience. "You don't have to."

"Leave?" Judy guessed.

It wasn't that simple. Left on her own, perhaps she would stay, even though Paul hadn't said anything to her about it. But there were deadlines to meet, and she had to face the fact that there was such a thing as beating a dead horse. If Paul had wanted her to stay here with him, he would have said something.

Judy sighed. "Yes, I do."

"No." Cynthia was in danger of twisting her fingers off. "I mean you don't have to miss me."

Judy gave her a curious look, lost.

Cynthia licked her lips, then broke into her rehearsed speech at a full gallop. "Take me with you, Judy." She caught hold of Judy's hand as if to anchor the woman to her. "I've got a little money put away. I could pay some of my way, and what I couldn't pay," she continued, gaining speed, "I'd make up for by taking care of Tina." Her eyes searched Judy's, pleading.

Judy studied the younger woman, surprised by the offer, and yet, not really surprised. Cynthia had made her longings known more than once. But Judy had written them off as just a young girl's wishful fantasy. Apparently there was more to it than that. "You'd come with me, just like that?"

Cynthia shook her head emphatically. "It's not 'just like that.' It's snatching my chance. My one chance." Her voice rose. A guilty look creased her brow as she glanced at the baby. She lowered her voice to a rushed whisper again. "I want to see someplace else before I die, just once." She shrugged helplessly. "I don't have enough money to make it on my own and I probably wouldn't ever go if I was by myself," she admitted, flushing, a pink hue rising to her pale cheeks. "I'm not as brave as you are." She clutched Judy's hand again. "But if you take me with you, I won't get in the way, I swear I won't. And you won't regret it."

Judy couldn't turn such eagerness down, even if she hadn't needed someone to help her care for Tina. Still, there were other things to consider. "Your mother would have to approve," Judy began tentatively.

Cynthia took Judy's words as tacit approval. Joy sprang into her eyes. She squeezed Judy's hand so hard, she nearly stopped the circulation.

"Oh, she will, she will." Cynthia was halfway to the door before she skidded to a halt. The look in her eyes was almost hesitant, afraid she had misunderstood. "Then you'll take me?"

Judy laughed softly and nodded. She glanced down at the sleeping infant. "I'll be grateful for the help."

Cynthia rushed back to hug Judy, then bolted from the room to find her mother. The door remained open in Cynthia's wake. Judy closed it and crossed to the crib once more.

"Now if only a certain other party would be half as eager to be with me," she mused aloud as she tucked the blanket around the dozing baby, "life would be pretty much perfect."

But life wasn't meant to be perfect, and she knew it. Perhaps never more than now.

* * *

The days whisked by too quickly, like streamers caught in the wind. All too soon, it was the evening before Judy's departure for Montreal. Through the captain's intervention, procedures involving Tina's guardianship had been sped up. Judy had been temporarily awarded custody of the baby. Reynolds assured her that, in the absence of any other relatives to contest the matter, and given Judy's background, Tina was as good as permanently hers.

To help matters along, after a marathon pleading session, Cynthia had finally gained her mother's blessings to spend the next six weeks in Montreal. After that, Hattie informed her, her eyes moist, they would see. It was all Cynthia needed.

Cynthia was ecstatic, and Judy was extremely relieved to have the girl's help. Everything, it seemed, was set.

Everything but her heart.

Judy fought an overwhelming sadness as they drove up to Paul's cabin for the last time. She had tried to store up every last shred of that day in her mind, but it wouldn't take the place of the real thing. It wouldn't take *his* place.

"Well," she said as she drew a long breath in and then let it out slowly, "I guess you're getting your wish."

He hadn't touched her even once today. Not a touch, not a kiss, nothing. It was as if he had already severed all ties with her.

Paul pulled up the emergency hand brake and turned off the ignition. How did she know what his wishes were? he wondered. How could she possibly even guess how much he ached inside, knowing that she was leaving tomorrow?

"How's that?" He tried his best to keep his feelings out of his words.

His voice was so cold, she thought. Just like the first time. Just as if they hadn't spent six weeks together, as if they hadn't saved two children between them and buried a girl that was hardly more than a child herself. He sounded as if they hadn't shared each other's bodies and found solace in that warmth.

He sounded like a stranger.

She wanted to hit him. To scream at him. To make him tell her that he loved her. But it wouldn't mean anything if she had to force the words out of him.

Still, she thought, nursing the gnawing, hollow feeling within her, at least she would have heard him say it just once.

She kept her practiced smile pasted in place. "I'm leaving, just like you wanted." She started to slowly climb out of the Land Rover. Her limbs felt like lead.

Damn her, didn't she know how hard this was for him? How much he wanted her to stay? But Grateful Bend wasn't a place for her. It would be like placing a diamond in a brass setting. And he wasn't the man for her to remain with. He'd always known that.

Paul turned slowly toward her. "Judy—"

There was something in his eyes, something dark and foreboding that held her transfixed. "Yes?"

He had made her a promise, and it was time to live up to it. He measured his words. "I told you I'd tell you before you left."

She knew what he was referring to. She saw the vulnerability in his eyes, though he tried to hide it. She wanted to place her arms around him and comfort him. To tell him that whatever it was didn't matter. But she knew he wouldn't let her. "Not if it hurts you."

His smile was incredulous. She was really something else. "After all these weeks of prodding and probing, you'd let me keep it to myself?"

She shrugged. Something was stopping him from being with her and would continue to stop him whether he said it aloud or not. It didn't seem to matter now, it only mattered that it was.

"I don't want you hurting any more than you already are."

He believed her. Which was why he had to tell her all the more. He owed her. Paul looked past her head, staring at the peak of his roof. He chose his words carefully. "I told you why I became a Mountie. Because my father was one." This was hard for him. He wasn't used to opening himself up. But he pressed on, because she mattered. "Because in my heart, even though he was dead, I wanted his approval. I guess I needed it. I lost my father when he died and my mother when she went into mourning. When she married, she wasn't the same woman anymore. Becoming a Mountie was all I had to keep me going. It was like an ongoing goal."

Judy's heart ached for him, for the boy who had lost everything and needed so much just to be held and told that he was all right. Without thinking, she laid her hand on his arm in mute comfort.

He covered her hand with his own, knowing it was for the last time. "I couldn't live up to what was required of me." He paused.

Judy waited, aware that he had to cleanse himself, to bring this demon to the light. Then maybe, just maybe, they'd have a chance.

"I was on the force three and a half years when I went undercover to infiltrate a drug ring." His mouth twisted as he remembered the grueling months, the lies. The fear that became a part of every day. But he was doing something good, and that had kept him going. "I spent six months getting entrenched. Six months, and then someone blew my cover. But I didn't know it."

He could see it in front of him as clearly as if it were happening now. His skin prickled, just as it had that day. "I walked right into an ambush, taking my partner with me." He remembered Harry sweating, worrying. Harry, with a wife and three kids. "He didn't want to go, said he had a bad feeling. I kidded him out of it." His throat was completely dry. The words felt like cotton. "He was killed."

Paul told her the details as if he were reciting a grocery list. Any closer, and he would break down.

"I escaped unharmed."

It was evident to Judy that Paul would gladly have traded his life for his partner's.

There was sawdust in his mouth as he continued. "But not before a girl was caught in the crossfire. I found out later she'd been playing hide-and-seek in the alley. She came running out, screaming. The bullet that was meant for me slammed into her chest. Her name was Sally Blake." He looked angry and stricken at the same time. Paul echoed the words Sally's mother had shouted at him. "She died instead of me."

Horrified for him, for the burden he had carried with him for so long, Judy touched her fingertips to his face. She wished with all her might that she could somehow erase his guilt, his pain.

"It wasn't your fault, Paul."

He pulled away from her, angry at her words, angry at himself. "How can you say that?" He slammed his fist into the car door. His knuckles stung. It was nothing compared to the pain he felt within. "If I hadn't been there, she would still be alive somewhere, laughing, doing things a girl her age should be doing."

He whirled on Judy, his eyes dark with unfathomable grief. "She was only eleven years old. Eleven. A child died because of me!"

He looked away, trying to rein in his emotions. Unleashed, they were tangling inside of him, overwhelming him. He knew it would happen if he ever let go. And he had. For her.

More in control, he continued, his voice flat. "I couldn't live with the guilt. Everything I had tried to build for myself turned to ashes after that. I asked for a transfer and came out here."

There was no need to mention that he had given Harry's widow the money in his savings account. It didn't absolve him of anything or begin to rectify things.

He shrugged, knowing how silly it probably sounded. Maybe it was. "I thought I could make up for it somehow, being here. But she's still dead."

Judy wanted to shake him, to tell him that he had lived with his guilt too long. And he shouldn't have. She forced him to look at her. "And little Tina's alive because of you."

He looked at her quizzically.

How could he not see it? "If you weren't there, the baby would have died. It's that simple." She pressed her lips together. The wall was still up. How could she get through to him? "I think the debt is paid, don't you?"

He shook his head. He appreciated what she was trying to do, but it didn't change anything. "It doesn't work like that."

"Oh, yes, it does." She grabbed his arm, desperate, angry at him for having wasted so much of his life like this. "You can't blame yourself for one and ignore the other. If you're to be blamed for the one, then you're to be praised for the other." He just continued to look at her, his eyes expressionless. Damn him, he made her so angry. "It's all or nothing. Which way do you want to play it?"

She was making this so difficult for him. He didn't want to see her go, but she had to. He loved her too much to ask her to stay. "It's not a game, Judy. Sally's dead because of me. What right do I have to enjoy anything when she can't?"

Frustrated, she balled up her fist and punched him in the arm. When he stared at her, she fought to keep her angry tears back.

"The right of a human being, you idiot. What makes you think that your being out here, wearing sackcloth and ashes under your uniform, is going to make any difference to her?" He opened his mouth to answer, but she wouldn't let him. "But it makes a world of difference to the living. To Tina, to the people here." Her eyes held his, imploring. "To me. Think about that when you're trying to cut yourself up into little pieces. Think of the difference you've made in the lives of the people out here."

Out of breath, she stopped only long enough to suck in air. "Nobody said life was fair, but it should be the best that we can make it. You're not making it anything if you keep berating yourself for something you had no control over. You didn't fire that damn bullet, some thug did. You didn't kill that girl *or* your partner!''

She let out a long sigh, hoping she wasn't going to cry. She could see that her words had made no impression whatsoever. It was as if he had just shut off his ears.

It was over.

Suddenly she felt worn-out and tired. ''Will you come to see me off?''

God, they'd been with each other, warm and giving, making love by the fireplace, and now she was talking to him as if they were total strangers who had bumped into one another at a cocktail party.

It was better if they just parted now. ''I can't. I have something to do.''

She knew he was lying, but she wasn't going to beg. She had done all she could. Pride had to kick in sometime. ''Then I guess this is goodbye.''

He nodded, his face expressionless. Distant. ''Looks that way.''

She bit her lip to keep from crying. ''Don't forget to read your book.''

He raised a brow, confused. She got into her vehicle. He wanted to pull her out, to take her in his arms and make her stay. He remained standing where he was.

''*Don Juan in Hell,* remember?'' Bitterness fought for control. She pushed it back. ''Although I think you might have a few things you could teach the poet about creating a hell.''

She whistled for Raymond and patted the seat next to her. The dog looked reluctant to take his place beside her. Finally, after barking at Paul, he jumped in, and Judy closed the car door.

She gunned the engine and pulled away as fast as she could.

He didn't come. Just as he said he wouldn't.

A man true to his word, Judy thought as she climbed into

the four by four. Her insides felt as if a porcupine had gotten loose and was capriciously cavorting all through her. Her face muscles hurt as she attempted to maintain her smile.

Paul hadn't come, but it appeared everyone else had. They were all out in force to see her off. She had made friends so easily here, so quickly. Judy knew it was going to be difficult to leave this all behind her and face the more sophisticated rigors of Montreal.

She was going to miss this quaint town where the denizens were struggling with the present and coming to terms with the future.

Judy concentrated on allowing Cynthia's excitement to seep into her. She tried to think about that and the baby and her work. And not about the man who didn't come. The man who didn't care.

Trying to work around the huge lump in her throat, Judy waved again at the large gathering. She wiped her tears away with the back of her hand and started the four by four. She would leave the vehicle with the rental agency in Yellowknife. They would make the rest of the trip to Montreal by air. Raymond would ride in the baggage area. Everything was all neatly mapped out.

Except what she was going to do with her heart now that it was broken.

Driving toward the road that would connect her with Mackenzie Highway, Judy didn't see the lone figure parked on the incline that looked down on the outskirts of Grateful Bend. Looking straight ahead, she didn't see Paul watching her. Didn't know that he had come to silently tell her goodbye.

All she knew was that he wasn't there. He hadn't cared enough to even see her leave.

She was an idiot for loving him.

She let Cynthia's chatter fill her head and told herself that no one had ever died from a broken heart. They weren't fatal.

But this felt damn close.

She couldn't give in to it, couldn't even allow herself the luxury of feeling sorry for herself. She had responsibilities to live up to. There was her promise to Tina and her deadline. She couldn't just turn her back on that and wallow in grief because she had been foolish enough to fall in love with a man who couldn't give of himself.

But she had been so sure she could change him. So very sure.

Pride, Judy reminded herself, always went before a fall.

Chapter Seventeen

Judy felt exhausted as she stepped into the glass-walled elevator and pressed for her floor. It had been a long day, far longer than the days she had spent in Grateful Bend. Maybe she was out of practice for fast-paced city life after staying in a small town. Putting in a twelve-hour day with Paul had never left her feeling so drained, or so tired.

Problem was, she thought, she had started her day out that way.

She had barely leaned against the thick glass wall, oblivious to the opulently decorated floors that floated past her, when the elevator stopped. The doors drew apart, and she forced herself to step out on her floor.

The hotel she was staying in was only two years old. It was sleek and stylish, the last word in comfort and technology. Its tall, thin frame fit right into Montreal's cosmopolitan silhouette.

It made her yearn for Hattie's boarding house, with its smell of pine cleaner and its frayed runners on the stairs. She missed the sound of floors creaking beneath her feet, above her head.

She missed Paul.

Judy clenched her hand around her entry card as she shoved it into the slot. She had to get over it. Over him. She had to move on with her life.

Judy leaned her head against the door before opening it. The cool metal felt as good as anything did these days. She sighed and straightened. Maybe it was going to take longer than two weeks, she mused with half a smile.

A lot longer.

Jiggling the card in the lock, Judy let herself into the three-room suite her publisher had put her up in. There was a room for her and the baby and one for Cynthia. The small sitting room was where she had intended to set up all her chemicals and equipment for developing her photographs. Two weeks, and everything was still in boxes.

She had to stop moping like this and pull herself together. He wasn't worth it.

With visions of a hot bath to soothe her ragged nerves as much as possible, Judy began shedding her clothes at the door.

If she hadn't felt like a limp dishrag to begin with, Sergeant Hobbs would have turned her into one by the end of the day. The Mountie the commander here in Montreal had assigned to her had all but talked off her ears today. Four years with the RCMP, and he was still full of idealism. After observing him and his enthusiasm for the last two weeks, Judy had come to the conclusion that Hobbs was very good at what he did. The perfect Mountie. But today, just when she had wished she could be a tortoise hiding in her shell, he had overwhelmed her with rhetoric.

It was probably the way Paul had felt those six weeks they were together, she thought, unbuttoning her blouse and yanking it out of the waistband of her black skirt.

She thought of Hobbs. He was bright, witty, charming, good-looking and knew his field cold. Everyone at headquarters had a good word to say about him. Everyone she spoke to liked him. He was a joiner, a team player.

Except for being capable, he was almost the complete antithesis of Paul, she thought. The differences in the two men's approach to their job would be very good for the book.

She bit her lower lip. *Good for the book, rotten for me.*

"Cynthia, I'm back," she called out. Letting her blouse hang open, she uncinched her belt. "How was your day?" One shoe landed in the tiny foyer as she kicked it off. The other went under a writing desk. "Mine was awful."

There was no answer. Maybe Cynthia had taken the baby out for a walk. Usually when Tina fussed and all else failed, the swaying of a carriage seemed to soothe her. It was the first thing Judy had purchased when they arrived in Montreal.

Her fingers had grasped the zipper on her skirt and pulled it halfway down by the time she entered the sitting room. She stopped abruptly.

There was a man sitting on the sofa, his back to her. He hadn't turned around when she called out to Cynthia. For one second, her heart constricted, then went into double time.

No, it couldn't be him.

The man was wearing a full dress Mountie uniform. The bright red jacket brought a cheerfulness to the room that she didn't feel.

Another Mountie, not hers.

She'd seen her fill of bright red uniforms today. There'd been an official parade, and Mounties in full dress regalia from all over Canada had participated. The exuberance she would have normally felt at such a display was missing even as she worked to preserve the event on film for her book.

Damn his hide. He'd sucked out everything from her, all of her enthusiasm, all of her joy. There seemed to be nothing left inside her anymore. This was worse than the accident. Much worse.

She was going to have to reinvent herself piece by tiny piece.

Judy closed her eyes for a second, despair moistening her eyes. She had no time to pull herself together, no desire to.

There was no choice. She had to do it.

She cleared her throat and tossed her hair over her shoulder as she took another step into the room. With a quick yank, she pulled her zipper up. This was obviously one of the men she'd seen marching this morning. Maybe he wanted more exposure in the book and thought he'd get it by coming to her room. There had been no end to the volunteers she had encountered since the purpose of her photographs had come to light. They were coming out of the woodwork. Not like a certain reticent Mountie she knew in the Northwest Territories.

She clenched her hands until her nails dug into her palms. She had to stop doing this to herself. She had to stop comparing every detail of what was happening in her life to what had gone before.

There was no before, there was only now and the future. The sooner she got that through her head, the better off she'd be.

She couldn't understand why the Mountie hadn't turned around yet. Surely he'd heard her come in. Maybe he had suddenly gotten cold feet.

Well, cold feet or not, she didn't want to talk to anyone else tonight. She was off duty. "I'm afraid that I'm not—"

Judy's words backed up in her throat as she moved closer to the sofa.

The set of the shoulders, the tilt of the head...

Paul.

Get a grip, Judy. For two weeks, she'd fantasized that he'd come looking for her, like Rhett Butler storming through Tara, looking for Scarlett, Heathcliff calling Catherine. Damn, she would have settled for Mickey Mouse looking for Minnie.

It couldn't be him.

And yet—

Judy didn't know if she was just hallucinating—letting her tired imagination transform what she saw into what she wanted to see. But... nobody else's shoulders were that broad. Nobody else's hair was that shade of blond.

Tears threatened to choke her as she rushed into the room.

He hadn't been certain how much longer he could just sit there, waiting for her to come in. Waiting for her to realize that it was him. Half of him was frozen with fear that she'd tell him to get out and go to hell. But he had to take that chance. He was in hell as it was.

Paul rose to his feet just as she reached him. Only vaguely noting that her blouse was hanging open, he enveloped her in his arms, emotions scrambling wildly through him.

God, it felt so good to hold her, just to hold her. He felt as if he had been dead these last two weeks and was only now coming back to life.

For a moment, Judy did nothing but let herself absorb his presence. He was here, really here. She wasn't just conjuring him up this time.

And then her euphoria faded. He'd trained her too well to see the half-empty, not the half-full. She realized that he wasn't here because of her. There were Mounted Policemen from every province of Canada in the city. He had come for the parade. He was here to represent the Northwest Territories, not to see her. Stopping by was probably just a way to kill time until he was due back. Nothing more than that.

She wanted it to be more. Damn him, she wanted more.

No, she wasn't going to break down in front of him. Pride was all she had left, and she would hang on to it, no matter what.

Judy backed off and looked at him. She looked down at the neat row of buttons, afraid to look into his eyes. "Wow, what a surprise." She forced herself to sound cheery, impersonal. "I guess you're here for the parade."

He realized that she was backing away from him. Was he too late? Of course he was. What did he expect after the way he had treated her? There was no one but himself to blame.

"Captain Reynolds asked for volunteers." Paul picked up his hat from the sofa, needing to do something with his hands.

He was leaving. Hello and goodbye, just like that. What did he think she was, a yo-yo to jerk around? She wondered how stiff the penalty was for beating a Mountie. Two weeks of being absolutely miserable had her temper detonating without warning.

"You volunteered?" She raised her brows in mock surprise. "Aren't you out of your league here, Sergeant? There aren't many trees to hide behind in the center of Montreal." Because she suddenly didn't trust herself alone with him, didn't trust her temper, she looked toward the closed bedroom door. "Cynthia?"

He saw her temper flare in her eyes. Temper he understood. He could work with that. Temper meant that there were other emotions swirling beneath. Maybe he still had a chance after all. "I asked for a few minutes alone with you. Cynthia took the baby out for a walk. She said she'd be back around seven."

She wasn't going to hope. Hope was for people who had a shred of optimism left. She didn't, not when it came to Paul.

His courage was faltering. There was so much riding on this. "You always enter the room with your blouse hanging open?"

Flustered, she looked down and realized her oversight. She started to close it, but he caught her hand.

"No, don't. Let me look at you."

Confused, she blew out a breath. "What are you doing here, anyway? Changed your mind about seeing me off?" she bit off. She began rebuttoning her blouse.

"Yes." He took her hands. She tried to twist away, but he held them firmly in his. "Yes, I have."

There was something in his tone that had her staring at him. Despite her efforts, a tiny sliver of hope was breaking through, like a flower pushing its way through a crack in the concrete.

This was hard, harder than anything he'd ever done. But if he didn't do it, he was dooming himself to a life of solitude. He might deserve it, but he couldn't stand it anymore. Not after having been with her.

Paul took a long breath. "After you left Grateful Bend, I kept waiting for you to get out of my blood. Out of my head. But you didn't."

He wanted to touch her face, to run his hands through her hair. He wanted to press her close to him, but he remained where he was. Holding her hands would have to do.

"Everywhere I looked, everywhere I went, I'd remember being there with you." His mouth curved a little. "Your damn scent's still in my towels, my pillow, my sheets. My cabin. Even the Land Rover smells like you."

She wanted to cry. The tension that had riddled her body began to unclench its hold. She smiled. "Industrial-strength cologne."

He shook his head. "Nothing's right without you anymore. Nothing fits without you anymore." Not his clothes, not his skin. Not his life. "And it never will again." He'd never begged before. He knew he was begging now. "I love you, Judy. I know I've got no right to say it, no right to want it, but I love you and I need you back in my life."

Her eyes were bright with tears. "Of course you have the right, you big dope. Everyone's got the right to happiness. It's in the constitution." One tear slid down her face, and he wiped it gently away with his thumb. She sniffed, trying not to melt against his hand. "Mine, anyway. I'll share it with you if it's not in yours."

Standing on her toes, Judy wrapped her arms around his neck.

"You can't bring Sally back no matter what you do anymore than I can bring Tina back. But you can make it a better world for others by being in it, by rejoining the living." She raised her mouth to his and brushed a soft, fleeting kiss over his lips. The need that sprang up within him echoed within her. "I know you can make mine a whole lot better by being in it."

He searched her face and knew that she believed it. Still, he had his doubts. No one had ever made him believe that he mattered before.

"Can I, Judy?" he asked quietly. "Can I?"

She smiled into his eyes. "I'm going to enjoy making my point over and over again for as long as you let me."

This time, she kissed him harder. Passion erupted. She sighed as the excitement mingled with a comfort she had never known before.

Paul rested his chin on top of her head as he held her to him. "How does forever sound?"

Her breath felt warm and teasing against his chest as her words floated out. "Sounds good for openers." Judy pulled her head back and looked at him as his words actually sank in. "Does that mean you're going to marry me?"

Paul could only laugh softly and shake his head. "Never let me get anything out first, do you?"

He *was* going to ask her to marry him. Joy rushed through her veins like a raging river. "You've got to be fast, Sergeant, to keep up with me." *Soon, Paul, make it soon.*

"I'm learning that." He combed his fingers lightly through her hair. She was accepting him. Warts and all, she was accepting him. He couldn't believe it. But it was true. He only had to look at her to know it was true. "You've made everything good, Judy. Without you, there's no reason to go on anymore."

She hesitated. "What about Tina?" She couldn't abandon the baby, even at the cost of her own happiness. "We're a package deal."

He smiled. "I could never resist a bargain." He wiped away another tear from her cheek. "She'll be needing a father, won't she?"

"Yes, oh, yes." Plans began evolving in her head with the speed of a high-powered drill. "Think Grateful Bend could use a new teacher?" He raised a quizzical brow. "I've al-

ready got all the credentials—couldn't be that hard to get a
license in Canada.''

He thought of the days they had spent together. He'd
never seen anyone with such enthusiasm for their work.
"But your photography, it means so much to you." He
shook his head. "I can't ask you to give it up."

His thoughtfulness touched her. God, she did love this
man. "I can still do some work in the summertime." She
grinned. "That's what's so great about being a teacher. The
vacations." She curved her body toward his. "And I'll split
my haul of apples with you."

He still couldn't believe what she was telling him. "You'd
go back to Grateful Bend with me?"

He didn't understand, did he? When she loved, she loved
completely. "Sergeant, I love you. I'd go to the moon with
you if that's what it took."

She would, too, he realized. Maybe sometimes in life, a
man did get a second chance. "Grateful Bend's closer."

She laughed. "Grateful Bend it is. Right after my assignment's finished."

He arched a brow. He'd made it a point to find out just
who she was teamed with. Sergeant Hobbs was too damn
good-looking and eager for Paul's comfort. "I've got a lot
of leave I've never used, I can stay here with you until you're
finished." He wasn't going to take any foolish chances now
that she was his. "Make sure you're not just being dazzled
by the uniform."

She sighed as she lifted her mouth to his. "I've seen you
out of it. It's not just the *uniform* that's got me dazzled,
Sergeant."

"Good." He bent his head to kiss her, and then stopped.
"Oh, and Judy?"

Her body was already vibrating, anticipating. "Hmm?"

He still hadn't figured out how he had gotten so lucky.
This time, he decided not to think about it. It was better to
enjoy than dissect. "I think you can stop calling me Sergeant now."

She laughed as she rose up on her toes, ready to meet him more than halfway. "About time, Paul."

"Yes," he said just before he kissed her. "Yes, it is."

* * * * *

ONE WEDDING...

FOUR LOVE STORIES

Where better to fall in love than at a resplendent June wedding? As Nick and Diane walked down the aisle together little did they know how their most cherished of days would set the scene for four life-long love affairs.

AVAILABLE NOW

PRICED: £3.99

Silhouette Special Edition

COMING NEXT MONTH

WALK AWAY, JOE Pamela Toth

Emma Davenport was just the sort of woman Joe Sutter avoided: She was sweet, sincere and pretty as a picture. Getting involved with Emma wouldn't be fair, yet something wouldn't let him walk away...

HIGH COUNTRY RANCHER Judith Bowen

Nola Snow knew what she wanted from life—to marry a Native American man and follow the old traditions. She longed for a real family, for roots. Carson Harlow was a prospector with whom she had nothing in common—except attraction!

UNMARRIED WITH CHILDREN Victoria Pade

Lexi Kincaid and Jess Haley were perfect for each other—they just didn't know it yet. But their five-year-old daughters did. This was one time when the children knew best.

GRAND PRIZE WINNER! Tracy Sinclair

That Special Woman!

Kelley McCormick intended to have the trip of a lifetime when she won the lottery, but even she had never envisaged that she would meet a man like Grand Duke Erich Von Graile Und Tassburg. He really was Prince Charming material.

BROOMSTICK COWBOY Kathleen Eagle

Enchanting Amy Becker had chosen his best friend over him, so Tate Harrison had cut his losses and lit out. But now Amy was a widow, a very pregnant widow, and she needed help. Would she ever admit she needed him?

THE WAY OF A MAN Laurie Paige

Wild River Trilogy

Dinah St. Cloud's instinct for self preservation told her to stay far away from Paul McPherson this time. He was just too handsome for his own good...

COMING NEXT MONTH FROM

Silhouette

Desire

*provocative, sensual love stories
for the woman of today*

TWEED Lass Small
NOT JUST ANOTHER PERFECT WIFE Robin Elliott
WILD MIDNIGHT Ann Major
KEEGAN'S HUNT Dixie Browning
THE BEST REVENGE Barbara Boswell
DANCLER'S WOMAN Mary Lynn Baxter

Sensation

*romance with a special mix of adventure,
glamour and drama*

BABY MAGIC Marion Smith Collins
DEFYING GRAVITY Rachel Lee
STAND-OFF Lee Magner
SECOND-HAND HUSBAND Dallas Schulze